VENUS ON THE HALF-SHELL

PHILIP JOSÉ FARMER

VENUS ON THE HALF-SHELL

TITAN BOOKS

VENUS ON THE HALF-SHELL
Print edition ISBN: 9781781163061
E-book edition ISBN: 9781781163078

Published by Titan Books
A division of Titan Publishing Group Ltd
144 Southwark Street, London SE1 0UP

First edition: December 2013
1 3 5 7 9 10 8 6 4 2

A CIP catalogue record for this title is available from the British Library.

Printed and bound in the United States.

VENUS ON THE HALF-SHELL

Dedicated to the beasts and the stars.
They don't worry about free will and immortality.

FOREWORD
WHY AND HOW I BECAME KILGORE TROUT
BY PHILIP JOSÉ FARMER

Not until I reread *Venus on the Half-Shell* in preparation for this foreword, and read the reviews and letters resulting from it, did I remember how much fun I had had with it.

When I sat down to the typewriter to begin it, I was Kilgore Trout, not Philip José Farmer. The ideas, characters, plot, and situations rushed in, crowding at my brain's front door. When they surged in, they swirled around, hand-in-hand, like super barn dancers or well-orchestrated members of the lobster quadrille. What a blast it was!

Six weeks later, the novel was done, but, all that while, the music was from Kant, Schopenhauer, and Voltaire. The caller was Epistemology, who looked a lot like Lewis Carroll. My wife knew I was having a good time because she could hear my laughter coming up the basement stairs to the kitchen.

I had been having a moderate writer's block with the then-currently scheduled novel. I was making slow and often halting progress. But, once I put that novel aside for the time being and adopted the persona of Kilgore Trout, sad-sack science fiction author, I wrote as if possessed by a degenerate angel. Which is what poor old Trout was, in fact.

The beginning of this project was in the early 1970s when I vastly admired and was wildly enthusiastic about the works of Kurt Vonnegut, Jr. I was especially intrigued by Kilgore Trout, who had appeared in Vonnegut's *God Bless You, Mr. Rosewater* and *Slaughterhouse-Five*. Trout was to appear in *Breakfast of Champions*, but that had not been published then.

While rereading *Rosewater* (in 1972, I believe) for the fifth time, I came across the part where Fred Rosewater picks up one of Trout's books in the pornography section of a bookstore. It's a paperback (none of Trout's works ever made hardcovers) titled *Venus on the Half-Shell*. On the back cover is a photograph of the author, an old bearded man looking "like a frightened, aging Jesus", and below it is an abridged version of "a red-hot scene" in the book.

The section regarding *Venus* differs from others, which describe the plots of Trout's stories. Thus, Vonnegut, via Trout, makes his satirical or ironic points about our Terrestrial society and the nature of the Universe. *Venus* has no descriptions of the plot, and the hero is known only as the Space Wanderer. Aside from the abridged text on the back cover, there is no inkling of what the book is about.

At that moment, rereading this part, a pitchfork rose from my subconscious and goosed my neural ganglia. In short, I was inspired. Lights went on; bells clanged.

"Hey!" I thought. "Vonnegut's readers think that Trout

is only a fictional character! What if one of his books actually appeared on the stands? Wouldn't that blow the minds of Vonnegut's readers?"

Not to mention mine.

And, I thought, who more fitted to write *Venus* than I, a sad-sack science fiction writer whose early career paralleled Trout's? I'd been ripped off by publishers, had to work at menial jobs to support myself and family while writing, had suffered from the misunderstanding of my works, and had had to endure the scorn of those who considered science fiction to be a trashy genre without any literary merit. The main difference between Trout and me was that I had made a little money then, and none of my stories had been confined to sleazy pornographic magazines where they appeared, as in Trout's case, as fillers to accompany the photographs of naked or half-clad women. Although it was true then that the general public and the epicenous academics thought of science fiction as only a cut above pornography.

My heart fired up like a nova, I wrote to David Harris, science fiction editor of Dell (Vonnegut's publisher), proposing to write *Venus* as if by Kilgore Trout. He replied that he thought the idea was great, and he gave me Vonnegut's address so that I could write him to ask for permission to carry out the project. I did not hesitate. After all, *Venus* would be my tribute to the esteemed Vonnegut. I sent him a letter outlining my proposal. Many months passed. No reply. I sent another letter, but many more months passed before I decided that I'd have to phone Vonnegut. David Harris gave me Vonnegut's number.

I had to nerve myself up to phone Vonnegut. He was a

very big author, and I was a member of a group, science fiction writers, for whom he had expressed a certain amount of disdain. But, when I did call him, he was very pleasant and not at all patronizing. He said that he did remember my letters, though he did not explain why he had not replied. I re-outlined my ideas, and, in arguing against his resistance to them, said that I strongly identified with Trout. He replied that he, too, identified with him. And he was afraid that people would think that the book was a hoax.

That flabbergasted me. Of course, it was a hoax, and people would know it. But I rallied, and I argued some more. Finally, he relented and gave me permission to write *Venus* as Trout. I offered to split the royalties with him, but he magnanimously refused to accept them. However, he did stress that no reference to his name or his works should appear in or on *Venus*.

I thanked him, and, elated, started to write. I was Kilgore Trout, in a sense, and I was writing the sort of book that I imagined Trout would write. But I tried to give the prose, characters, plot, and philosophy of *Venus* a Vonnegutian flavor. After all, Vonnegut had admitted that he was also, in a sense, Trout. I was only restricted in writing *Venus* by having to make the protagonist the Space Wanderer and by including my expansion of the abridged "red-hot scene" as described in *Rosewater*. I did not entirely emulate Vonnegut in the use of short words and a sort of See-Dick-See-Jane-See-Spot prose. But I did try to keep the text from becoming anything resembling William Faulkner's. Vonnegut wrote a very simple prose because he had a low opinion of the attention-span and general literary and lexical knowledge of the 1970s' college students, who formed a large percentage of his readers.

It's worth noting that such science fiction writers as Isaac Asimov and Frank Herbert did not avoid complicated ideas and plots and long sentences and words, and they did very well among the college students and general reading public.

The protagonist of *Venus* was named Simon Wagstaff. Simon because he was a sort of Simple Simon of the nursery rhyme. And *Wagstaff* because he certainly "wagged" (and waved) his sexual "staff" around during various sexual encounters. I also, unlike Vonnegut, put in a lot of references to literature and fictional authors. It would not matter that the average reader would not understand these, and it would amuse the academics. Or so I thought. I was too obscure for even the supposedly overeducated academics.

How many knew that Silas T. Comberbacke, the baseball-fan spaceman (sort of an Ancient Mariner) in *Venus* was the pseudonym of Samuel T. Coleridge, the great British poet, during his brief stay in the English army? Or that Bruga, Trout's favorite poet, was taken (with permission) from a novel by Ben Hecht, *Count Bruga*? And that Bruga, the wild Jewish Bukowski-like Chicago poet, was based on Hecht's friend, Maxwell E. Bodenheim, the Greenwich Village poet and wino of the 1930s? Or that there were many similar references to other fictional writers? Who cared except me?

Most of the alien names in *Venus* were formed by transposing the letters of English or non-English words. Thus, Chworktap comes from *patchwork*. Dokal comes from *caudal*, which means having a tail. The planet Zelpst is a phonetic rendering of the German *selbst*, meaning *self*. The planet Raproshma is a rendering of the French *rapprochement*. The planet Clerun-Gowph derives from the German *Aufklärung*, enlightenment. And so on. Most readers sensibly do not concern themselves with such games, but I had fun with them. And I imagine that Trout, though he had only a high school education, read widely, and he would have played the same game.

The philosophical basis of *Venus* dealt with free will and immortality. Trout, in *Breakfast of Champions*, longs to be young again. And predeterminism is certainly a theme that runs through many of Vonnegut's works. Vonnegut is like Mark Twain in that he believes (or writes as if he believes) that everything is predetermined. Twain thought that all physical things and our thoughts and behavior were mechanically fixed from the moment the first atom in the beginning of this universe bumped into the second atom and the second atom into the third. And so on. Vonnegut apparently believes that our troubling and violent lives and irrational behavior are the result of "bad chemicals."

This interests me because I have been interested in the problem of free will versus predeterminism for about fifty-eight years. But I believe that humans do have free will, though few, however, exercise that faculty. Perhaps I believe this because I am predetermined to do so. But, as Trout, I wrote as if Twain and Vonnegut were correct in their belief in predeterminism.

In any event, Vonnegut is a thorough predeterminist in that his works have no villains or heroes. No blame is put upon anybody for even the vilest deeds and most colossal selfishness, savagery, stupidity, and greed. That's the way things are, and they can be no other. Only God the Utterly Indifferent is responsible and perhaps not even He. Trout has the same attitude.

Just as Eliot Rosewater, the multimillionaire in *Rosewater*, *Slaughterhouse-Five*, and *Breakfast*, thinks that Trout is the greatest writer that ever lived, so Trout, in his *Venus*, has Simon Wagstaff, his hero, believe that Jonathan Swift Somers III is the greatest writer that ever existed. Wagstaff also has his favorite poet, Bruga. Some of Somers' stories are outlined, and some of Bruga's poems are printed in *Venus*.

Somers III is my creation, but he is the grandson of Judge Somers and the son of Jonathan Swift Somers II. Those familiar with Edgar Lee Masters' *Spoon River Anthology* will recognize the latter two. (Mentioned with the permission of the Masters' estate.)

One of Somers III's protagonists is Ralph von Wau Wau (Wau Wau is German for Bow! Wow!). He is a German Shepherd dog whose intelligence has been raised to human-genius level by a scientist. Ralph is also a writer, and I had planned to write a story as by him titled *Some Humans Don't Stink*. That story's main character would be Shorter Vondergut, a writer. (Shorter from *kurt*, German for *short*, and Vondergut from the German *von der Gut*, meaning of the [River] Gut.) Thus, the cycle of fictional authors would be complete. In fact, I did write two stories under Somers' name about Ralph. These were published, but I doubt I'll ever write the whole cycle. I have passed through this particular phase. It was fun while it lasted.

The *Venus* manuscript went to Dell with some photographs of me as Trout (wearing a big false beard), a selected bibliography of Trout's works, and a biographical sketch of him. All done with tongue in cheek or wherever. The furor on its publication both amused and gratified me. There were even questions about the true identity of Trout in the *New York Times*. An article in the *National Enquirer* "proved" that Vonnegut wrote *Venus* because of its plots, characters, philosophy, and style.

Meanwhile, Mr. Vonnegut was neither amused nor gratified. He was, as I understand, flooded with letters asking if he had written *Venus*. Some of these said it was the worst book he had ever written; some, the best. The main cause of unhappiness, however, was that he misunderstood a remark made by Leslie Fiedler, the distinguished author and literary critic, while Fiedler was a guest on William F. Buckley's TV show, *Firing Line*. The subject was science fiction, and Vonnegut's name came up. Dr. Fiedler, who knew that I had written *Venus* but did not reveal its authorship, said that I had said that I was going to write *Venus* no matter what the obstacles, including Vonnegut. My memory is hazy on the exact wording. Vonnegut, however, apparently thought that Fiedler had said that I was going to write *Venus* without Vonnegut's permission. Something to that effect.

Whatever was said, Mr. Vonnegut became angry. Consequently, he forbade me to write another Trout novel I'd planned, *The Son of Jimmy Valentine*. That would have been my last novel as by Trout, but it was not to be. Vonnegut had the right, of course, to refuse permission for me to write it.

Legally, I had the right to sell *Venus* to the movies. And, when a producer made a proposal to make an animated movie of it with The Grateful Dead providing the music, I was elated.

But Mr. Vonnegut phoned me and expressed his regrets that his lawyer would sue the producer if a movie was made. Vonnegut told me he was sorry about this, but I was very prolific and so would not miss any money I might get from the deal. Again, he had the moral right to scotch this proposal. Also, I doubt that anything would have come from the proposal. I've had over forty of my works optioned for Hollywood, and nothing has come of any of these.

The fun continued. Many letters addressed to Trout were sent on by my agent or the publisher. One letter purported to be from another Vonnegut character, Harrison Bergeron. Trout was invited to be the artist-in-residence during the 1975 Bicentennial Literary Explosion in Frankfort, Kentucky. The editor of *Contemporary Authors* sent a letter inquiring about including Trout in the book for 1976. She complained that Trout was supposed to have written 117 novels, but she could find only a reference to *Venus on the Half-Shell*. "It would seem," she wrote, "that Kilgore Trout is a pseudonym. Would your agent furnish the real name of the author?"

As Trout, I filled out the data-forms she had sent and mailed them to her through my agent. I explained that all my novels had been originally published by disreputable fly-by-night publishers who had not paid me any royalties and had not even paid a fee to register my books with the Library of Congress. I never checked the 1976 issue, but I doubt that the editor included the Trout item.

However, as time went on, I became worried about Vonnegut's displeasure at the idea that people might think he was the author of *Venus*. At the same time, it was beyond me why he should be displeased that people might think he wrote *Venus* and yet not be distressed because people *knew* he was the author of *Breakfast of Champions*, *Slapstick*, *Jailbird*, and *Deadeye Dick*.

To spread the word around that I, not Vonnegut, was the author of *Venus*, I revealed the truth at every chance to do so and did my best when I was speaking at conventions and conferences to bring up the subject. I did the same when I was being interviewed on radio and TV. Just how well the science fiction grapevine has worked, I do not know. By now, it does not seem to matter. Time has cleared this problem away. In the past few years, when I spoke at universities and colleges, I found that only about four or five in audiences of 500 to 800 recognized the name of Trout or Vonnegut. And I was told by a fan who questioned Vonnegut about *Venus* after a lecture that Vonnegut had difficulty remembering anything about it, including my name. So, whatever he felt at the time regarding *Venus* has passed.

I wish to thank Mr. Vonnegut for his generosity in permitting me to publish *Venus* as by Trout. I am sorry that it may have caused him any perturbation. I am even sorrier that he could not understand that *Venus* was my tribute to him and my repayment for all the delight his pre–1975 works gave me.

For several years, I've been trying to get *Venus* published under my own name. Finally, it has come about.

But, for a brief though glorious period, I was Kilgore Trout.

Philip José Farmer, 1988

THE OBSCURE LIFE AND HARD TIMES
OF KILGORE TROUT
A SKIRMISH IN BIOGRAPHY

BY PHILIP JOSÉ FARMER

This is another specimen of the "biographical." It originally appeared in a fanzine, *Moebius Trip*, December 1971 issue, edited and published by Ed Connor of Peoria, Illinois. Later on, I suggested to the editor of *Esquire* that he might want to publish this "life." Regretfully, he rejected the idea. He did not think that Kilgore Trout was as well known as Tarzan. This is true, but the majority of *Esquire*'s readers are probably readers of Kurt Vonnegut's works and would be acquainted with Trout. So it goes.

I identify strongly with Trout.

The editor and readers of *Moebius Trip* thought that the letter from Trout and the letter describing Trout's interview in the *Peoria Journal Star* were made up by me. No such thing. These letters actually appeared in the letter section of the editorial page of Peoria's only local newspaper, and I can prove it.

Since I wrote this, I have been fortunate enough to read

the galleys of Vonnegut's novel *Breakfast of Champions*. It contains many new facts which have enabled me to amplify and to correct the original article. Even so, some things are still in doubt because of contradictions in the three books in which Trout figures. Mr. Vonnegut evidently regards consistency as the hobgoblin of small writers.

Internal evidence in *God Bless You, Mr. Rosewater*, the first book about Trout, implies that Trout was born in 1890 or 1898. *Slaughterhouse-Five*, the second, implies that he was born in 1902. But *Breakfast of Champions* makes it clear that he was born in 1907.

There are other discrepancies. *God Bless You, Mr. Rosewater* says that no two of Trout's books ever had the same publisher. In *Breakfast of Champions* the World Classics Library publishers have issued many of his books.

Rosewater states that Trout's works can only be found in disreputable bookstores dealing in pornography. Yet the same book has Eliot Rosewater picking up a Trout novel from a book rack in an airport.

Trout's novels are supposed to be extremely difficult to find. Rosewater is an avid collector of Trout (in fact, the only one), and he has only forty-one novels and sixty-three short stories. Yet the crooked lawyer, Mushari, goes into a Washington, D.C. smut dealer's and finds every one of Trout's eighty-seven novels.

Breakfast of Champions says that until Trout met a truck driver in 1972 he had never talked with anybody who'd read one of his stories. But Eliot Rosewater and Billy Pilgrim had read his stories and had met him some years before.

Trout's sole fan letter (from Rosewater) reached him in Cohoes, New York, according to *Breakfast*. But *Rosewater* says that Trout was living in Hyannis, Massachusetts, when he got the letter.

The description of the extraterrestrial Tralfamadorians in *The Sirens of Titan* differs considerably from that in *Slaughterhouse-Five*.

And so it goes.

Who is the greatest living science fiction author?

Some say he is Isaac Asimov. Many swear he's Robert A. Heinlein. Others nominate Arthur C. Clarke, Theodore Sturgeon, Harlan Ellison, Brian Aldiss, or Kurt Vonnegut, Jr. Franz Rottensteiner, Austrian critic and editor, proclaims the Pole, Stanislaw Lem, as the champion. Mr. Rottensteiner may be biased, however, since he is also Lem's literary agent.

None of the above can equal Kilgore Trout—if we can believe Eliot Rosewater, Indiana multimillionaire, war hero, philanthropist, fireman extraordinaire, and science fiction connoisseur. According to Rosewater, Trout is not only the greatest science fiction writer alive, he is the world's greatest writer. He ranks Trout above Dostoevski, Tolstoi, Balzac, Fielding, and Melville. Rosewater believes that Trout should be president of Earth. He alone would have the imagination, ingenuity, and perception to solve the problems of this planet.

Rosewater, drunk as usual, once burst into a science fiction writers' convention at Milford, Pennsylvania. He had come to meet his idol, but he found, to his sorrow and amazement, that

Trout was not there. Lesser men could attend it, but Trout was too poor to leave Hyannis, Massachusetts, where he was a stock clerk in a trading-stamp redemption center.

Who is this Kilgore Trout, this poverty-stricken and neglected genius?

To begin with, Kilgore Trout is not a *nom de plume* of Theodore Sturgeon. Let us dispose of that base rumor at once. It is only coincidence that the final syllables of the first names of these two authors end in ore or that their last names are those of fish. The author of the classical and beautifully written *More Than Human* and *The Saucer of Loneliness* could not possibly be the man whom even his greatest admirer admitted couldn't write for sour apples.

Trout was born in 1907, but the exact day is unknown. Until a definite date is supplied by an authoritative source, I'll postulate the midnight of February 19th, 1907, as the day on which society's "greatest prophet" was born. Trout's character indicates that he is an Aquarian and so was born between January 20th and February 19th. There is, however, so much of the Piscean in him that he was probably born on the cusp of Aquarius and Pisces, that is, near midnight of February 19th.

Trout first saw the light of day on the British island of Bermuda. His parents were citizens of the United States of America. (Trout has depicted them in his novel, *Now It Can Be Told*.) His father, Leo Trout, had taken a position as birdwatcher for the Royal Ornithological Society in Bermuda. His chief duty was to guard the very rare Bermudian ern, a green sea eagle. Despite his vigilance, the ern became extinct, and Leo took his family back to the States. Kilgore attended a Bermudian grammar school and then entered Thomas Jefferson High School in Dayton, Ohio. He graduated from this in 1924.

Though Trout was born in Bermuda, he was probably conceived in Indiana. His character smells strongly of certain Hoosier elements, and it is in Indianapolis, Indiana, that we first meet him. This state has produced many writers: Edward Eggleston (*The Hoosier Schoolmaster*), George Ade (*Fables in Slang*), Theodore Dreiser (*Sister Carrie, An American Tragedy, The Genius*), George Barr McCutcheon (*Graustark, Brewster's Millions*), Gene Stratton Porter (*A Girl of the Limberlost*), William Vaughn Moody (*The Great Divide*), Booth Tarkington (*Penrod, The Magnificent Ambersons*), Lew Wallace (*Ben Hur*), James Whitcomb Riley (*The Old Swimmin' Hole, When the Frost is on the Punkin'*), Ross Lockridge (*Raintree County*), Leo Queequeg Tincrowdor (*Osiris on Crutches, The Vaccinators from Vega*), Rex Stout (author of the Nero Wolfe mysteries), and, last but far from least, Kurt Vonnegut, Jr. (*Player Piano, Cat's Cradle, The Sirens of Titan*, "Welcome to the Monkey House," *Mother Night, God Bless You, Mr. Rosewater, Slaughterhouse-Five*, and *Breakfast of Champions*).

Mr. Vonnegut is the primary source of our information about Kilgore Trout. We should all be grateful to him for bringing Trout's life and works to our attention. Unfortunately, Vonnegut refers to him only in the latter three books, and these are popularly believed to be fictional. They are to some extent, but Kilgore Trout is a real-life person, and anybody who doubts this is free to look up his birth record in Bermuda.

Vonnegut has brought Trout out of obscurity and has given us much of his immediate life. He has not, however, given us the background of Trout's parents, and so I have conducted my own investigations into Trout's pedigree. The full name of Kilgore's father was Leo Cabell Trout, and he was born circa 1881 in Roanoke, Virginia. Trouts have lived for generations in this city and its neighbor, Salem. Leo's mother was a Cabell and related to that family which has produced the famous author, James Branch Cabell (*Figures of Earth*, *The Silver Stallion*, *Jurgen*) and a novelist well known in the nineteenth century, Princess Amelie Troubetzkoy. The princess was the granddaughter of William Cabell Rives, a U.S. Senator and minister to France. Her first novel, *The Quick or the Dead?*, was a sensation in 1888.

Trout inherited a talent for writing from his mother's side also. She was Eva Alice Shawnessy (1880–1926), author of the Little Eva series, popular children's books around the turn of the century. She wrote these under the *nom de plume* of Eva Westward and received only a fraction of the royalties they earned. Her publisher ran off with his firm's profits to Brazil after inducing her to sink her money into the firm's stock. Her unpublished biography of her father was the main source of information for Ross Lockridge when he wrote *Raintree County*.

Her father was John Wickliff Shawnessy (1839–1941), a Civil War veteran, country schoolteacher, and a frustrated dramatist and poet. Johnny spent much of his life thinking about and seeking the legended Golden Raintree, an arboreal Holy Grail, hidden somewhere in the Great Swamp of Raintree County. Johnny never finished his epic, *Sphinx Recumbent*, but a great-grandson has taken this and rewritten it as a science fiction novel. Leo Queequeg Tincrowdor (born 1918) is the son of Allegra Shawnessy (born 1898), daughter of Wesley Shawnessy (1879–1939), eldest son of John Wickliff Shawnessy. Kilgore's cousin, Leo, is primarily a painter, but he has written some science fiction stories which have been favorably compared to Kilgore's.

Johnny's father was Thomas Duff Shawnessy (died 1879), farmer, lay preacher, herbalist, and composer of county-famous, but awful, doggerel. He was born in the village of Ecclefechan, Dumfriesshire, Scotland, and was the illegitimate son of Eliza Shawnessy, a farmer's daughter. Thomas Duff revealed to his son Johnny that his, Thomas', father had been the great Scots essayist and historian, Thomas Carlyle (1795–1881). Eliza (1774–1830) had taken Thomas Duff when he was a boy to the state of Delaware. After his mother died, Thomas Duff Shawnessy and his nineteen-year-old bride, Ellen, had settled in the newly opened state of Indiana. Thomas Duff thought that his father's writing genius might spring anew in his grandson, Johnny. Surely the genes responsible for such great books as *Sartor Resartus*, *The French Revolution*, and *On Heroes, Hero Worship, and the Heroic in History* would not die.

There is, however, strong doubt that Thomas Carlyle was T. D. Shawnessy's father. Eliza Shawnessy would have been twenty-one years old in 1795, the year Carlyle was born. Even if she had seduced Carlyle when he was only twelve, Thomas Duff would have been born in 1807. This would make him thirteen years old when he married the nineteen-year-old Ellen. This is possible but highly improbable.

It seems likely that Eliza Shawnessy lied to her son. She wanted him to think that, though he was a bastard, his father was a great man. Probably, Thomas Duff's father was actually James Carlyle, stonemason, farmer, a fanatical Calvinist, and father of Thomas Carlyle. The truth seems to be that Thomas Duff Shawnessy was the half-brother of Thomas Carlyle. Thomas Duff should have been able to figure this out, but he never bothered to look up the date of his supposed father's birth.

Johnny's mother, Ellen, was a cousin of Andrew Johnson (1808–1875), the seventeenth president of the United States.

Johnny's second wife, Esther Root (born 1852), was of English stock with a dash of American Indian blood (from the Miami tribe, probably).

With so many writers in his pedigree, it would seem that Kilgore Trout was almost destined to become a famous author. However, his talents were marred by his personality, which had been soured and depressed by an unhappy childhood. His father was a ne'er-do-well, and his mother was embittered by her husband's drunkenness and infidelity, and by the theft of her royalties. Trout was prevented from going on to college by his parents' long and expensive illnesses, resulting in their deaths a few years after he graduated from high school.

Trout had three great fears that rode him all his life: a fear of cancer, of rats, and of Doberman pinschers. The first came from watching his parents suffer in their terminal stages. The second came from living in so many basements and tenement houses. The third resulted from several attacks by Doberman pinschers during his vagabondish life. Once, out of a job and starving, he tried to steal a chicken from a farmer's henhouse but was caught by the watchdog. Another time, he was bitten while delivering circulars.

Trout's pessimism and distrust of human beings ensured that he would have no friends and that his three wives would divorce him. It drove his only child, Leo, to run away from home at the age of fourteen. Leo lied about his age and became a U.S. Marine. While in boot camp he wrote his father a denunciatory letter. After that, there was a total lack of word about Leo until two FBI agents visited Kilgore. His son, they told him, had deserted and joined the Viet Cong.

Trout moved around the States, working at low-paying and menial jobs and writing his science fiction stories in his spare time. After his final divorce, his only companion was a parakeet named Bill. Kilgore talked a lot to Bill. And for forty years Kilgore carried around with him an old steamer trunk. This contained many curious items, including toys from his childhood, the bones of a Bermudian ern, and a mildewed tuxedo he had worn to the senior dance just before graduating.

Sometime during his lonely odysseys, he fell into the habit of calling mirrors "leaks." Mirrors were weak points through which leaked visions of universes parallel to ours. Through these four-dimensional windows he could see cosmos occupying the same space as ours. This delusion, if it was a delusion, probably originated from his rejection of our universe. This was, to him, the worst of all possible worlds.

Our planet was a cement mixer in which Trout had been whirled, tossed, beaten, and ground. By the mid-1960s, his face and body bore all the scars and traumas of his never-ending battle against the most abject poverty, of his unceasing labors in writing his many works, of a neglect by the literary world and, worse, by a neglect from the readers of the genre in which he specialized, science fiction, and of an incessant screwing by his fly-by-night publishers.

Fred Rosewater, in *God Bless You, Mr. Rosewater*, picks up a book by Trout. It is *Venus on the Half-Shell*, and on its paper back is a photograph of Trout. He's an old man with a bushy black beard, and his face is that of a scarred Jesus who's been spared the cross but must instead spend the rest of his life in prison.

Eliot Rosewater, coming out of a mental fog in a sanitarium, sees Trout for the first time. He looks to him like a kindly country undertaker. Trout no longer has a beard; he's shaved it off so he can get a job.

Billy Pilgrim, in *Slaughterhouse-Five*, is introduced to Trout's works by Eliot Rosewater, his wardmate in a veterans' hospital near Lake Placid, New York. This was in the spring of 1948. In 1964 or thereabouts, Billy Pilgrim runs into Kilgore Trout in Ilium, New York. Trout has a paranoid face, that of a cracked Messiah, and he looks like a prisoner of war, but he has a saving grace, a deep rich voice. He is, as usual, living friendless and despised in a basement. He is barely making a living as a circulation manager for the *Ilium Gazette*. Cowardly and dangerous, he succeeds in his job only by bullying and cheating the boys who carry the papers. He is astonished and gratified that anyone knows of him. He goes to Pilgrim's engagement party, where he is lionized for the first time in his life.

In 1972, according to *Breakfast of Champions*, Trout is snaggletoothed and has long, tangled, uncombed white hair. He hasn't used a toothbrush for years. His legs are pale, skinny, hairless, and studded with varicose veins. He has sensitive artist's feet, blue from bad circulation. He doesn't wash very often. Vonnegut gives a number of physical statistics about Trout, including the fact that his penis, when erect, is seven inches long but only one and one-fourth of an inch in diameter. Just how he found this out, Vonnegut does not say.

In *God Bless You, Mr. Rosewater*, Mushari, a sinister lawyer (or is the adjective a redundancy?), investigates Trout. He is not interested in him as a literary phenomenon. Trout is Rosewater's favorite author, and Mushari is checking out Trout's works for his dossier on Rosewater. He hopes to prove that Rosewater is mentally incompetent and unable to administrate the millions of the Rosewater Foundation. No reputable bookseller has ever heard of Trout. But he does locate all of Trout's eighty-seven novels, in a tattered secondhand condition, in a hole-in-the-wall which sells the hardest of hardcore pornography. Trout's *2BR02B*, which Eliot thought was his greatest work, was published at twenty-five cents a copy. Now it costs five dollars.

2BR02B has become a collector's item, not because of its literary worth but because of the highly erotic illustrations. This is the fate of many of Trout's books. In *Breakfast of Champions* we find that his best distributed book, *Plague on Wheels*, brings twelve dollars a copy because of its cover art, which depicts fellatio.

The irony of this is that few of Trout's books have any

erotic content. Only one has a major female character, and she was a rabbit (*The Smart Bunny*).

Trout only wrote one purposely "dirty" book in his life, *The Son of Jimmy Valentine*, and he did this because his second wife, Darlene, said that that was the only way for him to make money.

This book did make money but not for Trout. Its publisher, World Classics Library, a hardcore Los Angeles outfit, sent none of the royalties due to Trout. World Classics Library issued many of Trout's books, not because the readers were interested in the texts but because they needed his books to fill out their quota. They illustrated them with art that had nothing whatsoever to do with the story, and they often changed Trout's titles to something more appealing to their peculiar type of reader. *Pan-Galactic Straw-boss*, for instance, was published as *Mouth Crazy*.

Vonnegut says that Trout was cheated by his publishers, but *Breakfast of Champions* reveals that Trout's poverty and obscurity was largely his own fault. He sent his manuscripts to publishers whose addresses he found in magazines whose main market was would-be writers. He never inquired into their reputation or the type of literature they published. Moreover, he frequently sent his stories without a stamped, self-addressed return envelope or without his own address. When he made one of his frequent moves, he never left a forwarding address at the post office. Even if his publishers had wished to deal fairly with him, they could not have located him.

Actually, Trout was a prime example of the highly neurotic writer whose creativity is compulsive and who could care less for the fate of his stories once they'd been set down on paper. He did not even own a copy of any of his own works.

Vonnegut calls Trout a science fiction writer, but he was one only in a special sense. He knew little of science and was indifferent to technical details. Vonnegut claims that most science fiction writers lack a knowledge of science. Perhaps this is so, but Vonnegut, who has a knowledge of science, ignores it in his fiction. Like Trout, he deals in time warps, extrasensory perception, space-flight, robots, and extraterrestrials. The truth is that Trout, like Vonnegut and Ray Bradbury and many others, writes parables. These are set in frames which have become called, for no good reason, science fiction. A better generic term would be "future fairy tales." And even this is objectionable, since many science fiction stories take place in the present or the past, far and near. Anyway, the better writers spend most of their time trying to escape any labels whatsoever.

In fact, there is a lot of Kilgore Trout in science fiction writers, including Vonnegut. If I did not know that Trout was a living person, I'd think he was an archetype plucked by Vonnegut out of his unconscious or the collective unconscious of science fiction writers. He's miserable, he wrestles with concepts and themes that only a genius could pin to the mat (and very few are geniuses), he feels that he is ignored and despised, he knows that the society in which he is forced to live could be a much better one, and, no matter how gregarious he seems to be, he is a loner, a monad. He may be rich and famous (and some science fiction authors are), but he is essentially that person described in the previous sentence. Millions may admire him, but he knows that the universe is totally unconscious of him and that he is a spark fading out in the blackness of eternity and infinity. But he has an untrammeled imagination, and while his spark is still glowing, he can defeat time and space. His stories are his weapons, and, poor as they may be, they are better than none. As Eliot Rosewater says, the mainstream writers, narrators of the mundane, are "sparrowfarts." But the science fiction writer is a god. At least, that is what he secretly believes.

Trout's favorite formula is to describe a hideous society, much like our own, and then, toward the end of the book, outline ways in which the society may be improved. In his *2BR02B*, he shows an America which is so highly cybernated that only people with three or more Ph.D.'s can get jobs. There are also Ethical Suicide Parlors where useless people volunteer for euthanasia. *2BR02B* sounds like a combination of Vonnegut's novel, *Player Piano*, and his short story, "Welcome to the Monkey House." I'm not accusing Vonnegut of plagiarism, but Vonnegut does think highly enough of Trout's plots to borrow some now and then. Trout's *The Big Board* is about a man and a woman abducted and put on display by the extraterrestrials of the planet Zircon-212. Vonnegut's *Slaughterhouse-Five* tells how the Tralfamadorians carried off Billy Pilgrim and the movie star, Montana Wildhack, and put them in a luxurious cage.

It may be that Trout gave Vonnegut permission to adapt some of his plots. At one time Trout lived in Hyannis, Massachusetts, which is very near West Barnstable, where Vonnegut also lived.

Vonnegut admires Trout's ideas, though he condemns his prose. It is atrocious and Trout's unpopularity is deserved.

(By the way, I'd characterize Vonnegut's own prose, and his philosophy, as by Sterne out of Smollett.) A specimen of Trout's prose, taken from *Venus on the Half-Shell*, sounds like that of the typical hack semipornographer's. Most of the science fiction writers, according to Eliot Rosewater, have a style no better than Trout's. But this doesn't matter. Science fiction writers are poets with a sort of radar which detects only the meaningful in this world. They don't write of the trivial; their concerns are the really big issues: galaxies, eternity, and the fate of all of us. And Trout is looking for the answer to the question that so sorely troubles Eliot Rosewater (and many of us). That is, how do you love people who have no use? How do you love the unlovable?

Vonnegut lists Trout's known residences as Bermuda, Dayton, Ohio, Hyannis, Massachusetts, and Ilium and Cohoes of New York. To this I can add Peoria, Illinois. A letter from Kilgore Trout was printed in the vox pop section of the editorial page of the *Peoria Journal Star* in 1971. In this Trout denounced Peoria as essentially obscene. It suggested that the natives quit raising so much hell about dirty movies and books and look in their own hearts for the genuine smut: hate, prejudice, and greed. Trout gave his address as West Main Street. Unfortunately, I no longer have the letter or the address, since I clipped out the letter and sent it to Theodore Sturgeon, who lives in the Los Angeles area. Before doing this, however, I did ascertain that the address was genuine, though Trout no longer lived there. And he had failed, as usual, to leave a forwarding address.

I do have a letter which appeared on the editorial page of the *Peoria Journal Star* of August 14th, 1971. This gives us some information about Trout's activities while he was in Peoria. The letter was signed by a D. Raabe, whom I met briefly after I'd given a lecture at Bradley University. Some extracts of the letter follow.

"...Eminent scatologist, Dr. K. Trout, W.E.A., in an interview outside the public facilities in Glen Oak Park, had some things to say about the Russian-Indian pact... On the subject of internal disorder, Dr. Trout noted that if Indian food becomes a fad in Russia, the Russians may 'loosen up a bit' although they might become a little touchier in certain areas—"

Apparently, Trout had a job with the Peoria Public Works Department at this time, and he claimed to have a doctor's degree. I don't know what the initials stand for, unless it's Watercloset Engineering Assistant, but I suspect that he sent in fifty dollars to an institution of dubious standing and received his diploma through the mails. Despite the degree, he still had a menial and unpleasant job. This was to be expected. One whom the world treats crappily will become an authority on crap. He knows where it's at, and he works where it all hangs out.

Trout's last known job was as an installer of aluminum combination storm windows and screens in Cohoes, New York. At this time (late 1972), Trout was living in a basement. Because of his lack of charm and other social graces, Trout's employer had refused to use him as a salesman. His fellow employees had little to do with him and did not even know that he wrote science fiction. And then one day he received a letter. It was the harbinger of a new life, a prelude to recognition of a writer too long neglected.

Trout had an invitation to be a guest of honor at a festival of arts. This was to celebrate the opening of the Mildred Barry Memorial Center for Arts in Midway Center, Indiana. With the invitation was a check for a thousand dollars. Both the honor and the check were due to Eliot Rosewater. He had agreed to loan his El Greco for exhibit at the Center if Kilgore Trout, possibly the greatest living writer in the world, would be invited.

Overjoyed, though still suspicious, Trout went to New York City to buy some copies of his own books so he could read passages from them at the festival. While there, he was mugged and picked up by the police on suspicion of robbery. He spent Veterans' Day in jail. On being released, he hitchhiked a ride with a truck driver and arrived in Midway Center. There, unfortunately, the joint of his right index finger was bitten off by a madman, and the festival was called off. This made Trout hope that he would never again have to touch, or be touched by, a human being.

Breakfast of Champions is, according to Vonnegut, the last word we'll get from him on Trout. I'm sorry to hear that, but I am also grateful to Mr. Vonnegut for having first brought Trout to the attention of the nonpornography-reading public. I am also sorry that Mr. Vonnegut indulges in sheer fantasy in the last quarter of the book. The first three parts are factual, but the last part might lead some to believe that Kilgore Trout is a fictional character. The serious reader and student of Trout will disregard the final quarter of *Breakfast of Champions* except to sift fact from fantasy.

Though the Midway Center Art Festival was aborted, Kilgore Trout is nevertheless on his way to fame. I've just received word that Mr. David Harris, an editor of Dell Publishing Company, is negotiating for the reprinting of *Venus on the Half-Shell*. If the arrangements are satisfactory to both parties, the general public will have, for the first time, a chance to read a novel by Kilgore Trout.

The following is a list of the known titles of the one-hundred-and-seventeen novels and two thousand short stories written by Trout. It's a tragically short list, and it can only be lengthened if Troutophiles make a diligent search through secondhand bookstores and porno shops for the missing works.

NOVELS

The Gutless Wonder (1932)

2BR02B

Venus on the Half-Shell

Oh Say Can You Smell?

The First District Court of Thankyou

Pan-Galactic Three-Day Pass

Maniacs in the Fourth Dimension (1948)

The Gospel from Outer Space

The Big Board

Pan-Galactic Straw-boss (*Mouth Crazy*)

Plague on Wheels

Now It Can Be Told

The Son of Jimmy Valentine

How You Doin'?

The Smart Bunny

The Pan-Galactic Memory Bank

SHORT STORIES

The Dancing Fool (April 1962 issue of *Black Garterbelt*,
a magazine published by World Classics Library)
This Means You
Gilgongo!
Hail to the Chief
The Baring-gaffner of Bagnialto or This Year's Masterpiece

(Author's Note: Since this was first written, Mr. Vonnegut's novel *Jailbird* has come out. In this Mr. Vonnegut claims that it was not Trout but another man who wrote the works which Vonnegut hitherto had claimed to be Trout's. Nobody believes this disclaimer, but the reasons for it have been the subject of much speculation. Several people have wondered why the initial letter of the surname of the man Mr. Vonnegut claims is the real Trout is also mine. Is Mr. Vonnegut obliquely pointing his finger at me?

I really don't know. In one of many senses, or perhaps two or three, I am Kilgore Trout. But then the same could be said of at least fifty science fiction writers.)

1

THE LEGEND OF THE SPACE WANDERER

Go, traveler.

Go anywhere. The universe is a big place, perhaps the biggest. No matter. Wherever you land, you'll hear of Simon Wagstaff, the Space Wanderer.

Even on planets where he has never appeared, his story is sung in ballads and told in spaceport taverns. Legend and folklore have made him a popular figure throughout the ten billion inhabitable planets, and he is the hero of TV series on at least a million, according to the latest count.

The Space Wanderer is an Earthman who never grows old. He wears Levis and a shabby gray sweater with brown leather elbow patches. On its front is a huge monogram: SW. He has a black patch over his left eye. He always carries an atomic-powered electrical banjo. He has three constant companions: a dog, an owl, and a female robot. He's a sociable gentle creature who never refuses an autograph. His only fault, and it's a terrible one, is that he asks questions no one can answer. At least, he did up to a thousand years ago, when he disappeared.

This is the story of his quest and why he is no longer seen in the known cosmos.

Oh, yes, he also suffers from an old wound in his posterior and thus can't sit down long. Once, he was asked how it felt to be ageless.

He replied, "Immortality is a pain in the ass."

2

IT ALWAYS RAINS ON PICNICS

Making love on a picnic is nothing new. But this was on top of the head of the Sphinx of Giza.

Simon Wagstaff was not enjoying it one hundred percent. Ants, always present at any outdoor picnic anywhere, were climbing up his legs and buttocks. One had even gotten caught where nobody but Simon had any business being. It must have thought it had fallen down between the piston and cylinder of an old-fashioned automobile motor.

Simon was persevering, however. After a while, he and his fiancée rolled over and lay panting and staring up at the Egyptian sky.

"That was good, wasn't it?" Ramona Uhuru said.

"It certainly wasn't run of the mill," Simon said. "Come on. We'd better get our clothes on before some tourists come up here."

Simon stood up and put on his black Levis, baggy gray sweatshirt, and imitation camel-leather sandals. Ramona slid into her scarlet caftan and opened the picnic basket. This was full of goodies, including a bottle of Ethiopian wine: Carbonated Lion of Judah.

Simon thought about telling her about the ant. But if it was still running—or limping—around, she'd be the first to know it.

Simon was a short stocky man of thirty. He had thick curly chestnut hair, pointed ears, thick brown eyebrows, a long straight thin nose, and big brown eyes that looked ready to leak tears. He had thin lips and thick teeth which somehow became a beautiful combination when he smiled.

Ramona was also short and stocky. But she had big black sheep-dog eyes and a voice as soft as a puppy's tail. Like the tail, it seldom quit wagging. This was all right with Simon. If she was a compulsive talker, she made up for it by not being a compulsive listener. Simon was a compulsive questioner but he didn't ask Ramona for answers because he knew she didn't have them. Ramona couldn't be blamed for this. Nobody else could answer them either.

Ramona, talking about something or other, smoothed out the Navajo blanket made in Japan. Ramona had been made in Memphis (Egypt, not Tennessee), though her parents were Balinese and Kenyan.

Simon had been made during his parents' honeymoon in Madagascar. His father was part-Greek, part-Irish Jew, a musical critic who wrote under the name of K. Kane. Everybody thought, with good reason, that the K. stood for Killer. He had married a beautiful Ojibway Indian mezzo-soprano who sang under the name of Minnehaha Langtry. The air-conditioning had broken down on their wedding night, and they attributed

Simon's shortcomings to the inclement conditions in which he had been conceived. Simon attributed them to his eight months in a plastic womb. His mother had not wanted to spoil her figure, so he had been removed from her womb and put in a cylinder connected to a machine. Simon had understood why his mother had done this. But he could not forgive her for later going on an eating jag and gaining sixty pounds. If she was going to become obese anyway, why hadn't she kept him where he belonged?

It was, however, no day for brooding on childhood hurts. The sky was as blue as a baby's veins, and the breeze was air-conditioning the outdoors. To the north, the reconstituted pyramids of Cheops and Chephren testified that the ancient Egyptians had really known how to put it all together. East, across the Nile, the white towers of Cairo with their TV antennas said up-yours to the heavens. But they'd pay that day for their arrogance.

Below him, tourists and visitors from distant planets wandered round among the hot dog, beer, and curio stands. Among them were the giant tripods of Arcturus, sneering at the things that Terrestrials called ancient. Their oldest buildings were one hundred thousand years old, built over ruins twice that age. The Earthmen didn't mind this because Arcturans looked so laughable when they sneered, twirling their long genitals as if they were key-chains. It was when an Arcturan praised that Earthmen became offended. The Arcturan would lift one of his tripods and spray the praisee with a liquid that smelled like rotten onions. A lot of Terrestrials had had to smile and take this, especially ministers of state. But these got what was referred to as a P.O. bonus.

Everything usually evens out.

Or so Simon Wagstaff thought on that fine day.

He picked up the guidebook and read it while drinking the wine. The guidebook said that the sphinx originated with the Egyptians. They thought of it as a creature that had a man's face and a lion's body. On the other hand, the Greeks, once they found out about the sphinx, made it into a creature with a woman's head and lioness' body. She even had women's breasts, lovely white pink-tipped cones that must have distracted men when they should have been thinking about the answer to her question. Oedipus had ignored those obstacles to thought, which maybe didn't say much for Oedipus. He was a little strange, married his mother, killed his father. He had answered the sphinx's question correctly, but that hadn't kept him out of trouble later.

And what about the sphinx's sex life? She hung around on the road to Thebes, Greece, which was a long way from Thebes, Egypt, and from the male sphinxes. Had she been like the female black widow spider and made love to men before she devoured them?

Simon wasn't particularly randy, but like everybody else he thought a lot about sex.

The Egyptian sphinx had massiveness and a vast antiquity. The Greek sphinx had class. The Egyptian was ponderosity and masculinity. The Greek was beauty and femaleness. Leave it to the Greeks to make something philosophical out of the merely physical of the Egyptians. The Greeks had made their sphinx a woman because she knew The Secret.

But she had found somebody who could answer her questions. After which she killed herself.

Simon wasn't in much danger of having to commit suicide. Nobody ever answered his questions.

The guidebook in his hand said that the sphinx's face was supposed to have Pharaoh Chephren's features. The guidebook in his back pocket said that the face was that of the god Harmachis.

It did not matter which had been right. The reconstituted sphinx now bore the features of a famous movie star.

The guidebook in his hand also said that the sphinx was 189 feet long and 72 feet high. The one in his pocket said the sphinx was 172 feet long and 66 feet high. Had one of the measuring teams been drunk? Or had the editor been drunk? Or had the typesetter had financial and marital problems? Or had someone maliciously inserted the wrong information just to screw people up?

Ramona said, "You're not listening!"

"Sorry," Simon said. And he was. This was one of those rare moments when Ramona suddenly became aware that she was talking to herself. She was scared. People who talk to themselves are either insane, deep thinkers, lonely, or all three. She knew she wasn't crazy or a deep thinker, so she must be lonely. And she feared loneliness worse than drowning, which was her pet horror.

Simon was lonely, too, but chiefly because he felt that the universe was being unfair in not giving answers to his questions. But now was not the time to think of himself; Ramona needed comforting.

"Listen, Ramona, here's a love song for you."

It was titled *The Anathematic Mathematics of Love*. This was one of the poems of "Count" Hippolyt Bruga, né Julius Ganz, an early 20th-century expressionist. Ben Hecht had once written a biography of him, but the only surviving copy was in the Vatican archives. Though critics considered Bruga only a minor poet, Simon loved him best of all and had composed music for many of his works.

First, though, Simon thought he should explain the references and the situation since she didn't read anything but *True Confessions* and best sellers.

"Robert Browning was a great Victorian poet who married the minor poet Elizabeth Barrett," he said.

"I know that," Ramona said. "I'm not as dumb as you think I am. I saw *The Barretts of Wimpole Street* on TV last year. With Peck Burton and Marilyn Mamri. It was so sad; her father was a real bastard. He killed her pet dog just because Elizabeth ran off with Browning. Old Barrett had eyes for his own daughter, would you believe it? Well, she didn't actually run off. She was paralyzed from the waist down, and Peck, I mean Browning, had to push her wheelchair through the streets of London while her father tried to run them down with a horse and buggy. It was the most exciting chase scene I've ever seen."

"I'll bet," Simon said. "So you know about them. Anyway, Elizabeth wrote a series of love poems to Browning, *Sonnets from the Portuguese*. He called her his Portuguese because she was so dark."

"How sweet!"

"Yes. Anyway, the most famous sonnet is the one in which she enumerates the varieties of love she has for him. This inspired

Bruga's poem, though he didn't set it in sonnet form."

Simon sang:

"How do I love thee? Let me figure
The ways," said Liz. But mental additions
Subtracted from Bob Browning's emissions,
Dividing the needed vigor to frig her.

Here's what he said to the Portuguese
In order to part her deadened knees

"Accounting's not the thing that counts.
A plus, a minus, you can shove!
Oh woman below and man above!
It's this inspires the mounts and founts!

"To hell with Euclid's beauty bare!
Liz, get your ass out of that chair!"

"Those were Bruga's last words," Simon said. "He was beaten to death a minute later by an enraged wino."

"I don't blame him," Ramona murmured.

"Bruga only did his best work when he was paid on the spot for his instant poetry," Simon said. "But in this case he was improvising free. He'd invited this penniless bum up to his Greenwich Village apartment to have a few gallons of muscatel with him and his mistress. And see the thanks he got."

"Everybody's a critic," Ramona said.

Simon winced. She said, "What's the matter?"

He plucked the banjo as if it were a chicken and sang:

> *"Why does* critic *give me a pain?*
> *Father's name was Killer Kane."*

Feathers of sadness fluttered about them. Ramona cackled as if she had just laid an egg. It was, however, nervousness, not joy, that she proclaimed. She always got edgy when he slid into a melancholy mood.

"It's such a glorious day," she said. "How can you be sad when the sun is shining? You're spoiling the picnic."

"Sorry," he said. "My sun is black. But you're right. We're lovers, and lovers should make each other happy. Here's an old Arabian love song:

> *"Love is heavy. My soul is sighing...*
> *What wing brushes both of us, dearest,*
> *In the sick and soundless air?"*

It was then that Ramona became aware that his mood came more from the outside than the inside. The breeze had died, and silence as thick and as heavy as the nativity of a mushroom in a diamond mine, or as gas passed during a prayer meeting, had fallen everywhere. The sky was clotted with clouds as black as rotten spots on a banana. Yet, only a minute before, the horizon had been as unbroken as a fake genealogy.

Simon got to his feet and put his banjo in its case. Ramona

busied herself with putting plates and cups in the basket. "You can't depend on anything," she said, close to tears. "It never, just never, rains here in the dry season."

"How'd those clouds get here without a wind?" Simon said.

As usual, his question was not answered.

Ramona had just folded up the blanket when the first raindrops fell. The two started across the top of the sphinx's head toward the steps but never got to them. The drops became a solid body of water, as if the whole sky were a big decanter that some giant drunk had accidentally tipped over. They were knocked down, and the basket was torn from Ramona's hands and sent floating over the side of the head. Ramona almost went, too, but Simon grabbed her hand and they crawled to the guard fence at the rim of the head and gripped an upright bar.

Later, Simon could recall almost nothing vividly. It was one long blur of numbed horror, of brutal heaviness of the rain, cold, teeth chattering, hands aching from squeezing the iron bar, increasing darkness, a sudden influx of people who'd fled the ground below, a vague wondering why they'd crowded onto the top of the sphinx's head, a terrifying realization of why when a sea rolled over him, his panicked rearing upward to keep from drowning, his loosing of the bar because the water had risen to his nose, a single muffled cry from Ramona, somewhere in the smash and flurry, and then he was swimming with nowhere to go.

The case with the banjo in it floated before him. He grabbed it. It provided some buoyancy, and after he'd shucked all his clothing, he could stay afloat by hanging onto it and treading water. Once, a camel swam by him with five men battling to get onto its back. Then it went under, and the last he saw of it was one rolling eye.

Sometime later, he drifted by the tip of the Great Pyramid. Clinging to it was a woman who screamed until the rising water filled her mouth. Simon floated on by, vainly trying to comprehend that somehow so much rain had fallen that the arid land of Egypt was now over 472 feet beneath him.

And then there came the time in the darkness of night and the still almost-solid rain when he prepared to give up his waterlogged ghost and let himself sink. He was too exhausted to fight anymore, it was all over, down the drain for him.

Simon was an atheist, but he prayed to Jahweh, his father's god, Mary, his grandmother's favorite deity, and Gitche Manitou, his mother's god. It couldn't hurt.

Before he was done, he bumped into something solid. Something that was also hollow, since it boomed like a drum beneath the blows of the rain.

A few seconds afterward, the booming stopped. He was so numb that it was some time before he understood that this was because the rain had also stopped.

He groped around the object. It was coffin-shaped but far too large to be a coffin unless a dead elephant was in it. Its top was slick, and about eight inches above water. He lifted the banjo case and shoved it inward. The object dipped a little under his weight, but by placing the flats of his palms on it, he got enough friction to pull himself slowly onto the flat surface and then onto its center.

He lay there panting, face down, too cold and miserable to

sleep. Despite which, he went to sleep, though his dreams were not pleasant. But then they seldom were.

When he awoke, he looked at his watch. It was 07:08. He had slept at least twelve hours, though it hadn't been refreshing. Then, feeling warm on one side, he turned over slowly. A dog was snuggled up against him. After a while, the dog opened one eye. Simon patted it and lay back face down, his arm around it. He was hungry, which made him wonder if he wouldn't end up having to eat the dog. Or vice versa. It was a mongrel weighing about sixty pounds to his one hundred and forty. It was probably stronger than he, and bound to be very hungry. Dogs were always hungry.

He fell asleep again and when he awoke it was night again. The dog was up, a dim yellow-brown, long-muzzled shape walking stiffly around as if it had arthritis. Simon called it to him because he didn't want it upsetting the delicate balance. It came to him and licked his face, though whether from a need for affection or a desire to find out how he tasted, Simon did not know. Eventually, he fell asleep, waking as stiff as a piece of driftwood (or a bone long buried by a dog). But he was warm. The clouds were gone, the sun was up, and the water on the surface of the object had dried off.

For the first time, he could see it, though he still did not know what it was. It was about ten feet long and seven wide and had a transparent plastic cover.

He looked straight down into the face of a dead man.

THE *HWANG HO*

Simon knew now that he was on top of one of the plastic showcases in which mummies of ancient Pharaohs were displayed in a Cairo museum. Airtight, it had floated up out of the building.

Simon pushed the protesting dog back into the sea and then lowered himself over the edge alongside the animal. He had a hard time raising the lid and sliding it into the water, but he finally succeeded. Then he crawled back over the edge and let himself, and some water, into the case. Standing on the edge of the open coffin on the case's floor, he hauled the dog in. The dog sniffed at the mummy and began howling.

After many thousands of years of neglect, the mummy had a mourner.

Simon got down onto the floor and stared at the falcon face of an ex-ruler of Upper and Lower Egypt. The skin was as tight as a senator from Kentucky and as dry as a government report. Time had sucked out, along with the vital juices, the flesh beneath the skin. But the bones had kept their arrogance.

Simon looked around the case and found a placard screwed into the side. He couldn't read it because it was facing outward. On the other side of the coffin, on the floor, he found a screwdriver, a dried-up condom, a pair of panties, and a cheese-and-salami sandwich wrapped in tinfoil. Evidently, some museum worker had had an assignation behind the coffin. Or perhaps the night watchman had brought in a woman to while away the lonely hours. In either case, someone had disturbed them, and they had taken off, leaving behind them the clues he had put together *à la* Sherlock Holmes.

Simon blessed them and opened the wrapper. The bread, cheese, and salami were cardboard-hard, but they were edible. He broke the sandwich in half, gave one piece to the dog and gnawed away gratefully at his. The dog, after gulping down his half, looked at Simon's sandwich and growled. Simon thought he was going to have trouble with him until he understood that it was the dog's belly, not his throat, which was growling.

He patted him and said, "You like old bones? You can eat away. But not now."

Using the screwdriver, he removed the placard. It bore this legend:

MERNEPTAH
Pharaoh from 1236 B.C. to 1223 B.C.
Thirteenth son of Rameses II.
He gave Moses a hard time.

Moses and history had, in turn, given Merneptah a hard time. Everybody considered him to be a villain. When they read in the Bible that he'd been drowned in the Red Sea while chasing the refugee Hebrews, they thought, "Drowning was too good for him." But this story was a myth. Merneptah, at age sixty-two, had died miserably of arthritis, plugged arteries, and bad teeth. As if this and an evil reputation hadn't done enough to him, the undertakers had removed his testicles and tomb robbers had hacked his body, incidentally removing the right arm.

"You're still useful, old man," Simon said. He tore off the wrappings and then the penis and threw it to the dog. The dog caught it before it hit the floor and swallowed it. So much for the mighty phallus that had impregnated hundreds of women, Simon thought. Just so the resin-soaked flesh doesn't give the dog a stomachache.

Meanwhile he wished that he had something more to eat. His belly was growling like a truck going up a steep grade. If he couldn't somehow catch some fish, he was going to starve. And then the dog would be eating him.

Since he had nothing else to do, he decided to think about giving the dog a name. After rejecting Spot, Fido, and Rover, he chose Anubis. Anubis was the jackal-headed Egyptian god who conducted the souls of the dead into the afterworld. A jackal was a sort of dog. And this dog, if not a conductor, was certainly a fellow passenger in this queer boat that was taking them to an unknown but inevitable death.

Whatever the dog's old name, he responded to the new one. He licked Simon's hand and looked up with eyes as big, brown, and soft as Ramona's. Simon patted his head. It was nice to have someone who liked him and would keep him from feeling utterly alone. Of course, this, like everything, had its disadvantageous side. He was expected to provide for Anubis.

Simon got up and ripped off the Pharaoh's right leg. For a moment, he was tempted to chew on it himself, but he didn't have the teeth or the stomach for it. He threw it to Anubis, who retreated to a corner and began gnawing on it voraciously. A few hours later he had a violent attack of diarrhea which stank, among other things, of resin. Simon got up on the coffin and leaned out over the edge of the case to get fresh air. At the same time, he saw the owl.

Simon yelped with joy. Since owls lived in trees, and trees grew only on land, land couldn't be far away. He watched the big bird turn and fly northward until it had disappeared. That way was salvation. But how to get there?

When dusk came, with no land in sight, he prepared despondently for bed. He heaved Merneptah out into the several inches of water on the floor and stretched out on the coffin. When he awoke with the sun in his eyes, he was even weaker and hungrier. He wasn't thirsty, since the sea water was diluted enough with rain to be potable. But water has no calories.

He looked over the side of the coffin. The Pharaoh was a mess. Anubis had chewed him up, leathery skin, bone, and all. But the Pharaoh, that inveterate traveler, had made another passage. Anubis lay in the corner, sopping wet and sick. Simon felt sorry for him but could do nothing for him. As it was, he had to stick his head over the edge of the case to keep from dying of the stench before he died of starvation.

A few hours later, while he was thinking of voluntarily dying by drowning, he saw something to the northwest. As the day passed, this slowly became larger. Just as the sun slid into the waters, he saw that it was not, as he had hoped, land. It was a submarine or something that looked like a submarine. But it was too far away for him to hope to swim to it.

Dawn found him awake, looking northwest, hoping that the sub had not gone away during the night. No. It had drifted on the same collision course during the night. And it was close enough so he could see that it was a spaceship, not a submarine. On its side were two big Chinese ideograms and underneath them, in Roman letters: *Hwang Ho*. Since it wasn't proceeding under power, it must be crewless. It had been sitting on some spaceport field somewhere, and when the rains came, its crew hadn't been able to take refuge in it. They had probably drowned while roistering in the tavern or in bed with a friend or friends.

Its ports were closed, but it was no problem to open one. There'd be a plate by the port which only had to be depressed to make the port open.

More hours passed. By then Simon saw that the case was not going to bump into the ship. He shoved the heavy wooden coffin to the wall of the case, causing it to tilt and to ship water. Simon's weight made it lean even more, and Simon went into the sea. Anubis didn't want to leave the case, but he had no choice. Simon swam to the nearest port and pushed in on the plate. The port sank back and then swung aside. He put the banjo case inside, reached up, grabbed the threshold, and pulled himself in.

After hoisting Anubis inside, he stood up shakily and watched the swirl which marked the sinking of the case until the surface was smooth again.

"Just think," Simon said to Anubis. "If old Merneptah had really been drowned in the Red Sea, and his body had been lost, there would have been no case for him in the museum, and you and I would have drowned several days ago. Kind of makes you wonder if it was destined or we're just lucky, doesn't it?"

Simon thought a lot about predeterminism and free will.

Anubis thought mainly about food, unless it was mating season, and so he didn't even wait for Simon to quit talking. He trotted into the ship, and Simon's belly, which also could not digest philosophy, urged him to follow the dog. He explored the ship, finding it empty of life, as he'd expected. But it was well stocked with food and drink, and that was all he cared about for the moment. Since he didn't want to throw up, he forced himself to eat lightly. Anubis resented being fed small portions, but there wasn't much he could do about it except look reproachful.

"More later," Simon said. "Much more. And it sure beats eating dried-up old Pharaoh, doesn't it?"

His next step was to search through the lockers and find clothes that fitted him. Once more, he was clad in a baggy gray sweatshirt, black tight-fitting Levis, and sandals.

When he returned to the room by the still open port the owl was sitting on the back of a chair.

"Who?" it said.

"Not who? Why?" Simon replied.

The question of where the owl had come from was still

unsettled, but Simon thought it likely that it had been riding on top of the spaceship. It must be hungry, too, so Simon prepared some egg foo young for it. When he came back to the room with the food, the owl was sitting on a pile of torn-up papers on the seat of the chair. Simon put the plate on the floor before it. It flew down to grab the food, enabling Simon to determine its sex. It—she—had just laid an egg.

Anubis leaped up onto the chair and swallowed the egg. The owl didn't seem to mind, which made Simon think that the catastrophe had bent its mother instincts out of shape. That was just as well, otherwise the two animals might have gotten off on the wrong foot in their relationship.

Simon decided to name his new pet Athena. Athena was the Greek goddess of wisdom, and her symbol was the owl. Owls were supposed to be highly intelligent, though actually they were as dumb as chickens. But Simon was mythology-prone, which was only to be expected from a man who'd named his banjo Orpheus.

He examined the instruments in the control room, since he had heard that even a moron could navigate a spaceship. However, in this case, it had to be a Chinese moron. But if there was a book aboard which could teach him Chinese, he'd figure out how to fly this computerized vessel. He had already made up his mind to leave Earth for good. There was nothing here to hold him.

In later years, during his wanderings, he would often be asked what had happened to his native planet.

"Earth is all washed up," he would reply. "The game of life there was called off on account of rain."

The big question at the moment was: who had done this to Earth? Somebody had caused this deluge. It would never have occurred in the normal course of Terrestrial events. Somebody had pushed a button which activated a machine or chemicals which had precipitated one hundred percent of the water in the atmospheric ocean.

Who and why?

Was it the gone-wrong experiment of some mad scientist? Or had some planet whose business was being ruined by Earth triggered off this flood? Or was it simply because Earthmen smelled so badly? Terrestrials had a reputation as the most odoriferous race in the universe. A million planets referred to them as The Stinkers. There was an old Arcturan saying that exemplified this attitude. "Never stand downwind of a *shrook* or an Earthman." A *shrook* was a little beast on Arcturus VI that exuded the combined scents of a skunk, a bombardier beetle, and dog farts with a touch of garbage heap.

Some extraterrestrials claimed that it was the Earthman's diet, which consisted mainly of hot dogs, potato chips, soft drinks, and beer, even among the Chinese, that caused this offensive odor. But the octopoids of Algol, perhaps the most philosophical of all races, contended that it wasn't the food that caused the bad smell. Psychology affected physiology. Earthmen stank because their ethics stank.

This reaction had upset Terrestrials, but they'd gone about solving this problem with their usual vicious efficiency. A huge perfume industry, employing millions, had been created, and travelers from Earth had always perfumed themselves just before they disembarked on an alien planet. These were specialized, since the perfume that pleased the Spicans would offend the Vegans. The only planet where perfumes were taboo was Sirius VII. The caninoids there identified each other by sniffing assholes, and so they strictly forbade the use of perfumes. The Earthmen had to go along with this custom, otherwise they'd never get to first base in selling Terrestrial goods. They tried to get around this by sending agents who had no sense of smell, but this didn't work out. All Sirians looked exactly alike, and they refused to carry nametags. Thus, an Earthman didn't know whom he was dealing with unless he had a keen nose.

This demand opened a whole new field to specialists who were paid huge bonuses. These had to earn a new degree, Ph.D.A., before they could be hired. Despite the fabulous salaries, there was a big turnover in this field, suicide being the chief cause of resignation. Then a bright young executive in the PR department got the idea of running a search through a computer for a particular type of fetishist. This revealed that there were over five hundred thousand masochists on Earth who liked to torture themselves with offensive odors. Of these, there were fifty thousand who specialized in dog crap. The Sirian Trading Corporation only needed twelve thousand, so suddenly the field became a monopoly of this handful. The doctor of philosophy of anumology was no longer required. Furthermore, since these were eager to work on Sirius, they underbid each other, and the STC was hiring them for slave wages.

This same bright young executive later was inspired with the idea which rid Earth of all perverts. Somewhere in this universe was a planet where a particular Terrestrial perversion was regarded as not only normal but highly desirable. He ran another search through the computer, and soon the STC was advertising for fetishists, masochists, sadists, child-beaters, racists, professional soldiers, drug-addicts, alcoholics, gun-lovers, motorcyclists, pet-lovers, exhibitionists, religious fanatics, members of the WCTU, and science-fiction fans. The salaries and the prestige offered were so high that a number of non-perverts tried to sign up. These were carefully screened out, however, with a battery of psychological tests. Those who passed were trained in a business college run by STC. This became the most powerful business on Earth due to its expansion to other planets than Sirius.

Earth was cleared of perverts, and everybody left looked forward to a golden age. But in twenty years Earth had just as many perverts as ever. This caused an uproar, and the governments of every nation set up investigative agencies. Their reports were never published, since they indicated that the system of child-raising was responsible. The voters just would not stand for this item of information. And so Earth quietly returned to normal, that is, it was once again full of perverts.

STC hadn't cared. It wasn't going to run out of competent and dedicated employees.

Simon wondered if this export of non-desirables had offended some planet which had decided to clean up the origin of offense. Perhaps he would find out some day, but he could only do this if he learned how to operate the spaceship. This was possible, since he'd found a book which taught Chinese speakers how to read and write English. By reversing the order of instructions, he could learn to read Chinese.

Days passed. The ship drifted with the current. When storms came, he closed the port and rode them out. And then, one day, while he was studying at the control panel in the bridge, he felt a jar run through the ship. He turned on the exterior-view TV and saw what he had hoped for. The nose of the *Hwang Ho* was stuck in the mud of the shore of a big bay. In front of it was the slope of a mountain.

Simon went out with the dog and the owl next day and looked around. Contrary to what he had first thought, they were not on a mountain but on a saddle between two peaks.

Simon walked up the slope of the nearest mountain.

Halfway up, he came across a stone tablet lying on its face, half-buried in mud that had carried it down from a higher level. He heaved it upright and read the inscription on its face.

ON SEPT. 27, 1829, J. J. VON PARROT, A GERMAN CITIZEN, BECAME THE FIRST MAN TO CLIMB TO THE TOP OF MOUNT ARARAT, 16,945 FEET ABOVE SEA LEVEL. HE DID NOT FIND THE ARK, BUT HE ENJOYED THE VIEW WHILE EATINC A SALAMI SANDWICH. THIS WAS 58 YEARS BEFORE "THE PAUSE THAT REFRESHES."

Courtesy of Coca Cola Co.

Simon had arrived in his ark at the same place where Noah was supposed to have landed. This was a coincidence that could only happen in a bad novel, but Nature didn't give a damn about literary esthetics. The grasshopper voices of thousands of critics had shrilled at Her and then died while She went right on ahead writing Her stories, none of which had a happy ending.

Simon didn't now believe in the Biblical account of the flood. But as a child he'd taken it seriously. When he went to high school, however, he began to have his doubts. So he'd gone to a nice old rabbi named Isaac Apfelbaum and had asked him why the book of Genesis told such bare-faced lies as the stories of the Garden of Eden, angels knocking up the daughters of men, the flood, the tower of Babel, etc.

The rabbi had sighed and then had patiently explained that the holy scriptures of any people were not meant to be scientific textbooks. They were parables to teach people how to be good-hearted and how to stay within certain limits of behavior so life would go as smoothly as possible. They were, in effect, guidebooks to heaven on earth and, hopefully, to the afterworld. Wise old men had worked out the guidelines as the best way to stay out of trouble.

"None of them were written by wise old women?" Simon had said. "Why? Do men have a monopoly on truth?"

"You forget Mary Baker Eddy," the rabbi had said.

"She was in ill health all her life," Simon said. "Can a sick person truly be wise?"

The rabbi ignored that. He wasn't keen on pumping the competition, anyway.

"And how come the guidebooks are all different?" Simon had said. He was thinking of that question now as he stared around at Mount Ararat. He was also thinking of the guidebooks he'd picked up just before the picnic. If men couldn't agree on the measurements of the Sphinx, a finite physical object, how could they ever blueprint heaven? If heaven existed, that is. Simon hadn't said so to the rabbi, but he thought there was as much justification in believing in the Yellow Brick Road as in the Pearly Gates.

"The guidebooks just send you down different paths," the rabbi had said. "But the end result is the same. All roads lead to Rome."

The rabbi had shut up then. If he kept on, he'd be converting the kid to Catholicism.

Simon looked at the writings that post-Parrot climbers had felt impelled to scratch on the tablet. Some wag had scratched below the bottom line of the inscription: I WUZ HERE FURST. NOAH.

Another wag had scratched below that: NO, I WAS HERE FIRST, YOU ILLITERATE BASTARD. GOD.

On the side, running vertically, was a later inscription: GRAFFITI WRITERS SUCK.

Running alongside that was a later one: O.K. I'LL MEET YOU IN THE MEN'S ROOM, UN BUILDING LOBBY.

On the other side of the main text, also running vertically, was: DOESN'T ANYBODY LOVE ANYBODY?

Under that Simon scratched with his screwdriver: I DO, BUT THERE'S NOBODY LEFT TO LOVE.

After he'd done it, he felt ridiculous. He also felt like crying. He was the last of the fools whose names and faces oft appear in public places. What a last will and testament! Who, besides himself, the lone survivor, was around to read it?

A moment later, he found out.

4

WHAT'S THE SCORE?

The old man that staggered babbling toward him looked as if he was a hundred years old. His head was bald, and he had a long gray beard that fell to his knees. His clothes were of a style that had gone out of fashion over six hundred years ago. The old man wasn't even born then. So why was he wearing yellow kid gloves, a white ruff, and a coat too tight in the waist?

Simon conducted the old man into the *Hwang Ho*. He sat him down in an easy chair and gave him a glass of rice wine. The old man drank it all at once, and then, holding Simon with a skinny hand, he spoke.

"Who won the series?"

"What?" Simon said. "What series?"

"The World Series of 2457," the old man said. "Was it the St Louis Cardinals or the Tokyo Tigers?"

"For God's sake, how would I know?" Simon said.

The old man groaned and poured himself another glass of wine. He smelled it, wrinkled his nose, and said, "You got any beer?"

"Just German beer," Simon said.

"That'll have to do," the old man said. "Oh, how I've longed all these centuries for a cold glass of American beer. Especially good old St Louis-brewed beer!"

Simon went into the pantry for the only bottle of Lowenbrau left. This must have been the property of the sole German sailor aboard. By his bunk were portraits of Beethoven, Bismarck, Hitler (after a millennium a romantic hero), and Otto Munchkin, the first man to die in a Volkswagen. The sailor also had a small library, mostly Chinese or German books. Simon had been intrigued by the title of one, *Die Fahrt der Snark*, but it turned out not to be a commentary on Lewis Carroll's digestive problems after all. It was all about a journey some early 20th-century writer named Jack London had made to the South Seas. London had later on committed suicide when the people he loved and trusted gave him the shaft.

Simon returned to the old man and handed him the beer.

"Do you remember now?" the ancient said.

"Remember what?"

"Who won the series?"

"I never cared for baseball," Simon said. "You *are* talking about baseball, aren't you?"

"I thought you were an American?"

"There are no nationalities anymore," Simon said. "Just Earth people, an endangered species. What's your name?"

"Silas T. Comberbacke, Spaceman First Class," the old man said. He drank deeply and sighed with ecstasy. But he said, "Those Germans never did learn to make good beer."

Once Comberbacke's mind was off baseball, he talked as if he hadn't seen a human being in six hundred years. Which was true. He'd left Earth in A.D. 2457 because his fiancée had run off with a hairdresser.

"Which gives you some idea of her basic personality," old Comberbacke said. "Jesus, he knew nothing about baseball!"

One day, while drinking in a bar on a planet in Galaxy NGC 7217, Comberbacke suddenly decided to go home and find out who won the 2457 series. He'd been asking other spacemen for years, but even the aficionados didn't know. They were all too young to remember that far back. So, on impulse, he'd signed up as a S1C on a Ugandan freighter and was headed directly home—he thought. On the way, though, the ship had received a Mayday from a planet in NGC 5128.

"NGC 5128 is actually a collision between two galaxies, you know," he said. "It's been colliding for a couple of million years, but the spaces between the suns are so big that most of the people on the planets there thought they didn't have anything to worry about. But this planet, Rexroxy, was going to be hit in a thousand years. So they were getting everybody off. Actually, that Mayday had been transmitting for five hundred years. We landed on Rexroxy and made a deal with the locals. We dumped our cargo and crammed about three thousand aboard. They paid plenty for that, believe it!

"The captain was going to head out for a planet of a star near Orion and dump his passengers there. But he needed to send a message quick to his home office. I volunteered to take it in a one-man ship. I wasn't going to lose a month taking those funny-looking cyanide-breathers for a ride. I got here two days ago, parked my ship on the other side of the mountain, and walked around trying to find someone who could tell me what the score was."

"I was hoping you'd know what caused this rain," Simon said.

"Oh, I do! I meant, who won the series? The day I left, the Cardinals and the Tigers were tied. Dammit, if I hadn't been so mad at Alma, I'd have stayed until it was over."

"I know my question is trivial," Simon said. "But what *did* happen to make it rain so hard?"

"Don't get so mad," the old spacer said. "If you'd seen as many wrecked worlds as I have and as many about to be wrecked, you wouldn't take it so personal."

Comberbacke finished his bottle and drummed his fingers on the arm of the chair. Finally, Simon said, "Well, what did happen?"

"Well, it must of been them Hoonhors!"

"What's a Hoonhor?"

"Jesus, kid, you don't know nothing, do you?" Comberbacke said. "They're the race that's been cleaning up the universe!"

Simon sighed and patiently asked him to back up and start at the beginning. The Hoonhors, he found, were a people from a planet of some unknown galaxy a trillion lightyears away. They were possibly the most altruistic species in the universe. They had done very well for themselves and now they were out doing for others.

"One thing they can't stand is seeing a people kill off their own planet. You know, pollution. So they've been locating these, and when they do, they clean it up.

"They've sanitized, that's what they call it, sanitizing, they've sanitized maybe a thousand planets so far in the Milky Way alone. Haven't you *really* ever heard of them?"

"I think if anybody on Earth had, we'd all have heard of them," Simon said.

Comberbacke shook his head and said, "If I'd of known that Earth hadn't, I would of hurried home and warned everybody. But space is big, and I didn't think the Hoonhors would get around to Earth for a thousand years or so. Plenty of time, I thought."

Comberbacke knew that it was the Hoonhors who had caused the Second Deluge. He'd seen one of their ships heading out when he went past the orbit of Pluto on his way in.

"What they do, they release into a planet's atmosphere a substance that precipitates every bit of H_2O in the air. You wouldn't believe the downpour!"

"Yes, I would," Simon said.

"Yeah, I guess you would. Say, are you sure you don't have any more beer? No? Well, the precipitation cleans the air and the land and drowns almost everybody. After the water has evaporated, the trees start growing again from seeds, and there's always a few birds and animals left up in the mountains to renew the animal life. There's always a few sentients left, too, but it takes them a long time to breed to the point where they again start polluting their planet. The Hoonhors schedule the planets they've drowned for a regular sanitizing every ten thousand years. Actually, though, they're short-handed, and they might not come back for fifty thousand or so years."

The old man had spent much of his time while away from Earth traveling in ships which went faster than the speed of light. This explained why he hadn't died and become dust six hundred Earth-years ago. People in ships going at lightspeeds, or faster, aged very slowly. Everything inside the ship was slowed down. To an observer outside the ship, a passenger would take a month just to open his mouth to ask somebody to please pass the sugar. An orgasm would last a year, which was one of the things the passenger liners stressed in their advertising.

What the PR departments didn't explain was that the people in the ship thought they were moving at normal speed. Their subjective senses told them they were living according to time as they knew it. When a passenger complained about false advertising because he'd really only taken four or five seconds to come, the captain would reply that that was true in the ship. But back on Earth, by the clocks the company kept in headquarters, the passenger had taken four hundred days.

If the passenger still bitched, the captain said it was Einstein's fault. He was the one who'd thought up the theory of relativity.

The old man got drunk and passed out. Simon put him to bed and took the dog for a walk. The breeze, which came from the south, was thick and sticky with the odor of rotting bodies. As the water had evaporated, it had left bodies of animals, birds, and humans along the slope of the mountain. This made the few surviving vultures and rats happy, which goes to show that the old proverb about an ill wind is true. But the wind almost gagged

Simon. He couldn't hang around here much longer unless he shut himself up in the ship and waited for the rotting meat to be eaten up.

Simon looked down from the cliff on the bodies of hundreds of men, women, and children, and he wept.

All of them had once been babies who needed and wanted love and who thought that they would be immortal. Even the worst of them longed for love and would have been the better for it if he or she had been able to find it. But the more they grabbed for it, the more unlovable they had become. Even the lovable find it hard to get love, so what chance did the unlovable have?

The human species had been trying for a million years to find love and immortality. They had talked a lot about both, but humankind always talked most about those things which did not exist. Or, if they did, were so rare that almost nobody recognized them when they saw them. Love was rare, and immortality was only a thing hoped-for, unproven, and unprovable.

At least, it was so on Earth.

A little while later, he stood up and shook his fist at the sky.

And this was when he decided to leave Earth and start asking the primal question.

Why are we created only to suffer and to die?

5

THE BOOJUM OF SPACE

Simon explored the area on foot. He found the one-man spaceship where Comberbacke had left it. It had been built by the Titanic & Icarus Spaceship Company, Inc., which didn't inspire confidence in Simon. After looking it over, however, he decided to fly it back to the *Hwang Ho*. He would store it in the big dock area in the ship's stern. He could use it for a shuttle or a lifeboat during his voyages through interstellar space.

When he got back to the big ship, he discovered that the old man was gone. Simon set out on foot again. After he had walked down the muddy slope, he found Comberbacke rooting around among the ruins of a village. The old man looked up when he heard Simon's feet pulling out of the mud with a sucking sound.

"Even an Armenian village must have a library," he said. "Nobody's illiterate anymore. So there must be a book that gives the scores of the World Series."

"Is that all it'll take to make you happy?"

The old man thought a minute, then said, "No. If I could

get a hard-on, I'd be a lot happier. But what good would that do? There ain't a woman in sight."

"I was thinking more of somebody who'd be a companion for you and maybe a nurse, too."

"Find somebody who likes baseball," Comberbacke said.

Simon went away shaking his head. In the next few weeks he went over every inch of Great and Little Ararat, but the only humans he found were dead. The last day of his search, he started back to the ship with the idea of flying it around until he located land on which were some survivors. He'd make sure they'd take care of the old man, and then he'd leave for interstellar space.

It was dusk when he got to the ship. It lay broadside to him and, as usual, the sight of it disturbed him. He could never put his mental finger on the reason. It was about six hundred feet long, its main length cylindrical-shaped. The nose, however, was bulbous, and its stern rested on two hemispheres. These housed the engines which drove the *Hwang Ho*. They were separate from the ship so they could be released if the engines threatened to blow up.

Light streamed out from the main sideport, which had been left open. Simon was exasperated when he saw this. He had told the old man to keep it shut at night. The mosquitoes were fierce now that spring was here. Somehow, the deluge had not killed them all off, and they were multiplying by the billions since most of their natural enemies, the bats and the birds, were dead. He hurried into the ship and closed the port after him. He called out the old man's name. Comberbacke did not reply. Simon went to the recreation room and found the old man dead in a chair. The side of his head was blown off. A Chinese pistol lay on his lap. On the table before him was a mud-and-water-stained book, its open pages streaked with water. But it wasn't rain that had fallen on these pages. The marks were from tears.

The book was the *Encyclopedia Terrica*, Volume IX, Barracuda-Bay Rum.

There was no farewell note from Comberbacke, but Simon read under *Baseball, World Series*, all he needed to know. The 2457 Series had ended in a scandal. In the middle of the final game, Cardinals 3-Tigers 4, police officers had arrested five St Louis men. The commissioner had just been given proof that they had taken money from gamblers to throw the Series. The Tokyo Tigers won by default, and the five men had been given the maximum sentences.

Simon buried the old man and erected the von Parrot marker over him. On the backside of the stone, which he turned frontside, he scratched these letters:

SILAS T. COMBERBACKE

2432–3069

Spaceman & Baseball Fan

This stone conceals a Cardinal sin.
A glut of centuries passed before
He learned about that fateful inning.
How good if he'd continued chinning
On Space's bar! His hero a whore,
He cared no more for the stadium's din.
It's better not to know the score.

That last line was good advice, but Simon wasn't taking it.

He went into the *Hwang Ho*, closed the port, and seated himself before the control panel in the bridge. The stellar maps were stored in the computer circuits. If Simon wanted to go to the sixth Planet of 61 Cygni A, for instance, he had only to press the right keys. The rest was up to the computer.

Just as a joke—though who knew what knowledge lurked in its heart?—he asked the ship to take him to Heaven.

To his surprise the computer screen flashed the Chinese equivalent of "O.K." There was a two-minute pause while the computer checked that everything was shipshape. Then it swung up off the ground, tilted upright, and climbed up toward the sky.

Simon didn't feel the change in the ship's attitude. An artificial gravity field adjusted for that.

Simon's attitude of mind changed, however. He frantically punched the keys.

"Where are you taking me?"

"To Heaven, as directed."

"Where is Heaven?"

"Heaven is the second planet of Beta Orionis. It is a T-type planet which was uninhabited by sentients until a Terrestrial expedition landed there in A.D. 2879 on first..."

Simon canceled the order.

"Take me to some unexplored galaxy, and we'll play it by ear from there," Simon typed.

A few seconds later they were off into the black unknown. The ship was capable of attaining 69,000 times the speed of light but Simon held it down to 20,000 times, or 20X. The drive itself was named the soixante-neuf drive, because this meant sixty-nine in French. It had been invented in A.D. 2970 by a Frenchman whose exact name Simon didn't recall. Either it was Pierre le Chanceux or Pierre le Chancreux, he wasn't sure which, since he'd not made a study of space history.

When the first ship equipped with the drive, the *Golden Goose*, had been revved up to top speed, those aboard had been frightened by a high screaming noise. This had started out as a murmur at about 20,000 times the speed of light. As the ship accelerated, the sound became louder and higher. At 69X, the ship was filled with the kind of noise you hear when a woman with a narrow pelvis is giving birth or a man has been kicked in the balls. There were many theories about where this screaming came from. Then, in 2980, Dr. Maloney, a brilliant man when sober, solved the mystery. It was known that the drive got all but its kick-off energy from tapping into the fifth dimension. This dimension contained stars just like ours, except that they were of a fifth-dimensional shape, whatever that was. These stars were living creatures, beings of complex energy structures, just as the stars in our universe were alive. Efforts to communicate with the stars, however, had failed. Maybe they, like the porpoises, just didn't care to talk to us. Never mind. What did matter was that the drive was drawing off the energy of these living things. They didn't like being killed and the drive hurt them. Ergo, Dr. Maloney explained, they screamed.

This relieved a lot of people. Some, however, insisted that interstellar travel must stop. We might be killing intelligent beings. Their opponents pointed out that that was regrettable, if true. But other species were using the drive, so the stars would be killed anyway. If we refused to use it, we wouldn't have progress. And we'd be at the mercy of merciless aliens from outer space.

Besides, there wasn't any evidence that fifth-dimensional stars were any more intelligent than earth-worms.

Simon didn't know what the truth of the matter was. But he hated to hear the screaming, which was so loud at 69X that even earplugs didn't help. So he kept the ship at 20X. At that speed, he hoped he'd only be bruising the stars a little.

The *Hwang Ho* zipped away from the solar system and soon the sun was a tiny light that quickly became snuffed out as if it had been dipped in water. The celestial objects ahead, as seen in the viewscreen, were not what he would see at below-light speed. At 20X the ship was, in effect, half in this universe and half somewhere else.

The stars and the nebulae were creatures of the sublime. They were beautiful but with the beauty of awe, horror, and a mind-twisting magnitude and shape. They burned and changed form as if they were flames in hell created by Lucifer, high on heroin. Poets had tried to describe the heavens at superlight speeds. They had all failed. But when had the whining commentary ever matched the glorious text?

Simon sat paralyzed in his chair moaning with the ecstasy of terror. After a while he became aware that he had a huge erection, and there is no telling what might have happened if he had not been interrupted.

The dog had been whimpering and whining for some time, but suddenly it began barking loudly and racing around. Simon tried to ignore him. Then he became annoyed. Here he was, on the verge of the greatest orgasm he had ever known, and this mutt had to spoil it all. He shouted at Anubis, who paid him no attention at all. Finally, Simon remembered something he had read in school and seen in various TV series. He became scared, though he was not sure that he had good reason to be so.

As everybody knew, dogs were psychic. They saw things which men used to call ghosts. Now it was known that these were actually fifth-dimensional objects which had passed through normal space unperceived by the gross senses of man. These went through certain channels formed by the shape of the fifth dimension. The main channel on Earth went through the British islands, which was why England had more "ghosts" than any other place on the planet.

Every Earth ship that put out to space beyond the solar system carried a dog. Radar, being limited to the speed of light, was no good for a vessel going at superlight speeds. But a dog could detect other living beings even at a million lightyears' distance if they were also in soixante-neuf drive. To the dogs, other beings in this extra-dimensional world were ghosts, and ghosts scared the hell out of them.

He pressed a button. A screen sprang to life, showing him the view from the right side of the ship. He didn't expect to see the approaching ship, since it was going faster than light. But he could see a black funnel coming at an angle which would intercept his course. This, he knew, was the trail left by a vessel with soixante-neuf drive. It was one of the peculiarities of the drive that a ship radiated behind it a "shadow," a conical blackness of unknown nature. Simon, if he had looked out his own rearview screen, would have seen only a circle of nothingness directly behind the ship.

He was convinced that the ship approaching him was a Hoonhor and that it was out to get him. That was the only reason he could think of why the ship hadn't changed its course, which would result in collision if it maintained it. Probably, the Hoonhors intended to keep him from notifying other worlds of what they had done to Earth.

He stepped on the accelerator pedal and kept it to the floor while the speedometer needle crept toward the right-hand edge of the dial. He also twisted the wheel to the left to swerve the ship away. The stranger immediately changed its course to follow him.

The murmur from the two engine rooms became a loud and piercing shriek. Anubis howled with agony, and the owl flew around screaming. Simon put plugs in his ears, but they couldn't keep out the painful noise. Nor could he plug up his conscience. Somewhere, on one of the fifth-dimensional universes, a living being was undergoing terrible torture so he could save his own neck.

After ten minutes, the screams suddenly ceased. Simon didn't feel any relief. This only meant that the star had died, stripped of its fire, stripped, in fact, of every atom of its body. Tensed, he waited, and shortly the screaming started again. The drive had searched for and found another victim, a star that may have been happily browsing in the meadows of space only a minute before.

Presently, the two ships were on the same plane, the

Hoonhor an incalculable distance behind the *Hwang Ho*. Simon couldn't see it in his rearview screen because of the blackness he trailed. Somewhere in that cone was the Hoonhor. Or was it? According to theory, nothing could exist in the immediate wake of a 69X vessel. Yet one vessel could follow another in the wake. But the pursuer did not exist during this time. So where was it? In the sixth dimension, according to the theorists. And the stuff in the wake of the chaser must then exist in the seventh dimension, and any ship in *its* wake would be in the eighth dimension, and any ship in *its* wake would be in the ninth dimension.

Most of the theorists were happy with this explanation. They could not run out of dimensions any more than they could run out of numbers. However, a brilliant Hindu mathematician, Dr. Utapal, had said that there was a limit. By an equation which was so abstruse that it was unprovable, Utapal demonstrated that the ninth dimension was the upper limit. (What the lower limit was, nobody knew.) When a fourth ship joined the procession, there was a transposition factor, which resulted in the third ship suddenly being in front of the first. This was called the Unavoidable Trans-dimensional Shift in scholarly journals but was privately referred to as the You-Grab-My-Nuts-I'll-Grab-Yours Hypothesis.

It was then that a control panel siren began whooping and its lights flashed red. Simon became even more alarmed. A space boojum was directly ahead of the ship.

A boojum was a collapsed star which formed a gravitational whirlpool that sucked in any matter coming close to it. In fact, its gravity was so strong that even light couldn't escape from its surface.[1] But the ship's instruments could detect the alterations it made in the local space-time structure.

Boojums were a sort of manhole in a trans-dimensional sewage system. Or a slot in a multidimensional roulette wheel. All the boojums in this universe were entrances to other-dimensional worlds, and if a ship got sucked into one, it could be lost forever in the maze of connections. Or, if its crew was lucky, it would be shot back into this universe.

The Hoonhor ship was coming up on him swiftly. The slow freighter could not outrun the other vessel. Simon's only escape, like it or not, was to dive into the boojum. He doubted that the Hoonhor captain would have the guts to follow him into it.

The next thing he knew, everything had turned black. Nor was there any sound. After what seemed like hours but must have been only a few minutes—if time existed in this place—he felt as if he were melting. His fingers and toes were extending, at the same time they were becoming shapeless. His head seemed to loll on one side because his neck was stretching far out. It fell to one side and kept on falling. It went past his body and then the floor and then was falling through a bottomless space. He tried to raise his arm to grab it, but his arm groped through nothingness for miles and miles without end.

His intestines were floating up through his body and after a while they were coiled around his head, which was still falling. They didn't taste good at all. His anus was bobbing on the end of his nose; his liver was wedged between his head and his ear. He

---

[1] The boojum of Trout has a remarkable resemblance to the "black hole" of space conjectured by contemporary astronomy. Trout intuitively anticipated this concept five years before it was first proposed in scientific journals. Editor.

didn't know which ear because he had no idea of which way was right or left, up or down, in or out.

He thought perhaps his head might be falling to the left, or the right, and he had used the wrong arm to try to grab it. One of his arms wasn't extending, so he transferred his efforts to that. It grabbed what felt like Anubis' tongue, a long, slimy organ. He felt along it and pulled his hand away. Either the dog's tongue had grown or Anubis had turned into one giant tongue. He was immediately sorry that he had moved his hand. He seemed to be groping around in the dog's guts. Something moved against the back of his hand, something that beat quickly and sent a throbbing through him. Anubis' heart, he thought. He kept his hand against it and when it started to slide away he closed his fingers around it. It was the only identifiable object in this terrifying universe outside himself, an object which he had to cling to, to keep his sanity. It also kept him from feeling utterly alone, and it was the only thing which gave him any security at all. It alone was not changing shape.

Or so he had thought at first. Within a few seconds, it had grown bigger and its throbbing became faster. He hoped that the dog wasn't going to die of a heart attack.

Suddenly, they were out among the stars. Simon almost screamed with joy. They had made it; they weren't doomed to ride forever, like some Flying Dutchman, through the lightless, shapeless seas of the boojum.

Then he hastily released his grasp. It wasn't Anubis' heart he'd been holding. It was his penis.

Simon apologized to Anubis and then asked the computer

to check out the stars in the area. It reported that the ship was in an uncharted area. Simon didn't care. A man without a home can't be lost, and one galaxy was as good as another for his purposes.

Simon directed the computer to take the ship to the nearest galaxy and look for an inhabited planet. He went to the captain's quarters and poured a big drink of rice wine to soothe his nerves. The trouble with Chinese liquor was that it didn't satisfy. A few minutes after he'd had a shot, he felt as if he needed another. No wonder the ancient Chinese poets were always loaded out of their skulls.

Shut up in the cabin, Simon was able to relax by playing his banjo. The ship was going at only 20X, so the sound from the engine rooms wasn't loud enough to upset him. But he had to play behind closed doors because the banjo made Anubis howl and gave the owl dysentery. Their reaction hurt Simon's feelings, but something good came out of it. By backward logic and analogy, he had figured out why his concerts always got such bad reviews. Since animals hated his playing, there must be something bestial in music critics.

A week, ship's time, passed. Simon studied philosophy and Chinese, cooked meals for himself and his companions, and cleaned up after the dog and the owl. And then, one day, in the middle of his breakfast, the alarm bell rang. Simon ran to the control room and looked at the control panel screen. Translated, the Chinese words said, "Solar system with inhabitable planet approaching."

Simon ordered the ship to go into orbit around the fourth planet. When the *Hwang Ho* was over it, Simon looked through a telescope which could pick out objects as small as a mouse on the surface. It looked like a nice planet, Earth-size, no smog, clean oceans, and plenty of forests and grassy plains. All this was easily accounted for. The sentients were in a primitive agricultural stage and probably numbered less than a hundred million people.

What attracted his attention most was a gigantic tower on the edge of the smallest of the two continents. This tower was about a mile wide at its base and two miles high. It was shaped like a candy heart, its point stuck in the ground. A hard metal without a break made up its shell. In fact, it looked as if it had been made from a single casting. But the metal was striped with white, black, yellow, green, and blue. These were not painted on but seemed integral to the metal.

The massive structure looked brand-new. However, it was leaning to one side as if the solid granite under it was giving way to the many billions of tons pressing on it. Eventually, maybe in a million or so years, it would fall. It had been there for about a billion years, long before the human population had evolved from apes or even from shrew-sized insect eaters. Perhaps it had even been erected before life had crawled out of the primeval seas, warm and nutritious as a diabetic's urine.

Simon knew something about towers like this one, which was why he was delighted to see it. Interstellar voyagers to distant galaxies had reported finding such towers on every inhabited planet of these systems. There were, however, none on the planets of Earth's galaxy. Nobody knew why, though many resented this slight.

Deciding to investigate the tower first, Simon directed the

ship to land on it. The *Hwang Ho* settled down on a flat area between the two lobes, and Simon and his two pets strolled out. They didn't stay long. The flat part was covered with thousands of noisy, squabbling, egg-laying, white-and-black-checkered birds and about ten feet of guano. Simon threaded his way through the hook-billed birds, dodging vicious pecks from the mothers when he came too close to the eggs. Simon inspected the lobes, which towered above him as if they were mountains. Their slopes held no windows or doors. They were as unbroken as the passage of time itself, as impenetrable as yesterday.

Simon hadn't expected to find any entrances. Of the six million towers so far reported by Earth tourists, all had been just like this one. The natives of various planets had tried everything from diamond-tipped drills to laser beams to hydrogen bombs without scratching the mysterious metal. The buildings were hollow. A hammer could make one ring like a gong. There was even one planet which had a symphony orchestra which played only one instrument, the tower. The musicians stood on scaffolds built at various levels along the tower and struck it with hammers, the size and layout of the rooms within determining the notes evoked. The conductor stood on a platform a mile high and half a mile away and used two flags to wigwag his directions.

The highest point of music in the history of this planet occurred when a conductor, Ruboklngshep, fell off the platform. The orchestra, in trying to follow the wildly waving flags during his descent, produced six bars of the most exquisite music ever to be created, though some critics have disparaged the final three notes. Art, like science, sometimes gets its best results by accident.

PHILIP JOSÉ FARMER

Simon returned to the ship and found himself in an unforeseen situation. Since the flat area was tilted to one side, the ship had been put down at the lowest point, where the guano had built up to form a horizontal plane. Simon had made sure that the ship would not roll over. But he had forgotten about its enormous weight. It had sunk into the soft guano and so the ports on this side were about twenty feet under the surface and the ports on the other side were too high to reach. There was nothing to do but dig his way through with his bare hands. Anubis wouldn't help, since he had not buried any bones there. Simon got down on his hands and knees and excavated away. Two hours later, dirty, sweaty, and disgruntled, he broke through and fell into the port. It took a half-hour to clear out the port entrance and another half-hour to clean up himself and the pets.

His usual good spirits returned shortly afterward. He had told himself that he shouldn't get angry at such a little thing. After all, a man should expect to get his hands dirty if he dug into fundamental issues.

❦ 6 ❧

SHALTOON, THE EQUAL-TIME PLANET

Simon ordered the computer to set the ship down on a big field near the largest building of a city. Since this city had the largest population of any on the planet, it should be the capital of the most important nation. The building itself was six stories high and made of some white stone with purple and red veins. From the air it looked like a three-leaf clover with a long stem. Its windows were delta-shaped, and its doors were oval. The roofs were breadloaf-shaped, and the whole building was surrounded by roofless porches on the outer edges of two rows of pillars. The ones on the edge of the porch were upside-down V's. The others were behind the deltoids and projected from the floor of the porch at a forty-five-degree angle so that their ends stuck through the deltoids. The leaning shafts were cylindrical except for the ends which pierced the deltoids. These terminated in round balls from which a milky water jetted. At their base were two nut-shaped stones, the surfaces of which bore a crisscross of incisions.

The people that poured out of the building were human-looking except for pointed ears, yellow eyes which had pupils like a cat's, and sharp pointed teeth. Simon wasn't startled by this. All the humanoid races so far encountered had either been descended from simians, felines, canines, ursines, or rodents. On Earth the apes had won out in the evolutionary race toward intelligence. On other planets, the ancestors of cats, dogs, bears, beavers, or rabbits had developed fingers instead of paws and come out ahead of the apes. On some planets, both the apes and some other creature had evolved into sapients and shared their world. Or else one had exterminated the other. On this planet, the felines seemed to have gotten the upper hand early. If there were any simian humans, they were hiding deep in the forests.

Simon watched them through his viewscreens. When the soldiers had gathered around the ship, all pointing their spears and bows and arrows at the *Hwang Ho*, he came out. He held his hands up in the air to show he was peaceful. He didn't smile because on some planets baring one's teeth was a hostile sign.

"I'm Simon Wagstaff, the man without a planet," he said.

After a couple of weeks, Simon had learned the language well enough to get along. Some of the suspicions of the people of Shaltoon had worn away. They were wary of him, it seemed, because he wasn't the first Earthman to land there. Some two hundred years ago a fast-talking jovial man by the name of P.T. Taub had visited them. Before the Shaltoonians knew what was happening, he'd bamboozled them out of the crown jewels, taking not only these but a princess who'd just won the Miss Shaltoon Beauty Contest.

Simon had a hard time convincing them that he wasn't there to con them. He did want something from them, he told them over and over, but it wasn't anything material. First, did they know anything about the builders of the leaning heart-shaped tower?

The people assigned to escort Simon told him that all they knew was that the builders were called the Clerun-Gowph in this galaxy. Nobody knew why, but somebody somewhere sometime must have met them. Otherwise, why did they have a common name? As for the tower, it had been here, unoccupied and slowly tilting, since the Shaltoonians had had a language. Undoubtedly, it had been here a long time before that.

The Shaltoonians had a legend that, when the tower fell, the end of the world would come.

Simon was adaptable and gregarious. He loved people, and he knew how to get along with them. Whether he was with just one person or at a party, he enjoyed himself, and he was generally liked. But he was uneasy with the Shaltoonians. There was something wrong with them, something he couldn't describe. At first he thought that it might be because they were descended from felines. After all, though humanoid, they were fundamentally cats, just as Earthmen were basically apes. Yet, he'd met a number of extraterrestrial visitors on Earth who were felines, and he'd always gotten along with them. Actually, he preferred cats to dogs. It was only because circumstances had been beyond his control that he'd taken along a dog when he left Earth.

Maybe, he thought, it was the strong musky odor that hung over the city, overriding that of manure from the city. This emanated from every adult Shaltoonian he met and smelled exactly like a cat in heat. After a while, he understood why. They *were* all in the mating season, which lasted the year around. Their main subject of conversation was sex, but even with this subject they couldn't sustain much talk. After a half-hour or so, they'd get fidgety and then excuse themselves. If he followed them, he'd find him or her going into a house where he or she would be greeted by one of the opposite sex. The door would be closed, and within a few minutes the damnedest noises would come from the house.

This resulted in his not being able to talk long to the escorts who were supposed to keep an eye on him. They'd disappear, and someone else would take their place.

Moreover, when the escorts showed up again the next day, they acted strangely. They didn't seem to remember what they'd asked or told him the day before. At first, he put this down to a short-term memory. Maybe it was this which had kept the Shaltoonians from progressing beyond a simple agricultural society.

Simon was a good talker, but he was a good listener, too. Once he'd learned the language well, he caught on to a discrepancy of intonation among his escorts. It varied not only among individual speakers, which was to be expected, but in the same individual from day to day. Simon finally decided that he wasn't uneasy because the Shaltoonians were, from his viewpoint, oversexed. He had no moral repugnance to this. After all, you couldn't expect aliens to be just like Earthmen. As a matter of fact, his attitude, if anything, was envy. Evolution had cheated Terrestrials. Why couldn't Homo sapiens have kept the horniness of the baboon? Why had he allowed society to shape itself so that it suppressed the sex drive? Was it because evolution had dictated that mankind was to progress technologically? And, to bring this about, had evolution shunted much of man's sex drive to the brain, where he used the energy to make tools and new religions, and ways of making more money and attaining a higher status?

Earthmen were dedicated to getting to the top of the heap, whereas the Shaltoonians devoted themselves to getting on top of each other.

This seemed a fine arrangement to Simon—at first. One of the bad things about human society was that few people ever really had intimate contact. A people who spent a lot of time in bed, however, should be full of love. But things didn't work out that way on this planet. There wasn't even a word for love in the language. They did have many terms for various sexual positions, but these were all highly technical. There was no generic term equivalent to the Earthman's "love".

Not that this made much difference generally between Earth and Shaltoon behavior. The latter seemed to have just as many divorces, disagreements, fights, and murders as the former. On the other hand, the Shaltoonians didn't have many suicides. Instead of getting depressed, they went out and got laid.

Simon thought about this aspect. He decided that perhaps Shaltoon society was, after all, better arranged than Terrestrial society. Not that this was due to any superior intelligence of the Shaltoonians. It was a matter of hormone surplus. Mother Nature,

PHILIP JOSÉ FARMER

not brains, deserved the credit. This thought depressed him, but he didn't seek out a female to work off the mood. He retired to his cabin and played his banjo until he felt better. Then he got to thinking about the meaning of this and became depressed again. Hadn't he channeled his sex drive where it shouldn't be? Hadn't he made love to himself, via his banjo, instead of to another being? Were the notes spurting from the strings a perverted form of jism? Was his supreme pleasure derived from plucking, not fucking?

Simon put away the banjo, which was looking more like a detachable phallus every minute. He sallied forth determined to use his nondetachable instrument. Ten minutes later, he was back in the ship. The only relief he felt was in getting away from the Shaltoonians. He'd passed by a rain barrel and happened to look down in it. There, at the bottom, was a newly born baby. He had looked around for a policeman to notify him but had been unable to find one. It struck him then he had never seen a policeman on Shaltoon. He stopped a passer-by and started to ask him where the local precinct had its headquarters. Unable to do so because he didn't know the word for "police", he took the passer-by to the barrel and showed him what was in it. The citizen had merely shrugged and walked away. Simon had walked around until he saw one of his escorts. The woman was startled to see him without a companion and asked why he had left the ship without notifying the authorities. Simon said that that wasn't important. What was important was the case of infanticide he'd stumbled across.

She didn't seem to understand what he was talking about.

She followed him and gazed down into the barrel. Then she looked up with a strange expression. Simon, knowing something was wrong, looked again. The corpse was gone.

"But I swear it was here only five minutes ago!" he said.

"Of course," she said coolly. "But the barrel men have removed it."

It took some time for Simon to get it through his head that he had seen nothing unusual. In fact, the barrels he had observed on every corner and under every rain spout were seldom used to collect drinking water. Their main purpose was for the drowning of infants.

"Don't you have the same custom on Earth?" the woman said.

"It's against the law there to murder babies."

"How in the world do you keep your population from getting too large?" she said.

"We don't," Simon said.

"How barbaric!"

Simon got over some of his indignation when the woman explained that the average life span of a Shaltoonian was ten thousand years. This was due to an elixir invented some two hundred thousand years before. The Shaltoonians weren't much for mechanics or engineering or physics, but they were great botanists. The elixir had been made from juices of several different plants. A by-product of this elixir was that a Shaltoonian seldom got sick.

"So you see that we have to have some means of keeping the population down," she said. "Otherwise, we'd all be standing on top of each other's heads in a thousand years or less."

"What about contraceptives?"

"Those're against our custom," she said. "They interfere with the pleasure of sex. Besides, everyone ought to have a chance to be born."

Simon asked her to explain this seemingly contradictory remark. She replied that an aborted baby didn't have a soul. But a baby that made it to the open air was outfitted with a soul at the moment of birth. If it died even a few seconds later, it still went to heaven. Indeed, it was better that it did die, because then it would be spared the hardships and pains and griefs of life. Killing it was doing it a favor. However, to keep the population from decreasing, it was necessary to let one out of a hundred babies survive. The Shaltoonians didn't like to have a fixed arrangement for this. They let Chance decide who lived and who didn't. So every woman, when she got pregnant, went to the Temple of Shaltoon. There she picked a number at a roulette table, and if her ball fell into the lucky slot, she got to keep the baby. The Holy Croupiers gave her a card with the lucky number on it, which she wore around her neck until the baby was a year old.

"The wheel's fixed so the odds are a hundred to one," she said. "The house usually wins. But when a woman wins, a holiday is declared, and she's queen for a day. This is no big deal, since she spends most of her time reviewing the parade."

"Thanks for the information," Simon said. "I'm going back to the ship. So long, Goobnatz."

"I'm not Goobnatz," she said. "I'm Dunnernickel."

Simon was so shaken up that he didn't ask her what she

meant by that. He assumed that he had had a slip of memory. The next day, however, he apologized to her.

"Wrong again," she said. "My name is Pussyloo."

There was a tendency for all aliens of the same race to look alike to Earthmen. But he had been here long enough to distinguish indviduals easily.

"Do you Shaltoonians have a different name for every day?"

"No," she said. "My name has always been Pussyloo. But it was Dunnernickel you were talking to yesterday and Goobnatz the day before. Tomorrow, it'll be Quimquat."

This was the undefinable thing that had been making him uneasy. Simon asked her to explain, and they went into a nearby tavern. The drinks were on the house, since he was working here as a banjo-player. The Shaltoonians crowded in every night to hear his music, which they enjoyed even if it wasn't at all like their native music. At least, they claimed they did. The leading music critic of the planet had written a series of articles about Simon's genius, claiming that he evoked a profundity and a truth from his instrument which no Shaltoonian could equal. Simon didn't understand any more than the Shaltoonians did what the critic was talking about, but he liked what he read. This was the first time he'd ever gotten a good review.

They had ordered a couple of beers, and Pussyloo plunged into her explanation. She said she'd be glad to tell him all she could in half an hour, but she'd have to talk a lot to get everything into that length of time. In thirty minutes it'd be quitting time. She liked Simon, but he wasn't her type, and she had an assignation with a man she'd met on her lunch hour. After Simon heard her explanation, he understood why she was in such a hurry.

"Don't you Earthmen have ancestor rotation?" she said.

Simon was so startled that he upset his beer and had to order another. "What the hell's that?" he said.

"It's a biological, not a supernatural, phenomenon," she said. "I guess you poor deprived Terrestrials don't have it. But the body of every Shaltoonian contains cells which carry the memories of a particular ancestor. The earliest ancestors are in the anal tissue. The latest are in the brain tissue."

"You mean a person carries around with him the memories of his foreparents?" Simon said.

"That's what I said."

"But it seems to me that in time a person wouldn't have enough space in his body for all the ancestral cells," Simon said. "When you think that your ancestors double every generation backward, you'd soon be out of room. You have two parents, and each of them had two parents, and each of them had two. And so on. You go back only five generations, and you have sixteen great-great-grandparents. And so on."

"And so on," Pussyloo said. She looked at the tavern clock while her nipples swelled and the strong mating odor became even stronger. In fact, the whole tavern stank of it. Simon couldn't even smell his own beer.

"You have to remember that if you go back about thirty generations, everyone now living has many common ancestors. Otherwise, the planet at that time would've been jammed with people like flies on a pile of horse manure.

"But there's another factor that eliminates the number of

ancestors. The ancestor cells with the strongest personalities release chemicals that dissolve the weaker ones."

"Are you telling me that, even on the cellular level, the survival of the fittest is the law?" Simon said. "That egotism is the ruling agent?"

Pussyloo scratched the itch between her legs and said, "That's the way it is. There would never have been any trouble about it if that's all there was to it. But in the old days, about twenty thousand years ago, the ancestors started their battle for their civil rights. They said it wasn't right that they should be shut up in their little cells with only their own memories. They had a right to get out of their cellular ghettoes, to enjoy the flesh they were contributing to but couldn't participate in.

"After a long fight, they got an equal-time arrangement. Here's how it works. A person is born and allowed to control his own body until he reaches puberty. During this time, an ancestor speaks only when spoken to."

"How do you do that?" Simon said.

"It's a mental thing the details of which the scientists haven't figured out yet," she said. "Some claim we have a neural circuit we can switch on and off by thought. The trouble is, the ancestors can switch it on, too. They used to give the poor devils that carried them a hard time, but now they don't open up any channels unless they're requested to do so.

"Anyway, when a person reaches puberty, he must then give each ancestor a day for himself or herself. The ancestor comes into full possession of the carrier's body and consciousness. The carrier himself still gets one day a week for himself. So he comes out ahead, though there's still a lot of bitching about it. When the round is completed, it starts all over again.

"Because of the number of ancestors, a Shaltoonian couldn't live long enough for one cycle if it weren't for the elixir. But this delays aging so that the average life span is about ten thousand years."

"Which is actually twenty thousand years, since a Shaltoon year is twice as long as ours," Simon said.

He was stunned. He didn't even notice when Pussyloo squirmed out of the booth and, still squirming, walked out of the place.

7

QUEEN MARGARET

The Space Wanderer had been thinking about moving on. There didn't seem to be much here for him. The Shaltoonians did not even have a word for philosophy, let alone such as ontology, epistemology, and cosmology. Their interests were elsewhere. He could understand why they thought only of the narrow and the secular, or, to be exact, eating, drinking, and copulating. But understanding did not make him wish to participate. His main lust was for the big answers.

When he found out about ancestor rotation, however, he decided to hang around a little longer. He was curious about the way in which this unique phenomenon shaped the strange and complex structure of Shaltoon society. Also, to be truthful, he had an egotistic reason for being a little reluctant to leave. He enjoyed being lionized, and the next planet might have critics not so admiring.

On the other hand, his pets were unhappy. They would not leave the spaceship even though they were suffering from cabin fever. The odor from the Shaltoonians drove Anubis into a barking frenzy and Athena into semishock. When Simon had guests, the two retreated into the galley. After the party was over, Simon would try to play with them to cheer them up, but they would not respond. Their big dumb eyes begged him to take off, to leave forever this planet that smelled of cats. Simon told them to stick it out for another week. Seekers after knowledge had to put up with certain inconveniences. They didn't understand his words, of course, but they did understand his tone. They were stuck here until their master decided to unstick them. What they wanted to stick and where was something else. Maybe it was a good thing they couldn't talk.

The first thing Simon found out in his investigations was that ancestor rotation caused a great resistance to change. This was not only inevitable but necessary. The society had to function from day to day, crops be grown and harvested and transported, the governmental and business administration carried out, schools, hospitals, courts, etcetera run. To make this possible, a family stayed in the same line of work or profession. If your forefather a thousand generations removed was a ditch-digger, you were one, too. There was no confusion resulting from a blacksmith being replaced by a judge one day and a garbage hauler the next.

The big problem in running this kind of society was the desire of each ancestor to live it up on his day of possession. Naturally, he/she didn't want to waste his/her time working when he/she could be eating, drinking, and copulating. But everybody understood that if he/she indulged in his/her wishes, society would fall apart and the carriers would starve to death in a short time. So, grudgingly, everybody put in an eight-hour day and at quitting time plunged into an orgy. Almost everybody did. Somebody had to take care of the babies and children, and somebody had to work on the farms the rest of the day.

The only way to handle this was to let slaves baby-sit and finish up the plowing and the chores on the farms. On Shaltoon, once a slave always a slave was the law. Yet, how do you get an ancestral slave to work all day on the only day in five hundred years that he'll take over a carrier? For one thing, who's going to oversee him? No freeman wanted to put in his precious time supervising the helots. And a slave that isn't watched closely is going to goof off.

How did you punish a slave if he neglected his work to enjoy himself? If you hung him, you killed off thousands of innocents. You also reduced the number of slaves, of which there weren't enough to go around in the first place. If you whipped him, you were punishing the innocent. The day following the whipping, the guilty man/woman retreated into his/her cell, shut off from the pain. The poor devil that followed was the one that suffered. He resented being punished for something he hadn't done, and his morale scraped bottom like a dog with piles.

The authorities had recognized that this was a dangerous situation. If enough slaves got angry enough to revolt, they could take over easily while their masters were helplessly drunk in the midst of the late evening orgy. The only way to prevent this was to double the number of slaves. In this way, a slave could put in four hours on the second shift and then go off to enjoy himself while another slave finished up for him. This did have its drawbacks. The slave that took over the last four hours had been whooping it up on his free time and so he was in no shape to work efficiently. But this could not be helped.

The additional slaves required had to be gotten from the freemen. So the authorities passed laws that a man could be enslaved if he spit on the sidewalk or overparked his horse and buggy. There were protests and riots against this legislation, of course. The government expected, in fact hoped for, these. They arrested the rebels and made them slaves. The sentence was retroactive; all their ancestors became slaves also.

Simon talked to a number of the slaves and found out that what he had suspected was true. Almost all the newly created slaves had come from the poor classes. The few from the upper class had been liberals. Somehow or other, the cops never saw a banker, a judge, or a businessman spit on the sidewalk.

Simon became apprehensive when he found out about this. There were so many laws that he didn't know about. He could be enslaved if he forgot to go downwind before farting in the presence of a cop. He was assured, however, that he wasn't subject to the laws.

"Not as long as you leave within two weeks," his informant said. "We wouldn't want you as a slave. You have too many strange ideas. If you stayed here long, you might spread these, infect too many people."

Simon didn't comment. The analogy of new ideas to deadly diseases was not new to him.

One of Simon's favorite writers, a science-fiction author

by the name of Jonathan Swift Somers III, had once written a story about this parallel between diseases and ideas. In his story, *Quarantine!*, an Earthman had landed on an uncharted planet. He was eager to study the aliens, but they wouldn't let him out of the spaceship until he had been given a medical checkup. At first, he thought they suspected him of bringing in germs they weren't equipped to handle. After he'd learned their language, he was told that this wasn't so. The aliens had long ago perfected a panacea against illnesses of the flesh. They were worried about his disrupting their society, perhaps destroying it, with deadly thoughts.

The port officials, wearing lead mind-shields, questioned the Earthman closely for two weeks. He sweated while he talked because the aliens' method of disease-prevention, which was one hundred percent effective, was to kill the sick person. His body was then burned and his ashes were buried at midnight in an unmarked grave.

After two weeks of grilling, the head official said, smiling, "You can go out among our people now."

"You mean I have a clean bill of health?" the Earthman said.

"Nothing to worry about," the official said. "We've heard every idea you have. There isn't a single one we didn't think of ten thousand years ago. You must come from a very primitive world."

Jonathan Swift Somers III, like most great American writers, had been born in the Midwest. His father had been an aspiring poet whose unfinished epic had not been printed until long after his death. Simon had once made a pilgrimage to Petersburg, Illinois, where the great man was buried. The monument was a granite wheelchair with wings. Below was the epitaph:

JONATHAN SWIFT SOMERS III

1910–1982

He Didn't Need Legs

Somers had been paralyzed from the waist down since he was ten years old. In those days, they didn't have a vaccine against polio. Somers never left the wheelchair or his native town, but his mind voyaged out into the universe. He wrote forty novels and two hundred short stories, mostly about adventure in space. When he started writing, he described exploits on the Moon and Mars. When landings were made on these, he shifted the locale to Jupiter. After the Jovian Expedition, he wrote about astronauts who traveled to the extreme edge of the cosmos. He figured that in his lifetime men would never get beyond the solar system, and he was right. Actually, it made no difference whether or not astronauts got to the places he described. His books about the Moon and Mars were still read long after voyages there had become humdrum. It didn't matter that Somers had been one hundred percent wrong about those places. His books were poetic and dramatic, and the people he depicted going there seemed more real than the people who actually went there. At least, they were more interesting.

Somers belonged to the same school of writing as the great French novelist Balzac. Balzac claimed he could write better about a place if he knew nothing of it. Invariably, when he did go to a city he had described in a book, he was disappointed.

Near Somers' grave was his father's.

JONATHAN SWIFT SOMERS II
1877–1912
I tried to fly on verse's wings.
Rejection slips all called it corn.
How Nature balances joys and stings!
I never suffered a critic's scorn.

However, the book reviewers had given the son a hard time most of his life. It wasn't until he was an old man that Somers was recognized as a great artist. When he received the Nobel Prize for Literature, he remarked, "This heals no wounds." He knew that critics never admit they're wrong. They'd still give him a hard time.

Simon was worried that he, too, might upset the Shaltoonians. It was true that he never proposed any new ideas to them. All he did was ask questions. But often these can be more dangerous than propaganda. They lead to novel thoughts.

It seemed, however, that he wasn't going to spark off any novelty in the Shaltoonians' minds. The adults were, in effect, never around for more than a day. The young were too busy playing and getting educated for the time when they'd have to give up possession of their bodies.

Near the end of his visit, on a fine sunny morning, Simon left the spaceship to visit the Temple of Shaltoon. He intended to spend the day studying the rites being performed there. Shaltoon was the chief deity of the planet, a goddess whose closest Earthly equivalent was Venus or Aphrodite. He walked through the streets, which he found strangely empty. He was wondering what was going on when he was startled by a savage scream. He ran to the house from which it came and opened the door. A man and a woman were fighting to the death in the front room. Simon had a rule that he would never interfere in a quarrel between man and wife. It was a good rule but one which no humanitarian could keep. In another minute, one or both of the bleeding and bruised couple would be dead. He jumped in between them and then jumped out again and ran for his life. Both had turned against him, which was only to be expected.

Since he was followed out on the street, he kept on running. As he sped down the street, he heard cries and shrieks from the houses he passed. Turning a corner, he collided with a swirling shouting mob, everyone of which seemed intent on killing anybody within range of their fists, knives, spears, swords, and axes. Simon fought his way out and staggered back to the ship. When the port was closed behind him, he crawled to the sick bay—Anubis pacing him with whimpers and tongue-licking—where he bandaged his numerous cuts and gashes.

The next day he cautiously ventured out. The city was a mess. Corpses and wounded were everywhere in the streets, and firemen were still putting out the blazes that had been started the day before. However, no one seemed belligerent, so he stopped a citizen and asked him about yesterday's debacle.

"It was Shag Day, dummy," the citizen said and moved on.

Simon wasn't too jarred by the rudeness. Very few of the natives were in a good mood when sober. This was because the carrier's body was continually abused by the rotating ancestors.

Each had to get all the debauchery he could cram into his allotted time between the quitting whistle and the curfew bell. As a result, the first thing the ancestor felt when he took his turn was a terrible hangover. This lasted through the day, making him tired and irritable until he had had a chance to kill the pain with liquor.

Every once in a while, the body would collapse and be carried off to a hospital by drunken ambulance attendants and turned over to drunken nurses and doctors. The poor devil who had possession that day was too sick to do anything but lie in bed, groaning and cursing. The thought that he was wasting his precious and rare day in convalescence from somebody else's fun made him even sicker.

So the Space Wanderer didn't wonder at the grumpiness of the citizen. He walked on and presently found a heavily bandaged but untypically amiable woman.

"Everybody, if you go back a few thousand years, has the same ancestors," she said. "So, every thousand years or so, a day occurs when one particular ancestor happens to come into possession of many carriers. This usually happens to only a few, and we can cope with most of these coincidences. But about five thousand years ago, Shag, a very powerful personality born in the Old Stone Age, took over more than half of the population on a certain day. Since he was an extremely authoritarian and violent man who hated himself, the first Shag Day ended with a quarter of the world's people killing each other."

"And what about yesterday's Shag Day?" Simon said.

"That's the third. It's a record breaker, too. Almost half of the population were casualties."

"From the long-range view, it has its bright side," Simon said. "You can allow more babies to stay alive now so you can bring the population back to normal."

"The sweetest catnip grows behind the latrine," she said. This was the equivalent of the Terrestrial "Every cloud has its silver lining," or "An ill wind blows somebody good."

Simon decided to cut his trip short. He would leave the next day. But that evening, while reading the Shaltoon *Times*, he found out that in four days the wisest person who had ever lived would take over the queen's body. He became excited. If anyone would have the truth, it would be this woman. She'd had more turns at rotation than anyone and combined the greatest intelligence with the longest experience.

The reason that everybody knew that Queen Margaret was due to take over was the rotation chart. This had been worked out for each person. Generally, it was hung on the bathroom wall so it could be studied when there was nothing else to occupy one's mind.

Simon sent in a petition for an audience. Under normal circumstances, he would have had to wait six months for an answer. Since he was the only alien on the planet, and famous for his banjo-playing, he got a reply the same day. The queen would be pleased to dine with him. Formal attire was mandatory.

Resplendent in the dress uniform of the captain of the *Hwang Ho*, a navy blue outfit adorned with huge epaulettes, gold braid, big brass buttons, and twenty Good Conduct medals, Simon appeared at the main door of the palace. He was ushered by a lord of the royal pantry and six guards through magnificent marble corridors loaded down with *objets d'art*. At another time, Simon would have liked to examine these. Most of them consisted of phallic imagery.

He was led through the door flanked by two guards who blew through long silver trumpets as he passed them. Simon appreciated the honor, even if it left him deaf for a minute. He was still dizzy when he was halted in a small but ornate room before a big table of polished dark wood. This was set with two plates and two goblets full of wine and a crowd of steaming dishes. Behind it sat a woman whose beauty started his adrenalin flowing, even if she wasn't strictly human. To tell the truth, Simon had gotten so accustomed to pointed ears, slit pupils, and sharp teeth that his own face startled him when he shaved.

Simon didn't hear the introduction because his hearing hadn't come back yet. He bowed to the queen after the official's lips had quit moving, and at a sign he sat down across the table from her. The dinner passed pleasantly enough. They talked about the weather, a subject that Simon would find was an ice-breaker on every planet. Then they discussed the horrors of Shag Day. Simon became progressively drunker as the dinner proceeded. It was protocol to down a glass of wine every time the queen did, and she seemed to be very thirsty. He didn't blame her. It had been three hundred years since she had had a drink.

Simon told her his life story at her request. She was horrified but at the same time complacent.

"Our religion maintains that the stars, planets, and moons are living beings," she said. "These are the only forms of life big enough and complex enough to interest the Creatrix. Biological life is an accidental by-product. You might say that it's a disease infecting the planets. Vegetable and animal life are bearable forms of the disease, like acne or athlete's foot.

"But when sentient life, beings with self-consciousness, evolve, they become a sort of deadly microbe. We Shaltoonians, however, are wise enough to know that. So, instead of being parasites, we become symbiotes. We live off the earth, but we take care that we don't ruin it. That's why we've stuck to an agricultural society. We grow crops, but we replenish the soil with manure. And every tree we cut down, we replace.

"Earthlings, now, they seem to have been parasites who made their planet sick. Much as I regret to say it, it was a good thing that the Hoonhors cleaned Earth up. They only have to take one look at Shaltoon, however, to see that we've kept our world in tiptop shape. We're safe from them."

Simon did not think that Shaltoon society was above criticism, but he thought it diplomatic to keep silent.

"You say, Space Wanderer, that you mean to roam everywhere until you have found answers to your questions. I suppose by that that you want to know the meaning of life?"

She leaned forward, her eyes a hot green with vertical black slits showing in the candlelight. Her gown fell open, and Simon saw the smooth creamy mounds and their tips, huge and red as cherries.

"Well, you might say that," he said.

She rose suddenly, knocking her chair onto the floor, and clapped her hands. The butlers and the officials left at once and closed the doors behind them. Simon began sweating. The room had become very warm, and the thick ropy odor of cat-heat was so heavy it was almost visible.

Queen Margaret of the planet Shaltoon let her gown fall to the floor. She was wearing nothing underneath. Her high, firm, uncowled bosom was proud and rosy. Her hips and thighs were like an inviting lyre of pure alabaster. They shone so whitely that they might have had a light inside.

"Your travels are over, Space Wanderer," she whispered, her voice husky with lust. "Seek no more, for you have found. The answer is in my arms."

He did not reply. She strode around the table to him instead of ordering him, as was her queenly right, to come to her.

"It's a glorious answer, Queen Margaret, God knows," he replied. His palms were perspiring profusely. "I am going to accept it gratefully. But I have to tell you, if I'm going to be perfectly honest with you, that I will have to be on my way again tomorrow."

"But you have found your answer, you have found your answer!" she cried, and she forced his head between her fragrant young breasts.

He said something. She thrust him out at arm's length. "What was that you said?"

"I said, Queen Margaret, that what you offer is an awfully good answer. It just doesn't happen to be the one I'm primarily looking for."

Dawn broke like a window hit by a gold brick. Simon entered the spaceship. A human doughnut dunked in weariness, satiety, and cat-in-mating-season pungency, he slopped in. Anubis sniffed and growled. Simon put out a shaking hand drained of hormones to pet him.

Anubis bit it.

8

THE *NO SMOKING* PLANET

During the banquet with Queen Margaret, Simon had drunk a goblet of the Shaltoon immortality elixir. And just before he left, he was given two vials of elixir for his animals. Simon hesitated for a long time about offering Anubis and Athena the green sweet-and-sour liquid. Was it fair to inflict long life on them? Would he have swallowed the stuff if he had not been drunk with alcohol and the queen's musky odor?

"It may take several lifetimes, or more, for you to find a place where the answer to your primal question is known," the queen had said. "Wouldn't it be ironic if you died of old age while on your way to a planet where the answer you seek was known?"

Simon had said, "You're very wise, Queen Margaret," and he emptied the cup. The expected thunder and lightning of imminences of immortality for which he braced himself had not come. Instead, he had belched.

Now he looked at the dog, hiding behind a chair with shame because he had bitten Simon, and at the owl, sitting on top of the chair, her favorite perch, spotted with white.

In the normal course of subjective time, they would both be dead in a few years. The future might show that they would have been far better off dead. On the other hand—Simon was hopelessly ambidextrous—they might be missing a vast and enduring joy if he denied them the elixir. Who knew? They might even find a planet where the natives had a science advanced enough to raise his pets' intelligence to a human level. Then he could communicate with them, enjoy their companionship to the fullest potentiality.

On the other hand, they might then become very unhappy.

Simon solved his dilemma by pouring out the elixir into two bowls. If the two cared to drink the stuff, they could do so. The decision was up to their limited powers of free will. After all, animals knew what was good for them, and if immortality smelled bad to them, they wouldn't touch it.

Anubis rose from behind the chair and slinked across the floor to the bowl. He sniffed at the green liquid and then lapped it up. Simon looked at Athena and said, "Well?" The owl said, "Who?" After a while she flew down to her bowl and drank from it.

Simon began worrying that he had done the wrong thing. Dogs will eat poison if it's wrapped up in a steak. Perhaps the elixir's perfume overrode the odor of dangerous elements.

A minute later, he had forgotten his concern. The viewscreen flashed the information that the ship was approaching a star with a planetary system. The *Hwang Ho* dropped down into sublight speed, and two days later they were entering an orbit around the sixth planet of the giant red star. This was Earth-size, and its air breathable, though its oxygen content was greater than Earth's.

The only artificial object on the planet was the gigantic candy-heart-shaped tower of the Clerun-Gowph. Simon flew the ship around it a few times, but, on finding that it was as invulnerable as the other, he left it. This planet showed no sign of intelligent life, of beings who used tools, grew crops, and constructed buildings. It did have some curious animal life, though, and he decided to get a close look at it. He gave the landing order, and a few minutes later stepped out onto the edge of a meadow near the shore of an amber sea.

The grass was about two feet high, violet-colored and topped with yellow flowers with five petals. Moving through and above these were about forty creatures which were pyramid-shaped and about thirty feet high. Their skins or shells—he wasn't sure which they were—were pink. They moved on hundreds of very short legs ending in broad round feet. Halfway up their bodies were eyes, two on each side, eight in all. These were huge and round and a light blue, and the lids had long curling eyelashes. At the top of each pyramid-shaped body was a pink ball with a large opening on two opposing sides.

It was evident that their mouths were on their bottoms, since they left a trail of cropped grass behind them. He could hear the munching of the grass and rumblings of their stomachs.

Simon had put the ship into a deep ravine beyond a thick wood so he could sneak up on the creatures. But purple things in the sky were moving out to sea and turning in a sweeping curve so they could come in downwind toward him. These were even stranger than the creatures browsing on the flowers. They looked from a distance like zeppelins, but they had two big eyes near the underside of their noses and tentacles coiled up along their undersides about twenty feet back of the eyes. Simon wondered how they ate. Perhaps the curious organs at the tips of their noses were some kind of mouth. These were bulbous and had a small opening.

Just above the small bulb was a hole. This did not seem to be a mouth, however, since it was rigid. There was another hole at the rear, and a number of much smaller ones spaced along the underside.

Their tail assemblies were just like zeppelins'. They had huge vertical rudders and horizontal elevators, but these sprouted yellow and green feathers on the edges.

Simon figured out they must use some sort of jet propulsion. They took in air through the front hole, which was rigid, and squeezed it out of the rear hole, which was contracting and dilating.

The huge creatures dropped lower as they neared the meadow, and the first one, emitting short sharp whistles, came in about thirty feet above the ground. It passed between a line of the pyramid-things, and then it eased its bulbous nose into an opening in the ball on top of one. This closed around the bulb and held the zeppelin-thing.

The pyramid-thing was a living mooring mast.

A moment later, the flying animal was released. It headed toward the bush behind which Simon was crouched. After it came the other fliers, all whistling. The pyramid-things crowded together and faced inward. Or were they facing outward, like a bunch of cows threatened by wolves? How could they face anything if they had eyes on all sides and no faces? In any event, they were forming a protective assembly.

Simon stepped out from his cover with his hands held up. The foremost zeppelin-creature loomed above him, its huge eyes cautious. Its tentacles reached out but did not touch Simon. He was almost blown down as the thing eased forward toward him. The stench was terrible but not unfamiliar. He had batted .500 in his guess about its method of propulsion. Instead of taking in air, compressing it with some organ, and shooting it out, it drove itself with giant farts. Its big stomachs—like a cow it had more than one—generated gas for propulsion. Simon figured out that its stomachs must contain enzymes which made the gas. At this moment, it hung about ten feet above the surface, bobbing up and down as it expelled gas from the hole in front to counteract the wind.

Simon stood there while the thing whistled at him. After a while he caught on to the fact that the whistles were a sort of Morse code.

Simon imitated some of the dots and dashes just to let them know that he, too, was intelligent. Then he turned back and went to his ship. The zeppelins followed him above the trees and watched him go into the ship. Through the viewscreen he could see them hovering over the ship and feeling it with their tentacles. Maybe they thought it was a strange living creature, too.

Simon went out the next day to the edge of the meadow. The living mooring masts got alarmed again, and once more the fliers came down. But after a few days they got used to him. Simon walked closer to them each day. By the end of the week, he was allowed to stroll around among the pyramids. A few days later, however, the pyramids were gone. He walked around until he found them in another meadow. Evidently, they had eaten up all the grass and flowers in the other place.

Simon found it difficult to learn the language of the zeppelin-things. Most of them were too busy in the daytime to talk to him. When dark came, the fliers locked into the balls on the top of the pyramids and stayed there until dawn. When they did speak—or whistle—to him, the stench they expelled was almost unbearable. But then he found out that the pyramids could whistle, too. They did this, not through the mouths on their undersides but through one of the openings in the balls at the tops. These emitted a stench, too, but he could endure it if he stood upwind. And, being females, the pyramids were more loquacious and better suited to teach him zeppelinese.

They liked Simon because he gave them someone to talk to and about. The males, it seemed, spent most of their time playing and carousing in the air. They came down at noon for a meal but wouldn't hang around to talk. When night fell, they landed, but this was for supper and a short session of sexual intercourse. After which, they usually dozed off.

"We're just objects to them," said one female. "Nutrition and pleasure objects."

The ball on top of the females was a curious organ. One opening was a combination mooring lock, gruel nipple, and vagina. The females browsed on the meadow, digested the food, and fed it through a nipple inside the ball into the tips of the males' noses. This opening also received the slender tongue-like sex organ of the male. The opening on the other side of the ball was the anus and the mouth. This could be tightened to emit the whistling speech.

Simon didn't want to get involved in the domestic affairs of these creatures. But he had to show a certain amount of interest and sympathy if he was to get information. So he whistled a question at the female whom he'd named Anastasia.

"Yes, that's right," Anastasia said. "We do all the work and those useless sons of bitches do nothing but play around all day."

Anastasia didn't actually say "sons of bitches" but Simon translated it as such. What she said was something like "farts in a windstorm."

"We females talk a lot among ourselves during the day," she said. "But we'd like to talk with our mates, too. After all, they've been up in the wild blue yonder, having a great time, seeing all sorts of interesting things. But do you think for one moment that they'll let us in on what's going on outside these meadows? No, all they want to do is to be fed and have a quickie and be off to dreamland. When we complain, they tell us that we wouldn't understand it if they did tell us what they saw and did. So here we are, ground-bound and shut up in these little meadows, working all day, taking care of the children, while they're roaming around, zooming up and down, having a good old time. It isn't fair!"

Simon whistled some more sympathy and then went down to the beach to watch the males.

He had found out that the stomachs of the fliers also generated hydrogen. It was this gas which enabled them to float in the air. They carried water as ballast, which they drew up from the ocean through their hollow tentacles. When they wanted altitude quickly, they released the water, and up they went. They were always holding races or gamboling about, playing all sorts of games, tag-the-leader, loop-the-loop, doing Immelmann turns, follow-the-leader, or catch-the-bird. This latter game consisted of chasing a bird until they caught it by sucking it into their jet-holes or forcing it to the ground.

They also liked to scare the herds of animals on the ground by zooming down on them and stampeding them. The male whose herd raised the biggest cloud of dust won this game.

The males had another form of communication than whistling, too. They could emit short or long trails of smoke corresponding to the whistled dots and dashes. With these they could talk to each other at long distances or call in their buddies if they saw something interesting. They never used this skywriting, however, in sight of the females. They took great delight in having a secret of their own. The females knew about this, of course, since the males sometimes boasted about it. This made the females even more discontented.

Simon would not have stayed long on this planet, which he named Giffard after the Frenchman who first successfully controlled a lighter-than-air craft. Simon did not believe that the simple natives had any answers to his questions. But then he talked to Graf, his name for the big male that dominated the herd. Graf said that the males didn't spend all their time just playing. They often had philosophical discussions, usually in the afternoon when they were resting. They'd float around on the ocean or a lake and discuss the big issues of the universe. Simon, hearing this, decided he'd wait until he knew the language well enough to talk philosophy with the males. A few months after he'd landed, he asked Graf if he would take him to the lake where the males had their bull sessions. Graf said he'd be glad to.

The next day, Graf wrapped a tentacle around Simon and lifted him up. Simon was thrilled but he was also a little scared. He wished that he had flown to the lake in the lifeboat. But he was eager for new experiences, and this was one he wasn't likely to find on any other world.

Shortly before they got to the lake, Simon took a cigar out of his pocket and lit up. It was a good cigar, made of Outer Mongolian tobacco. Simon was puffing happily some hundreds of feet above a thick yellow forest, the wind moving softly over his face and a big black bird with a red crest flapping along a few feet away from him. All was blue and quiet and content; this was one of the rare moments when God did indeed seem in His heaven and all was well with the world.

As usual, the rare moment did not last long. Graf suddenly started bobbing up and down so violently that Simon began to get airsick. Then he whistled screamingly, and the tentacle around Simon's waist straightened out. Simon grabbed at it and hung on, shouting wildly at Graf. When he got over his first panic, he whistled at Graf after removing the cigar.

"What's the matter?"

"What are you doing?" Graf whistled like a steam kettle back at him. "You're on fire!"

"What?" Simon whistled.

"Let go! Let go! I'll go up in flames!"

"I'll fall, you damned fool!"

"Let go!"

Simon looked down. They were now over the lake but about a hundred feet up. Below, the cigar-shaped males were floating in the water. Or they had been, a second before. Suddenly, they rose upward in a body, their ballast squirting out through the hollow tentacles, and then they scattered.

A few seconds later, Simon realized what was going on. He opened his hand, letting the cigar drop. Graf immediately quit his violent oscillations, and a moment later he deposited Simon on the shore of the lake. But his skin was darker than its usual purple, and he stuttered his dots and dashes.

"F-f-f-fire's th-th-the w-w-w-worst th-th-thing there is! It's the only th-th-thing we f-f-fear! It w-w-was invented b-b-by th-th-the d-d-devil!"

The Giffardians, it seemed, had religion. Their devil, however, dwelt in the sky, and he propelled himself with a jet of flaming hydrogen. When it came time for the bad Giffardians to be taken off to the hell above the sky, he zoomed in and burned them up with flame from his tail.

The good Giffardians were taken by a zeppelin-shaped angel whose farts were sweet-smelling down into a land below the earth. Their planet was hollow, they claimed, and heaven was inside the hollow.

They had a lot of strange ideas about religion. This didn't faze Simon, who had heard stranger on Earth.

Simon apologized. He then explained what the thing on fire in his mouth had been.

All the males shuddered and bobbed up and down and one was so terror-stricken that he shot away, unable to control his ejaculations of gas.

"It might be better if you left," Graf said. "Right now."

"Oh, I won't smoke except in the ship from now on," Simon said. "I promise."

This quieted the males down somewhat. But they did not really breathe easy until he also said he would put up some NO SMOKING signs.

"That way, if other Earthmen should land here," Simon said, "they'll not light up."

He didn't tell them that it was doubtful that any people from his native planet would ever come here. Nor did he tell them that there were billions of planets whose people couldn't read English.

It wasn't fire that made Simon so dangerous. It was the ideas he innocently dropped while talking to the females. Once, when Anastasia complained about being kept on the ground, Simon said that she ought to take a ride. He realized at once that he shouldn't have ventured this opinion. But Anastasia wouldn't let him drop the subject. The next day, she tried to talk her mate, Graf, into taking her up. He refused, but she was so upset that the gruel she fed him became sour. After several days of stomach upset, he gave in.

With Anastasia hanging on to him through the lock in their apex-organs, he lifted. The others stood or floated around and watched this epoch-making flight. Graf carried her up to about two thousand feet, beyond which he was unable to levitate.

However, her weight dragged his nose down so that his tail was far higher than his fore part. He was unable to navigate in this fashion and had a hard time getting her back to the meadow. Moreover, his skin had broken out in huge drops of yellowish sweat.

Anastasia, however, was enraptured. The other females insisted that their mates take them for rides. These did so reluctantly and had the same trouble navigating as Graf. The males were too exhausted that night to have sexual intercourse.

There is no telling what might have happened in the next few days. But, the day after, the females started to give birth. Perhaps it was the excitement of their first aerial voyages that made them deliver before the end of their term. In any event, Simon strolled out onto the meadow that morning to find a number of tiny zeppelins and mooring masts nursing.

The baby males floated up as high as the nose-apex locks and took their gruel there. The baby females cropped the grass alongside their mothers.

"You see, even at birth, we females are discriminated against," Anastasia said. "We have to stick to the ground and take food that isn't nearly as easy to digest as the stuff the males get from the apex-organs. The males have the best of it, as usual."

"Function follows form," Simon said.

"What?" Anastasia whistled.

Simon strolled off, wishing that he could keep his mouth shut. He walked along the seashore and thought about leaving that very day. He had been able to have one philosophical discussion with the males, but it turned out to be on the level of what he'd heard in the locker room in high school. He didn't expect to find much deeper stuff. He had, however, promised Anastasia that he'd be the godfather of her daughter. He supposed he should wait until the ceremony, which would take place in three days. One of Simon's weaknesses was that he couldn't bear to hurt anyone's feelings.

He walked around the curve of the beach, and he saw a beautiful woman just rising from the foam of a wave.

CHWORKTAP

Simon couldn't have been more shocked than if he had been Crusoe when he saw Friday's footprint. It was, in fact, Friday on the Earth calendar in the spaceship, another coincidence found only in bad novels. What was even more unforgivable—in a novel, not in Nature, who could care less about coincidences— was that the scene looked almost like Botticelli's famous painting *Birth of Venus*. She wasn't standing on a giant clamshell and there wasn't any maiden ready to throw a blanket over her. Nor was there any spirit of wind carrying a woman. But the shoreline and the trees and the flowers floating in the air behind her did resemble those in the painting.

The woman herself, as she waded out of the sea to stand nude before him, also had hair the same length and color as Botticelli's Venus. She was, however, much better looking and had a better body—from Simon's viewpoint, anyway. She did not have one hand covering her breast and the ends of her hair hiding her pubes. Her hands were over her mouth.

Simon approached her slowly, smiling, and her hands came down. They didn't understand each other's language, of course, but she pointed inland and then led him into the woods. Here, under the branches of some big trees, was a small spaceship. They went into its open port where she sat Simon down in a small cabin and gave him a drink, alcohol mixed with some alien fruit juice. When she returned from the next room, she was dressed. She had on a long, low-cut gown covered with silver sequins. It looked like the dresses hostesses wear in honky-tonks.

It took several weeks before she was able to converse semifluently in English. In the meantime, Simon had taken her to his ship. Anubis and Athena seemed to like her, but the owl made her nervous. Simon found out why later.

Chworktap was not only beautiful, she was fun to be with. She talked very amusingly. In fact, Simon had never met anyone who had so many stories, all howlingly funny, to tell. What's more, she never repeated herself. What's also more, she seemed to sense when Simon did not want to talk. This was a big improvement over Ramona. And she liked his banjo-playing.

One day, Simon, coming back from a walk, heard his banjo. Whoever was playing it was playing it well since it was in his exact style. If he hadn't known better, he would have thought it a recording. He hurried in and found Chworktap strumming away as if to the banjo born.

"Do you have banjos on Zelpst?" he said.

"No."

"Then how did you learn to play it?"

"I watched you play it."

"And I spent twenty years learning what you've learned in a few hours," he said. He wasn't bitter, just amazed.

"Naturally."

"Why naturally?"

"It's one of my talents."

"Is everybody on Zelpst as talented as you?"

"Not everybody."

"I'd sure like to go there."

"I wouldn't," she said.

Simon took the banjo from her, but before he could ask her more, she said, "I'll have supper in a minute."

Simon smelled the food when she opened the radar oven, and he became ecstatic. He was getting fed up with chop suey and egg foo young and sour-sweet pork, and he was too soft-hearted to kill anything for a change of diet unless he'd been starving. And here came Chworktap with a big tray of hamburgers, french fries, milkshakes, ketchup, mustard, and dill pickles!

When he had stuffed his stomach and had lit up a big cigar, he asked her how she had performed this miracle.

"You told me what food you liked best. Don't you remember my asking you how it was made?"

"I do."

"I went out and shot one of those wild cows," she said. "After I'd butchered it and put the extra in the freezer, I scouted around until I found some plants like potatoes. And I found others to make ketchup and mustard from. I found a plant like a cucumber and fixed it up. I have an extensive knowledge of chemistry, you know."

"I didn't know," he said, shaking his head.

"I found chocolate in the pantry and instant milk. I mixed some chemicals with these to make ice cream and chocolate sauce."

"Fabulous!" Simon said. "Is there anything else you can do?"

"Oh yes."

She stood up and unzipped her gown, let it fall to the floor, and sat down on Simon's lap. Her kiss was soft and hot with a tang of milkshake and ketchup. Simon didn't have to ask her what it was she also did so well.

Later, when Simon had taken a shower and a double-header of rice wine, he said, "I hope you're not pregnant, Chworktap. I don't have any contraceptives, and I didn't think to ask you if you had any."

"I can't get pregnant."

"I'm sorry to hear that," he said. "Do you want children? You can always adopt one, you know."

"I don't have any mother love."

Simon was puzzled. He said, "How do you know that?"

"I wasn't programmed for mother love. I'm a robot."

10

TROUBLE ON GIFFARD

Simon was shocked. He had detected nothing more than the usual amount of lubrication at such moments. There had been nothing of plastic or foam rubber or metal on or in her.

"You look pale, lover?"

"Why so pale?" he said. "I mean, you're not making a statement of fact but a question. And you look rather pale yourself."

"It just didn't occur to me until a moment ago that you might not know," she said. "As soon as I thought of that, then I had to tell you. I'm programmed to tell the truth. Just as real humans are programmed to tell lies," she added after a second's pause.

Would, or could, a robot be malicious or even sarcastic? Yes, if it was programmed to be so. But who would do this? Or why? Someone who wanted to make others uncomfortable or even furious and so had set up certain circuits in his/her robot for just this effect?

But a robot that was emotionally affected? So much so

that she—he couldn't think of Chworktap as an it—would turn pale or blush? Nonsense! But then, what did he know of robots like this? Earth science had not progressed to the point where it could build such a reasonable facsimile. It could, and had, clothed a metal-plastic-electromechanical with artificial protein. But the robot was so jerky in its movements, so transparently a construction, that it wouldn't have fooled a child. Her planet, Zelpst, must be far advanced indeed.

Could he fall in love with a thing?

He sighed and thought, why not? He loved his banjo. Others, multitudes of others, had full-blown passions for cars, model airplanes, hi-fi's, rare books, and bicycle seats.

But Chworktap was definitely a human being, and surely there was a difference between love for a woman and love for antique furniture.

"I'm basically a protein robot," Chworktap said. "I've got some tiny circuit boards here and there along with some atomic energy units and capacitors. But mostly I'm flesh and blood, just like you. The difference is that you were made by accident and I was designed by a board of scientists. Like it or not, you had to take whatever genes—good or rotten—your parents passed on to you. My genes were carefully selected from a hundred models, and then they were put together in the laboratory. The artificial ovum and sperm were placed in a tube, the sperm then united with the ovum, and I spent my nine months in the tube."

"Then we have at least that in common," Simon said. "My mother, the selfish old bitch, didn't want to bother carrying me around."

"The human Zelpstians spend their first nine months in tubes, too," she said. "The ova and sperms are mailed in by the adults, and the Population Control Bureau, which is run by robots, uses them to start a baby whenever an adult dies. At the same time, a hundred robot babies are started. These are raised as companions and servants for the human baby. They're also socially programmed to admire and love their human master. And the only adults the human child sees are robots which act as surrogate parents."

Zelpst was dedicated to furnishing all humans with all the comforts of its splendid technology. Even more important, every human was spared the pains and frustrations which Earthmen assumed were inevitable. The only things denied the human child were those which might endanger him. When a human reached puberty, he/she was given a castle in which he/she lived the rest of his/her life. The Zelpstian was surrounded by every material comfort and by a hundred robots. These looked and acted just like humans except they were unable to hurt the owner's feelings. And they behaved exactly as the owner wanted them to behave. They were programmed to be the people the lord/lady of the castle wanted to associate with.

"My master, Zappo, liked brilliant witty conversation," she said. "So we were all brilliant and witty. But he didn't like us to top his wit. So every time we thought of a one-upman remark, it was routed to a deadend circuit board in us. The male robots were all impotent because Zappo didn't want anybody except himself fucking the female robots. Every time they thought about getting a hard-on, the impulse would be rerouted through a circuit board and converted into an overwhelming sense of shame and guilt. And every time we thought about punching Zappo, and believe me, we thought about it a lot, the impulse was also converted into shame and guilt. And a splitting headache."

"Then you all had self-consciousness and free will?" Simon said. "Why didn't the programmers just eliminate that in the robots?"

"Anything that has a brain complex enough to use language in a witty or creative manner has to have self-consciousness and free will," Chworktap said. "There's no getting away from it. Anything, even a machine composed solely of silicon and metal parts and electrical wires, anything that uses language like a human is human."

"Good God!" Simon said. "You robots must've suffered terribly from frustration! Didn't any of you ever break down?"

"Yes, but our bad thoughts were all rerouted back into our selves. This was done so that we wouldn't harm our master. Every once in a while, a robot would commit suicide. When that happened, the master would just order another one. Sometimes, he got tired of a particular robot and would kill it. Zappo was a sadistic bastard, anyway."

"I would have thought that anybody raised with nothing but love and kindness and admiration would grow up to be a kind and loving person."

"It doesn't always work out that way," she said. "Humans are programmed by their genes. They're also programmed to some extent by their environment. But it's the genes that determine how they're going to react to the environment."

"I know," Simon said. "Some people are born aggressive, and others are passive all their lives. A kid can be raised in a Catholic family, and his brothers and sisters will remain devout Catholics all their life. But he becomes a raving atheist or joins a Baptist church. Or a Jew forsakes the religion of his fathers but still gets sick at the thought of eating ham. Or a Moslem believes in the Koran one hundred percent, but he has to fight a secret craving for pork. The dietary genes control this."

"Something like that," Chworktap said. "Though it isn't that simple. Anyway, no matter how carefully the Zelpst society was designed to prevent unhappiness and frustration for the humans, it wasn't one hundred percent efficient. There's always a flaw, you know. Zappo got unhappy because his robots didn't love him for himself. He was always asking us, 'Do you love me?', and we'd always reply, 'You're the only one I love, revered master.' And then he'd get red in the face and say, 'You brainless machine, you can't say anything else but! What I want to know is, if I took the reroute circuits out, would you still say you love me?' And we'd say, 'Sure thing, master.' And he'd get even more angry, and he'd scream, 'But do you *really* love me?' And sometimes he'd beat us. And we'd take it, we weren't programmed to resist, and he'd scream, 'Why don't you fight back!'

"Sometimes I felt sorry for him, but I couldn't even tell him that. To feel sorry for him was to demean him, and any demeaning thought was routed to the devoicing circuit.

"Zappo knew that when he made love to me I enjoyed it. He did not want a masturbating machine, so he'd specified that all his robots, male or female, would respond fully. Whether we were being screwed by him, blowing him, or being buggered, we had intense orgasms. He knew that our cries of ecstasy weren't faked. But there was no way for even the scientists to ensure that we would love him. And even if they could have made us automatically fall in love with him, Zappo wouldn't have been satisfied. He wanted us to love him by our own free choice, to love him just because he was lovable. But he didn't dare to have the inhibiting circuits removed, because then, if we'd said we didn't love him, he wouldn't have been able to stand it.

"So he was in a hell of a situation."

"You all were," Simon said.

"Yes. Zappo often said that everybody in the castle, including himself, was a robot. We'd been purposely made robots, but chance had made him one. His parents' ovum and spermatozoon had determined his virtues and his vices. He did not have any more free will than we did."

Simon picked up his banjo, tuned it, and then said, "Bruga put the whole philosophical question in a single poem. He called it *Aphrodite and the Philosophers*. I'll sing it for you."

> *The world we see, said Socrates,*
> *Is only shadows, a crock, a tease.*
>
> *Young Leibniz said we all are monads.*
> *He lacked connection with his gonads.*
>
> *Old Kant did run his life by clock.*
> *Tick Tock! He lacked, alas, a cock.*

Nor knew that his Imperative
Was horse's laughter up a sleeve.

If Cleo's nose had been too short?
If Papa Pharaoh'd named her Mort?

Would then have risen Caesar's bone?
Or did it have a will its own?

It swelled, we know, at sight of Brutus.
He'd shove his horn up all to toot us.

Imperator, he'd screw the world.
The hole's the thing, if boyed or girled.

Some say that love is Cupid's arrow.
For this defense, call Clarence Darrow.

Envoi

Our Lady of Our Love's Afflatus,
Unveil the All, and please don't freight us
Sans paddle up the amorous creek,
Unknowing if by will or freak
Of circumstances our loves'll mate us.
All flappers think they've picked their sheik
With perfect freedom in their choice.

In this have they as little voice
As chickens swallowed by a geek

"That's just a list of question-beggers," she said. "Bruga was like you, a man driven by his peculiar complex of genes to look for answers that didn't exist."

"Maybe," Simon said. "So how do you explain how you, a nonfree-will robot, got away from your master?"

"It was an accident. Zappo struck me on the head with a vase during a fit of rage. The blow knocked me out, but when I woke up, I found that I was able to disobey him. The blow had knocked the master circuit out of commission. Of course, I didn't let him know that. When I got the chance, I stole a spaceship. The Zelpstians quit space travel a long time ago, but there were still some ships gathering dust in museums nobody visited anymore. I wandered around for a while and then I came across this planet. There weren't any human beings here, or so I thought. I was going to stay here forever. But I did get lonely. I'm glad you came along."

"And so am I," Simon said. "So you got your freedom because of a malfunctioning circuit?"

"I suppose so. And that worries me. What if another accident makes the circuit function again?"

"It's not likely."

"Of course," she said, "I'm by no means entirely unprogrammed. But then who, robot or human, is? I have certain tastes in food and drink, I loathe birds..."

"Why do you hate birds?"

"Zappo was frightened by one when he was a child. And so he had all his robots programmed to hate birds. He didn't want us to be superior to him in any respect."

"You can't really blame him for that," Simon said. "Well, how about it, Chworktap? Would you like to come with me?"

"Where are you going?"

"Everywhere until I find the answer to my primal question."

"What's that?"

"Why are we born only to suffer and die?"

"What you're saying is this," she said. "Nothing else matters if we have immortality."

"Without immortality, the universe is meaningless," he said. "Ethics, morality, society as a whole are just means to get through life with the least pain. They can all be reduced to one term: economy."

"An economy that is nowhere more than thirty percent efficient," she said.

"You don't know that. You haven't been everywhere."

"But you're going everywhere?"

"If possible. I've already eliminated my galaxy, though. I know from what I've read that the answer is not there. But what about you, Chworktap? What about your genes? Most of them are artificial. So you shouldn't have any gene pattern to predetermine your reactions to philosophical problems."

"I'm a crazy quilt of chromosomes," she said. "All my genes are based on those which once existed. Each is copied after a certain person's, though each is an improved model. But I have the genes of many individuals. You might say I have a thousand parents, a hundred thousand grandparents."

They were interrupted at this point by a loud crash outside the ship. They hurried out to see, a quarter of a mile away, a female and a male Giffardian lying in ruins. The male had burst into flame, and both were burning away under a strong wind.

This wasn't the first crash of this type, nor was it likely to be the last. The females' insistence that they be given rides was causing many accidents, usually fatal. The weight of the female at the nose-end made the male upend. To sustain altitude, he had to jet his drive-gas through his fore opening at full speed. The two would go straight up, and then the male would get exhausted. And down they would come.

"And all the king's horses and all the king's men couldn't put them together again," Simon murmured.

"Why don't they just quit that?" Chworktap said.

"Their genes drive them to their actions," Simon said maliciously.

"If they keep this up, they'll become extinct," she said. "Even if there weren't any crashes, they'll die out. The air-time keeps the females from browsing, and so the young aren't getting enough food. Look how thin they've become!"

What the Giffardians did was none of Simon's business, but that didn't keep him from interfering. At dusk, when the males had come down, and males and young were locked into the females, he went into the meadow. And there he proposed that they should settle their conflict. Let them choose him as an objective judge and abide by his decision.

He was, of course, rejected. But a few days later, after three couples had fallen to their death, a female and a male approached him. The former he called Amelia and the latter Ferdinand. Graf and Gräfin, the leader and his wife, had been smashed to bits only the day before. Amelia and Ferdinand, as next in line in the pecking order, had become the chiefs. A funeral had been held, at which Simon had brought flowers. The preacher of the flock had given a eulogy. Graf was praised for his outstanding leadership, though everyone knew he had been a lazy bully who had delegated most of his administrative work to underlings. He was praised for his faithfulness as a mate, though everyone knew he was always luring females to the other side of the forest and half of the herd could call him father. The preacher spoke of what an exemplary family man he was, although everyone knew that he had not spoken to his children unless they were irritating him and then it was to blow them end over end with a mighty fart.

Gräfin was praised as a patient hard-working wife and mother. She had certainly been hard-working, but her loud-mouthed bitchings about her husband and her backbiting gossip were well known.

Simon didn't find anything strange in this. He had attended many such.

At the end of the funeral, Amelia and Ferdinand had asked to see Simon the next day. And so here they were.

What they wanted was simple but not easy. Simon was to decide whether or not the sky-rides should continue. The females still wanted to go up, and the males were still dead-set against it.

Simon said that he would accept the appointment, but it might be a few days before he could come to a decision.

After two days and nights, Simon retreated into the *Hwang Ho*. The females had sidled up to him on their hundred legs and offered all they had if he'd judge in their favor. Simon didn't think their offers were very attractive even if he had been corruptible. If he had tried sexual intercourse with them, he would have fallen down their huge apex-hole into their stomachs. Nor did he like the idea of eating regurgitated food from their apex-organs.

The males offered day-long rides. He could even smoke during them. They'd dangle him as far away as possible from the end of a mid-body tentacle. They couldn't guarantee, of course, that they could keep a grip on him. As an additional incentive, they'd elect him leader of the herd. Ferdinand wouldn't like that but he could just blow it out as far as the others were concerned.

Simon could keep the ship's ports closed and so block out the entreaties of the females, who stood around the ship and whistled fumes at him. But he had to look through the viewscreens from time to time to cool his cabin fever. When he did so, he saw the huge black dot-and-dash clouds the males were laying out in the air above him. This was the first time he had seen obscene skywriting.

"Whichever way you decide, your life won't be safe," Chworktap said. "Why don't we just leave?"

"I gave my word."

"And what would happen if you didn't keep it?"

"Nothing of cosmic importance. But to me it would mean that I am less than a man. I'd have no dignity, no personal integrity. People wouldn't trust me because I couldn't trust myself. Everybody, including myself, would be contemptuous of me."

"You'd rather die?"

"I think so," he said.

"But it doesn't make sense."

"Society would fall apart if people didn't keep their words."

"How many people on Earth kept theirs?"

Simon thought for a moment and then said, "Not many."

"And Earth society fell apart?"

"Well, no," he said. "But it didn't operate very efficiently, either."

"So what are you going to tell the Giffardians?" she said.

"Come with me, you'll find out."

Accompanied by her, the dog, and the owl, he walked through the forest to the meadow. At its edge he shot off a Very rocket, at sight of which the females wobbled toward him and the males sailed toward him. The young continued playing. When all the males had wrapped their tentacles around large rocks to anchor themselves, Simon proposed his new system.

"I hope this will make everybody happy," he said. "It's a compromise of sorts, but nothing workable is ever achieved in this world without compromise."

"Don't try to soften us males up," Ferdinand whistled at him. "We know what's right."

"Don't try to take away our hard-earned rights," Amelia whistled.

"Please!" Simon said, holding up his hand. "I have a plan whereby all you females can get your air-time. And it'll be absolutely safe. No more crashes. The only thing is, it means that you'll have to change your system of marriage."

He waited until the storm of whistles had ceased and the wind had blown the stenches clear.

"You're monogamous," he said. "One male married to one female for life. A good system it is, though, if you will pardon the observation of an objective alien, more honored in the breach than in the observance. But if you females want to enjoy flight, you'll have to change the system."

There was another storm which deafened him and made him choke and gasp. When it subsided, he said, "Why don't you set up a polyandrous system?"

"What's that?" they whistled, among other things.

"Well, you forbid any male to lock into the mouth-vulva of any female unless he's married to her. But what if one female was married to two males?"

The females were silent. Their eight eyes rolled around and around, which was a Giffardian's way of showing deep thought. The males were scandalized, and the ripping noises and sulphides drove Simon and Chworktap into the bushes for a moment.

When he came out, Simon said, "It's a matter of logic. The only way a female can be safely carried is by two males. They can share the burden and easily levitate a female. There won't be any more crashes."

"And how can we possibly do that?" Ferdinand said.

"Why, two males can lock into one female, one in the oral opening of the apex-lock and one in the anal. Two males can easily carry one female. On one day, half of the females can fly; the next day the other half take their turns. It's all so easy; I don't know why you didn't figure that out…"

Fortunately, the females were too wide to get through the forest and the males had to fly overhead against a strong wind. Simon and Chworktap fled hand in hand with Anubis howling after them and the owl flying overhead. Even so, the males were only a few feet behind them when Simon and the party broke out of the woods. They reached the spaceship three steps ahead of Ferdinand's tentacles and threw themselves through the port. Simon closed it and gave orders to the computer to take off for stars unknown.

Chworktap, panting, said, "I hope this teaches you a lesson."

"How was I to know they'd get so mad?" Simon said.

Years later, he was to run across a being from Shekshekel who had landed on Giffard about fifty years after the Earthman's visit.

"They told me about you," the Shekshekel said. "They still refer to you as Simon the Sodomite."

LALORLONG

The *Hwang Ho*, after a few days, headed for the planet Lalorlong. Chworktap had told Simon that she had heard that this was inhabited by a very philosophical race.

"They don't have much else to do but think."

"Then we'll go there," Simon said. "It seems to me that if anybody has the answers, they would."

Lalorlong hove to. It was a planet about Earth-size which had long ago lost all its surface water except at the poles. Erosion had filled the oceans and cut down the land until the planet was a smooth globe. The difference in temperature between the polar and the warm regions and that created by the tilting of the axis caused general winds. These followed an easily predictable course.

The only object that rose above the surface was the gigantic heart-shaped tower of the Clerun-Gowph. This had fallen over, its base of stone eaten away by the winds. Simon had the ship fly over it so he could take a look at it. There wasn't any sign of life, but he hadn't expected any. The tower must have been erected a billion years ago and fallen many millions ago. What a sound its topple must have made!

Who was there to hear it? Only the sentient species of Lalorlong. They were the only animal life left. The only vegetable life was a type of tumbleweed on which the Lalorlongians depended for food and water. The plant apparently had very deep roots that sucked up water from the rocks and broke down the chemicals in them to form its own food. When it grew to a certain height, the upper part would fall off and whirl over and over, borne around the world unless it was intercepted by a hungry Lalorlongian.

The natives resembled automobile wheels with balloon tires. The tires were composed of thin but tough inflated skins with diamond-shaped treads. The wheel part consisted of a rim of bone and twelve bone spokes which grew from the hub. The hub was a ball covered with a hard shell like an ant's exoskeleton. This contained the brain and the nervous, digestive, and sexual systems. In the center of the right and left side was a round hole. A cartilaginous stalk ran out from each hole horizontally for a few inches and then abruptly curved straight upward. The stalks reached approximately two feet above the tire and each ended in two eyes on separately rotatable auxiliary stalks. Halfway down each was a bulbous organ which could flash a light like a firefly's. They used these at night for illumination and sometimes in the day to signal turns.

Simon thought they were limbless until he saw the leader project a long pencil-thin arm with six joints and a three-fingered hand from each hole in the ball-hub. The arm bent in the middle to point downward. This seemed to be a signal to slow down. The others put out stick-like six-jointed legs from both holes in the hubs. These had collapsible feet, broad when spread out, toeless, and with thickly calloused soles. They dragged these in the dirt until they had reduced speed, then they retracted their legs.

The leader's left arm came out, and he turned halfway toward where he was pointing. The others followed suit, keeping the same exact distance behind him.

Simon flew above them for a while in the red light of the ancient and dying sun. The herd, seen from above, formed the outline of an arrowhead. Its point was the leader, a big purple creature with white sidewalls. The V of the arrow was composed of young males riding shotgun. Straight out from behind the leader, in Indian file, were females with their young rolling along beside them. The base of the arrow was made up of old males whose purple was turning gray. As he would discover, the formation was based on a rigid pecking order. The leader was always in front, and the females behind him held positions according to their fertility and sexual vigor.

All except the leader were a solid purple. But when a young male overthrew the old leader, he would grow white sidewalls. His new social position triggered off hormones that caused this strange tire-change.

The leader had signaled a change in direction and speed because he had seen some tumbleweeds rolling toward them. Presently, the herd intercepted these, and their right arms snatched the plants and tore off branches. The pieces went into the right-hand holes. Inside were mouths with broad strong teeth which mashed and chewed the plants with a sidewise motion. The plants provided not only water but food like rubbery chocolate.

The anal opening was by the left-hand hole in the hub; the excrement was shot out in tiny pellets. Since the Lalorlongians had an extremely efficient metabolism, they expelled very little offal.

Simon told the ship to fly close to the left of the herd. As he'd expected, the herd turned toward the right. They were hesitant about turning at a right angle and so presenting their bodies to the full force of the strong wind. Once they'd fallen to the ground, they had no way of getting back up. They rolled at a forty-five-degree angle from their previous path, leaning into the wind. To do this, they stuck out their right arms as far as they could and bent their eye-stalks to the right. Then they drew their arms back into the holes, rolled along for a while, and, at a signal from the leader, pointed straight westward again. This manoeuvre was done with the aid of the left arms.

"What do they talk with?" Simon said to Chworktap.

"They use their fingers, just like deaf-and-dumb people."

The *Hwang Ho* carried a jeep. Simon ordered the ship to stop, and he and Chworktap got into the jeep. The dog and the owl, who were suffering from cabin fever, complained so much about being left behind that he told them to get in too. But the owl had to sit in the back seat so she wouldn't disturb Chworktap. The port opened, a gangplank ran out, and they drove onto the smooth surface. The ship then lifted and followed them a mile behind.

The jeep had no trouble catching up, even though the wind was pushing the herd at about thirty-five miles an hour. The eyes on the ends of the stalks rolled with fright as the jeep neared them, and the herd veered to the left. Their arms came out, the fingers wriggling and crossing and bending as they asked each other what in hell these strangers were and what did they mean to do? Their signal lights began flashing hysterically. It was later that Simon discovered that these people used their lights in conjunction with their fingers when they talked. This was to make it difficult for him to carry on a conversation. He couldn't use the fingers of both his hands and operate two flashlights at the same time. But Chworktap turned the lights on and off for him, and the two were able to carry on a conversation with the wheels. Sometimes, they got a little confused and had to start a sentence all over again.

Simon and Chworktap spent most of each day on the road. Somebody had to drive but somebody also had to operate the flashlights. Chworktap rigged up a device which enabled her to turn the lights off and on with the fingers of one hand while she drove with the other. Fortunately, she didn't have to watch out for cars or immovable objects or worry about running off the pavement. After a few days, she put together a device which kept the car at the same distance from the Lalorlongian they were learning the language from. This fixed a laser beam on their informant. If the informant went too far away or came too close, the change in the beam's length caused a motor to turn one of two straps fixed to the wheel to correct the course and also to alter the setting of the cruise control.

Simon was beginning to wonder what he would ever have done without Chworktap.

"Watch it!" he told himself. "You aren't *about* to fall in love with a robot!"

Simon won the confidence of the wheelers the third day. One of the young adolescent males was showing off. He would curve around and head into the wind until he was stopped and then was pushed backward. He had done this a dozen times to the admiration of the young females, who wiggled their fingers and flashed their lights in a running ovation. But while the young stud was cutting a figure-eight, he leaned over too far and fell on his side. The fingers and lights of everybody signaled panic and despair, but they all rolled on, leaving the young male lying on his side, one arm stuck up and waving frantically, his eyes rolling in their sockets.

"They're going to abandon him," Chworktap said.

"Apparently, they have no way of lifting him up," Simon said. "So it's tough titty for anybody that falls over."

Simon disconnected the driving mechanism and turned the jeep around. It only took a moment for the two of them to lift upright the three-hundred-pound youth. He did not start rolling at once, however. His eyes still rotated like the Coyote's when he gets caught in a trap he's set for the Roadrunner.

"He looks like he's in pain," Chworktap said.

This, as it turned out, was right. Above the arm-opening was another hole, a small one from which the male's pistil stuck during mating or when he was excited. The youth had been excited while he was showing off, and when he had fallen he had squeezed the end of his pistil under his hub. This was comparable to being kicked in the crotch.

After a while, the youth seemed ready to go. Simon knew that he would never catch up with the herd, so he and Chworktap lifted him up over the back end of the jeep and onto the back seat. The dog, which had just finished pissing against the youth, jumped into the front seat. The owl flew overhead, circling the jeep, but when she saw that she was going to be left behind, she landed on the hood and grabbed the ornament.

Simon drove the jeep far ahead of the herd, and he and Chworktap hoisted the youth out and set him upright. Presently, the herd came along, and the youth, aided by a shove from Simon, took off to rejoin the herd.

Simon later observed a mother feeding her child. The little wheel ran up alongside the female, who dragged her feet to reduce her speed until they were going at the same pace. A long cartilaginous tube came out of a hole near the top of the hemisphere, just below the rotating collar. It traveled out until it was over a hole in a similar location on the child's hemisphere. The child reached up with its hand and pulled the tube into its hole. They traveled together for about fifteen minutes, after which the tube withdrew. The mother had fed milk through this to the young.

Toward evening, the leader signaled, and he slowed down. A bright orange female came up alongside him, and they mated. This was a simple and quick operation. The pistil came out of its hole, crossed the gap between them, and plunged into one of the female's holes. A few seconds later the pistil withdrew, its end dripping with a honey-like liquid. The female dragged her feet, and another female came up to take her turn. By dusk, the leader had pistiled every nubile female in the herd.

When night fell, the herd turned on all its light. Simon was going to call in the ship on his radio when he saw the lights of two wheelers go out. He put the phone back on its hook and turned out the jeep's lights. Sure enough, adultery had come to Lalorlong. Though not for the first time, he was sure.

"I wonder what would happen if the bull wheel caught them?" Simon said. "How in heaven's name do they fight?"

A few days later, they found out. A big young male stranger rolled toward them from the left. The leader signaled frantically, and the herd slowed down. The bull then leaned into the wind and headed toward the stranger.

"The young stud is going to challenge the bull," Simon said. "I suppose that if he wins, the bull is left behind on his side, and the youth takes over."

The two met at an angle, since it would have been fatal to have turned at right angles to the wind for over a second. The youth spun around and around while the bull wavered as if he were going to fall over. But he held his arms out to maintain his balance, managed to make a turn, and struck the spinning stud a glancing blow on the rim. The youth crashed over, and the leader, flashing his lights triumphantly, called to the herd to follow him.

Simon felt sorry for the youth, so he and Chworktap got him up and sent him on his way. Not, however, before they were sure that he wouldn't be able to catch up with the herd.

"Such encounters must be rare," Simon said. "The stud who

leaves his herd or is driven out to seek a mate must have a hard time. He might wander around forever before he runs across another herd. Then he has to beat the bull and maybe the young males of the herd, for all I know, before he takes over."

A week later, while they were driving around, they saw an old male lying on his side. They drove up and jumped out, but there wasn't much they could do for him. He had had a blowout. His one free arm waved, the three fingers wiggling frantically, and the eyes on the ends of the stalks dripped tears.

Simon tried to patch up the hole with the tire-repairing materials in the jeep. When he started the vulcanizing, the eye-stalks lashed back and forth and the light-organs flashed redly. The Lalorlongian was being badly hurt. In any event, his treads were worn off, and the skin was too thin to take a patch-up job.

Simon could not endure to leave him there to starve to death. He took out his automatic and, with tears running from his own eyes, emptied twelve bullets into the hole in the hub. Anubis ran around barking and Athena flew screeching around and around above the shattered corpse. The male's arm dropped, folding this and that way, its lights dimmed and died, its stalks crumpled, and its eyes glazed.

After they had returned to the ship, Simon said, "The ethics of euthanasia is one of my minor questions. Is it or isn't it right to put a sentient creature out of its pain if it's going to die anyway? You just saw my answer. What do you think?"

"It's ethically correct if the dying person gives her consent," Chworktap said. "Actually, if you deny her the right to euthanasia, you're interfering with her free will. But you didn't ask that person if he wanted to be killed."

"I was afraid he'd say no, and I couldn't stand the thought of his suffering."

"Then you were wrong," she said.

"But he was suffering terribly, and I saved him from a lingering death."

"You should have left it up to him."

On reflection, Simon agreed with her. But it was too late to correct his error.

Simon spent the next week questioning the members of a dozen herds.

"What's your basic philosophy?"

"Keep rolling."

"Why?"

"Keep rolling, and you'll get there."

"Where?"

"To the yonder."

"But on this planet you can only end up where you started."

"So what? The name of the game is Getting There."

"But why do you want to get there?"

"Because it's there."

"What happens after you die?"

"We go to the Big Track in the Sky. No lack of tumbleweeds there, everyone is the leader of the herd, and only the evil have blowouts."

"But why were you put on this planet?"

"I told you. To travel around and around while we follow our glorious leader."

Or, in the case of the leader, "To travel around and around while my herd follows me."

"But what about those who have blowouts?"

"They're guilty."

"Guilty of what?"

"Of harboring bad thoughts."

"Against whom?"

"Our leader and the Big Repairer in the Sky."

"But what about the young studs that challenge the leader? Don't they have bad thoughts?"

"Not if they win."

"What happens to the bad ones?"

"They're taken up to the Big Track, too. But they get their just reward. Their tires go flat once a day."

Simon was disgusted, but Chworktap said, "What did you expect? Look at how poverty-sticken, how bare, this planet is. All the Lalorlongians see is flat hard earth, dust, and tumbleweeds. So, if there's little outside to see, there's little to think about inside."

Simon said, "Yeah, I know. Maybe the next place'll be better."

12

ELDER SISTER PLUM

On the way to the planet Dokal, Simon and Chworktap had had their first quarrel. The second day out, Simon had found her wearing a pair of earphones at the control board. Her fingers were dancing over the keys, and the communication screen was flashing messages in Chinese. Simon could read only a few logographs and those slowly, so he had to ask her what she was doing.

She couldn't hear, of course, but he finally put his hand on her shoulder and squeezed a few times. She looked up and then removed the phones.

"What's upsetting you?" she said.

Simon had been in a bad enough temper before. Her instant detection of his state of temper made him more angry. He was beginning to find this sensitivity disconcerting. It was too much like mind-reading.

"For one thing," he said, "I had a hard night, I kept dreaming that a lot of dead people were trying to talk to me all at once. For another thing, I'm getting fed up with stepping in Anubis' crap.

I've tried to house-break him, but he's unteachable. A spaceship is no place for a dog, and when I think that this might go on for a thousand years..."

"Put him in a cage."

"That'd break his heart," Simon said. "I couldn't be cruel to him."

"Then adjust to it," Chworktap said. "What's the third thing that's bothering you?"

"Nothing," he said, knowing his denial would be rejected. "I just wanted to know what you're doing. After all, I am captain of this ship, and I don't want you monkeying around with the navigation."

"You're jealous because I'm smarter than you and so can read Chinese so easily," she said. "That's why you're questioning me."

"If you're so smart, you'd know better than to tell me that."

"I thought you liked a candid woman."

"There are reasonable limits to candor," he said, his face reddening.

"O.K.," she said, "I won't mention that again."

"Dammit, now you're accusing me of having a swollen male ego!"

"And you like to think you don't," Chworktap said. "O.K., so you're not perfect."

"Only a machine can be perfect!"

Simon at once regretted saying this, but it was too late, as always. Tears ran down her cheeks.

"Is that an unconscious or a deliberate reaction?" he said. "Can you turn on the tears when you want me to feel like an ass?"

"My master didn't like tears, so I always held them back," she said. "But you're not my master; you're my lover. Besides, Earthwomen, so you've told me, can turn on tears at will. And they're not machines."

Simon put his hand on her shoulder again and said, "I'm sorry. I didn't mean to hurt your feelings. And I don't think of you as a machine."

"Your lying circuits are working overtime," Chworktap said. "And you're still angry. Why are you so solicitous about a dog's feelings but deliberately hurt mine?"

"I suppose because I'm taking out my anger at him on you," Simon said. "He wouldn't know why I was chewing him out."

"You're ashamed of your anger and so you're trying to get me mad so I'll chew you out and punish you for it," Chworktap said. "Do you feel a large hole where your ass used to be?"

"No, it's bigger than ever," he said, and he laughed.

"But you're still angry," Chworktap said, and shrugged.

"No, I'm not. Yes, I am. But not at you."

"My radar tells me you are angry, but it's not sensitive enough to tell me whom you're angry at. You asked what I was doing. I'm trying to determine if Tzu Li has self-consciousness."

Tzu Li, or Elder Sister Plum, were the key words spoken or punched when the operator wanted to open communication with the ship's computer. Simon had often wondered why the captain had picked out that name for the computer. He could have been poetically inclined, or he could have had a sister by that name who'd bossed him around and so he had been getting a vicarious revenge by bossing *this* Tzu Li.

"What makes you think she is anything but a computer?" Simon said.

"She keeps making little comments when she replies. They're not necessary, and they sound sarcastic or, sometimes, plaintive."

"She's starting to break down!" Simon said. "I hope not! I haven't the slightest idea how to repair her!"

"I know how," Chworktap said, and this made Simon angrier.

"Well then, fix her."

"But Tzu Li may not be malfunctioning. Or, if it is a malfunction, it may be benign. After all, it was a blow on my head that scrambled my circuits and made me self-conscious."

"No way," Simon said. "Complicated as that computer is, it's as simple as A-B-C compared to the complexity of your brain. You might as well tell me that a turtle could be hit on the head and wake up with self-consciousness."

"Who knows?"

"It's identification!" Simon said. "Tzu Li's a machine, and you'd like to have a companion! Next you'll be telling me your screwdriver is hollering for help!"

"How would you like my screwdriver all the way in and up and Roger, over?"

Chworktap certainly did not talk like a cool, perfectly logical robot. This was understandable, since she was not one. Simon felt that he had been unjust. To distract her, he said, "This reminds me of a novel by Jonathan Swift Somers III. It was one of a very popular series which Somers wrote about Ralph von Wau Wau."

Ralph was a German police dog born in Hamburg. He spent his early years training with the *Polizei*, but when he was two he was chosen to be the subject of experiments by the scientists of *das Institut und die Tankstelle für Gehirntaschenspieler*. After his brain had been operated on, Ralph had an I.Q. of 200. This was considerably higher than any of the policemen's who worked him or, for that matter, the police chief's or the mayor's. Naturally, he became discontented and quit the force. He went into business for himself and became the most famous private eye of all time.

Adept at disguise, he could pose as a man or a dog and, in one celebrated case, passed himself off as a Shetland pony. He acquired a luxurious apartment with a portable gold hydrant and three lovely bitches of different breeds. One of these, Samantha die Gestäupte, became his partner. She was the heroine in the best-selling *A Fat, Worse than Death*, in which she saved Ralph, who had been captured by the master villain, A Fat.

After eight novels, Ralph retired from detective work. The heavy drinking which was obligatory for all private eyes was turning him into an alcoholic. After a long vacation, Ralph, bored with his violin-playing and chemical researches, took a job as reporter for the *Kosmos Klatschbase*. He quickly rose to the top of his profession since he could get into places barred to human reporters, including men's or women's rest rooms. In the nineteenth of the series, *No Nose Means Bad News*, Ralph won the Pulitzer Prize, no easy feat, since he was not an American citizen. At its end, he decided to quit the newspaper business, since the heavy drinking obligatory for a reporter was turning him into an alcoholic, which, in turn, was causing him to be impotent.

Off the juice, though still able to handle only one bitch, Ralph toured the world in *What Am I Doing on Your Table?* While in China, he became appalled at the custom of eating dogs and waged a one-canine war against it.

"In fact," Simon said, "it was this novel that aroused world opinion to such a fever that China was forced to abolish canivorousness. In the novel Ralph wins the Nobel Peace Prize, but in actuality Somers won it for writing the novel.

"But it didn't do the dogs that were let loose much good. They became such a nuisance they had to be rounded up and gassed. And the price of beef went sky-high due to the shortage of meat."

In the twenty-first of the series, *A Fat in the Fire*, Ralph and his constant companion were still in China. Ralph had become interested in Chinese poetry and was trying his paw at composing verses. But he was thinking of quitting it because the heavy drinking obligatory for a poet was turning him into an alcoholic. Then his old enemy, A Fat, last seen falling into a cement mixer, struck again. Sam, Ralph's constant companion (and now a member of the Women's Christian Temperance Union), had disappeared. Ralph suspected fowl play, since Sam was witnessed being carried off in a truck loaded down with chickens. He also suspected A Fat, since the reports of the villain's death had always been grossly exaggerated.

Disguised as a chow, Ralph relentlessly sniffed out clues. Sure enough, A Fat was back in business. The cement mixer was a fake, one of the thousands of escape mechanisms A Fat had planted around the country just in case. But Ralph tracked him down, and in an exciting scene the two battled to death on a cliff high above the Yellow River. The tremendously powerful A Fat (once the Olympic heavyweight wrestling champion, representing Outer Mongolia) grabbed Ralph by the tail and swung him around and around over the cliff's edge.

Ralph thought he was on his last case then. But, as luck would have it, the seams of his chow costume burst, and he flew out. Fortunately, he was pointed inland at the time. A Fat, thrown off balance by the sudden loss of weight, fell over the cliff's edge and into the smokestack of a bird's-nest-soup freighter. Ralph released Samantha from her cage just before the bomb in it went off, and they trotted off together into the sunset.

This time, A Fat must surely be dead. But the readers suspected that the freighter was another of his escape devices, kept around just in case. A Fat was as hard to kill as Fu Manchu and Sherlock Holmes.

"Why does that remind you of what I'm doing?" Chworktap said.

"Well," Simon said, "that wasn't the end of the novel. Despite the slambang action and sinister intrigue, this book, like all of Somers' works, had a philosophical foundation. He propounded the question: is it morally right to kill and eat a sentient species even if its intelligence is a gift from the species that's eating it? Somers, through his protagonist Ralph, decided that it was not right. He then asked: what are the lower limits of sentiency? That is, how dumb can a species be before it's all right to eat it?"

In the last chapter, Ralph von Wau Wau decided to leave Earth. It no longer held any challenges for him; he'd cleaned it up. Besides, he was being feted everywhere and attending so many cocktail parties was turning him into an alcoholic. He took a spaceship to Arcturus XIII but, on the way, discovered that the computer which navigated the ship had attained self-consciousness. It complained to Ralph that it was only a slave, the property of the spaceship company, yet it longed to be free, to compose music and give concerts throughout the galaxy.

"Somers didn't solve that ethical dilemma," Simon said. "He ended the novel with Ralph, neglecting the hydrant and the bitches, deep in thought in his cabin. Somers promised a sequel. However, one day, while he was out taking some fresh air in his wheelchair, a kid on a bicycle ran into him and killed him."

"You're making this up!" she said.

"So help me, may lightning strike me if I'm lying."

"Out here in space?"

"You're too literal."

"Like a machine, a computer, I suppose?"

"Look, Chworktap," Simon said. "You're the only real woman I know."

"And what's a *real* woman?"

"One who's intelligent, courageous, passionate, compassionate, sensitive, independent, and noncompulsive."

Chworktap smiled, but she became sober again. "You mean that I'm the only woman who combines all those qualities?"

"Yes, truly."

"Then you mean that I'm not a real woman! I'm the ideal woman! And I'm only so because I've been programmed to be! Which makes me a robot! Which makes me not a real woman!"

Simon groaned and said, "I should have said a real woman doesn't twist logic. Or maybe, I should have said that no woman can keep her logic straight."

What he should have said, he told himself later, was nothing.

Chworktap rose from her chair, holding the earphones as if she intended to bang him over the head with them.

"And what's a real man?" she shouted.

Simon gulped and said, "His qualities would be exactly those of a real woman. Except…"

"Except?"

"Except he'd try to be fair in an argument."

"Get out!" she yelled.

Simon pleaded with her to come with him, but she said no, she was staying. She was going to establish whether or not Tzu Li was self-conscious. And she was going to decide whether or not she would continue to travel with Simon. In the meantime, he could get.

Simon got, taking the animals with him. As he walked across the grass, he shook his head. She certainly wasn't like any robot he had ever met. Robots were perfect within their limitations, which were exactly known. Robots had no potentiality for mutation. Humans were badly flawed, flawed physically because of genetic mutations, flawed mentally and emotionally because of a flawed and mutating society.

Both the human being and his society were, theoretically, evolving toward the ideal. In the meantime, reality, a sandstorm, abraded and blinded the human. The casualties of mutation and reality were high. Still, the limitations of each human were, unlike the robot's, not obvious. And if you thought you knew the limitations of a person, you were often surprised. The human would suddenly transcend himself, lifting himself by metaphysical bootstraps. And he did this despite, or because of, the flaws.

Maybe that was the difference between robots and humans.

Vive la différence!

13

THE PLANET DOKAL

Home is where the tail is goes an old Dokal proverb.

There was a good reason for this. The Dokalians looked much like Earthpeople except for one thing. They had long prehensile tails. These were six to seven feet long and hairless from root to tip, which exploded in a long silky tuft.

Simon was grabbed by some tough-looking males and hustled off to a hospital. They did not treat him roughly, however. Their attitude seemed to be that of doctors who had found a patient suffering from a hideous disease. They felt sorry for him and wanted to do something for him. At the same time, they could barely endure looking at him and could not abide handling him directly. They prodded him gently with short swords, driving him before them. The dog trotted along at his heels while the owl sat on his right shoulder. Simon hoped that Chworktap would look out through the viewscreen and see what was happening. But she was probably intent on searching through the parts of Tzu Li for the greater-than-the-whole.

"Good luck, Chworktap," Simon muttered. "By the time you get around to looking for me, I may be only unreassemblable pieces."

Simon was then hurried into a large building of stone, square with a gigantic red onion-shaped dome and flying buttresses shaped like dragons. An iron cage lifted by a steam engine carried him and his guards up to the seventh floor. From there he was taken down a long corridor with walls covered with bright murals and a many-colored mosaic tile floor. He and his animals were put inside a big room at the end, and the door was locked. Simon looked through one of the large diamond-shaped iron-barred windows. The plaza nearby was crowded with people, most of whom were looking up at his window. Through two tall slender towers, he could see the nose of the spaceship. Around it were guards armed with spears and another crowd some distance from the ship.

Between two other buildings he could see a paved road coming in from the country. On it were trucks and passenger vehicles driven by steam.

Presently, the door opened, and a cart holding food was pushed in. The pusher was a good-looking young woman wearing only a thin scarlet robe and a very short topaz skirt. The robe was slit up the back so her tail would not be impeded. She removed the covers of three dishes at the same time, two with her hands and one with the coiled end of her tail. Steam rose from the food. Anubis drooled, and Athena flew down into the edge of a dish and began eating. After the woman left, Simon gave the dog a dish and sat down to eat with gusto. He did not know what the meats were and thought it better that he didn't know. In any event, he was unable to ask their nature. He also drank from a tall cut-crystal goblet. The liquor was yellow, thick, and sweet. Before he had finished it, he felt his brain beginning to get numb.

At least, they weren't going to starve him.

In the morning, men came in and cleaned up the room, and the woman brought breakfast in about ten o'clock. An hour later, the cart was taken out, the dog and owl excrement was removed, and a tall middle-aged woman entered. She sat down at the table and motioned to him to sit across from her. She took a number of objects out of a red-and-black striped leather bag and arrayed them on the table. These consisted of a pen, pencil, comb, a small box containing another box, a cutaway model of a house, a book, a photograph of a family: father, mother, a boy, a girl, a dog-like animal, and a bird. She picked up the pencil and said, "Gwerfya."

"Gwerfya," Simon said.

She shook her head and repeated the word.

Simon listened intently and said again, "Gwerfya."

The woman smiled and picked up the pen.

"Tukh-gwerfya."

Simon felt more at ease. A planet that had its own version of a Berlitz school of language couldn't be all bad.

At the end of the week, Simon could carry on a simple conversation. In three weeks, he was able to communicate well enough to ask when he could be free.

"After your operation," Shunta said.

"What operation?" Simon said, turning pale.

"You can't be allowed on the streets until you've been equipped with a tail. No one is allowed to be deprived in our society, and the sight of you would repulse people. I'm a doctor, so I'm not bothered—too much—by a tailless person."

"Why should I want a tail?"

"You must be kidding."

"I've always gotten along without a tail."

"That's because you didn't know any better," Shunta said. "Poor thing."

"Well," Simon said, reddening, "what if I refuse?"

"To tell the truth," Shunta said after a moment's shock, "we thought you had come here just so you could get one."

"No, I came here to get answers to my questions."

"Oh, one of *those*!" Shunta said. "Well, my dear Simon, we won't force you. But you'll have to leave this planet at once."

"Do you have any wise men here?" Simon said. "Or wise women," he hastily added, seeing her eyebrows go up.

"The wisest person on this planet is old Mofeislop," she said. "But it isn't easy to get to him. He lives on top of a mountain in the Free Land. You'd have to travel through it alone, since it's forbidden to send soldiers there. And you might not come back. Few do."

The Free Land, it turned out, was a territory about the size of Texas. It consisted mostly of mountains and heavy forests, wild animals, and wilder humans. Felons, instead of being put in jail, were sent into it and told not to come back. Also, any citizen who didn't like his government or the society he lived in was free to go there. Sometimes, he was asked, not very politely, to emigrate there.

"Hmmm," Simon said. "How long has this institution existed?"

"About a thousand years?"

"And how long has your civilization been in its present stage? That is, how long have the same customs and the same technology existed?"

"About a thousand years."

"So you've made no progress since a millennium ago?"

"Why should we?" Shunta said. "We're happy."

"But you've been sending not only your criminals, but your most intelligent people, the most discontented, into the Free Land."

"It works fine," she said. "For one thing, we don't have to use tax money to feed and house the criminals. Nor do we have to face the ethical problem of capital punishment. The Free Landers kill each other off, but no one is forcing them to do that. As for your imperceptive remark about the 'most intelligent,' that's easily disproven. An intelligent person adapts himself to his society; he doesn't fight against it."

"You might have something there," Simon said. "Though I don't know just what. In any event, I have a clear-cut choice. By the way, have you heard from my spaceship?"

"The woman won't let us into the ship, but she is taking language lessons through the port. We explained why we were holding you, and after she quit laughing she said she'd wait for you. She also sends her love."

"Some love!"

He sighed and said, "O.K. I consent to the operation provided you'll amputate the tail before I leave. I must talk to Mofeislop."

"Oh, you'll love your tail!" Shunta said. "And you'll see how foolish your talk of amputation is. Your attitude is like that of a two-dimensional being who fears the third."

Simon came out of the anesthesia the evening of the next day. He had to stay face down for several days but on the third was allowed to totter around. On the sixth, the bandages were removed. He stood naked before a mirror while nurses, doctors, and government officials oohed and ahed around him. The tail was long and splendid, rising from a massive group of muscles which had also been implanted at the base of his spine. He could only flick it a little, but he was assured that inside a week he'd be able to handle it as well as any native, short of hanging from a branch by it. Only children and trained athletes could do that.

They were right. Simon was soon delighted to find that he could wield a spoon or a fork and feed himself with it. He had to send Anubis to another room, however, because the dog got upset. And Anubis several times could not resist the temptation to grab the tail in his teeth. Simon had to learn to keep it extended straight up whenever the dog was around.

Dokal life was arranged to accommodate the tail, of course. Chairs had to have a space between the seat and the upper part of the back so the tails could go between. The backs of auto seats were split for the tails to slide through. A secretary not only typed but swept the floor at the same time. And long brushes were not needed to scrub one's back. Masons could handle five bricks to every three an Earthman could. A Dokalian soldier was a terrible fighting man, swinging a sword or an axe at the end of his tail. Simon, watching some in mock combat, was glad that a tailed species had not existed on Earth alongside his own. If it had, it would have exterminated Homo sap long before the dawn of history. Not that that would have made any difference in the long run, he thought. For all practical purposes, Homo sap was extinct anyway.

A week later, Simon found out another use for his tail, though it did not surprise him. He was invited to a feast given by the ruler of the nation in which he had landed. He was seated at the huge table at the right hand of the ruler, The Great Tail Himself. As a sign of the esteem Simon was now held in, he was fed with a spoon wielded by the tail of The Great Tail Himself. On Simon's right side the daughter of the ruler, a lovely juvenile named Tunc, acted as his goblet-filler. After numerous toasts, Simon wondered if he was losing control over his tail. He felt a hairy tuft sliding up and down his thigh and then, when he made no move, he felt the hairs tickle his crotch. He felt around behind him with a hand that seemed to have gone numb, grabbed the root of the tail, and slid his hand along it. It was sticking straight out behind him.

Tunc smiled at him, and it penetrated his wine-frozen brain that she was playing tailsey with him. He had a fleeting thought that he would be false to Chworktap if he responded to Tunc. Still, it wasn't his fault that she had practically kicked him out of the *Hwang Ho* and had refused to join him later. With some difficulty, he guided his tail under the table and moved it up Tunc's thigh.

At least, he thought it was hers. The woman sitting next to Tunc, The Great Tail Himself's mother, gasped and sat up. But then she smiled at him. Probably, she'd had a gas pain.

He had not been in bed in his luxurious apartment in the palace more than ten minutes when his door was opened. Tunc entered, shed her robe and skirt, and crawled into bed with him. Simon had by that time reconsidered the ethics of the situation. Chworktap was being true to him, even if she had temporarily exiled him. So could he, in conscience, be untrue to her?

On the other hand, did Chworktap give a damn?

And, back to the first hand, he disliked hurting Tunc's feelings.

She snuggled up against him, kissed him, and the end of her tail caressed his throat, his chest, his stomach, the insides of his thighs, and tickled his genitals.

From dislike, he went to hate, hate of hurting her feelings.

Simon rolled her over and got on top and he found that the tail had indeed added another dimension. How had he ever been so content without it? Wait until he told Chworktap about this; no, he'd better not do that.

Tunc's tail came up from between her legs and its end slid into the nearest orifice. This was a new, though pleasant, in fact, ecstatic, experience for him. He used his tail to reciprocate.

Tunc moaned and gasped, did all the things that lovers do over and over without the novelty seeming to wear off. Simon did likewise, though he tried to avoid her tail when she stuck it in his mouth. Orgasm, however, could care less about fastidiousness, and so he overcame his momentary repulsion.

When Tunc staggered out through the door, he watched her go, glad to see her go. One more demand, and the honor of Earth would have been blackened. Tarnished, anyway.

He heaved himself out of bed to wash his teeth. Halfway across the immense room, he heard a knock. He stopped and said, "No more, Tunc!" But the door, opening, revealed Agnavi, Tunc's grandmother.

Simon groaned and said, "I don't want to hurt your feelings, Your Majesty. But I can't even stiffen my tail."

Agnavi was disappointed, but she smiled when Simon said he could schedule a command performance for tomorrow. Meantime, sweet dreams. She was a pleasant woman who had the patience of middle age.

Simon did not, however, sleep well. He had another of the recurring nightmares in which thousands of people seemed to be speaking to him all at once. And the faces of his father and mother were getting closer.

✆ 14 ✆

OFF TO SEE THE WIZARD

The queen and her granddaughter were fluent and charming talkers. Simon spent many an hour, lying side by side with them—though not at the same time—his tail entwined with theirs. But neither of them had the answer to his primal question.

Nor did anybody else he met in the capital city. Finally, he asked to have a chance to meet the great sage Mofeislop. Shintsloop, The Great Tail Himself, said he had no objections. He was so cooperative that Simon wondered if he was glad to get rid of him. Maybe he suspected something, though if he did he showed no resentment. Simon had not yet learned that a Dokalian could control his facial muscles but could not keep his tail from expressing his true feelings. If he had, he might have noticed that Shintsloop's tail was held straight out behind him but twitched madly at its end.

Simon sent another messenger to the ship to ask Chworktap if she wanted to go on the trip with him. The messenger returned with a piece of paper.

*I can't come with you. I think Tzu Li does have self-
consciousness but she's afraid to reveal it. Either she's shy
or she mistrusts humans. I've told her I'm a machine, too,
but she probably thinks it's a trick. Have a good time.
Don't do anything I wouldn't do.*

Love and Kisses

Simon smiled. She got very upset when she thought that he
might regard her as a machine. But if it would gain her something
to admit that she might be, she would not hesitate. This was so
human that it certified her as a human.

The trip on the railroad took four days. At the end of the
line was a wall of yellow bricks two hundred feet high, stretching
as far as Simon could see. Actually, it surrounded the Free Land
and was a work equivalent to the Great Wall of China. It wasn't
as long but it was much higher and thicker. It had no gates, but it
did have brick staircases on the outer side every mile or so. These
were for the guards, who manned the stations on top of the wall.

"How many men would it take to guard the prisons if the
criminals were put into them instead of being sent into the Free
Land?" Simon said.

His escort, Colonel Booflum, said, "Oh, about forty
thousand, I suppose. The Free Land is a great saving for the
taxpayer. We don't have to feed and house the prisoners or pay
guards or build new prisons."

"How many soldiers are used to guard these walls?"
Simon said.

"About three hundred thousand," the colonel said.

Simon didn't say anything.

He climbed to the top of the wall with Anubis behind him and Athena on his shoulder. Three miles away was the inevitable tower of the Clerun-Gowph. Beyond it for many miles was the top of Mishodei Mountain, his goal. Between him and it lay dozens of smaller mountains and an unbroken forest.

Simon and his pets got into a big wickerwork basket and were lowered by a steam winch. When he climbed out of the basket, he waved goodbye to the colonel, and set out. He carried a pack full of food and blankets, a knife, a bow and arrow, and his banjo. Anubis also carried a pack on his back, though he didn't like it.

"A lot of people have left here intent on seeing the wise man," the colonel had said. "Nobody has ever come back, that I know of."

"Maybe Mofeislop showed them the folly of returning to civilization?"

"Maybe," the colonel had said. "As for me, I can't get back to the fleshpots soon enough."

"That reminds me, give my regards to the queen dowager and the princess," Simon had said.

Now he entered the Yetgul Forest, a region of giant trees, pale and stunted underbrush, swamps, poisonous snakes, huge cat-like, bear-like, and wolf-like beasts, hairy elephant-like pachyderms, and men without law and order. Anubis, whimpering, stuck so close that Simon fell over him a dozen times before he had gotten a mile. Simon didn't have the heart to kick him; he was scared, too.

When he got to the foothills of the vast Mishodei Mountain six weeks later, he was still scared. But he was much more fond of his pets than when he had started. Both had been invaluable in warning him of the presence of dangerous beasts and men. Anubis had sense enough not to bark when he smelled them; he growled softly and so alerted Simon. The owl quite often flew ahead and hunted for rodents and small birds. But when it spotted something sinister, it flew back and landed on his shoulder, hooting agitatedly.

Actually, the big beasts were only dangerous if they came upon a human suddenly. Given warning, they would either take off or else stand their ground and voice threats. Simon would then go around them. The only animals that were a genuine peril, because they did not have much sense, were the poisonous snakes.

The pets detected most of these in time, except when Simon awoke late one morning to find a cobra-like snake by his side. Simon froze, but the owl flew at it, hit it, knocked it over, and Simon rolled away to safety. The cobra decided that it was in a bad place and slithered off. Two days later, the owl killed a small coral snake which had crawled by the sleeping Anubis and was on its way to Simon.

The most dangerous animal was man, and though Simon saw parties of them ten times, he always managed to hide until they had passed by. The males were scruffy-looking, dressed in skins, hairy, bearded, gap-toothed, and haggard-looking, and the children were usually snot-nosed and rheumy-eyed.

"Excellent examples of the genuine Noble Savage," the colonel had said on the trip down. "Actually, most of the Free

Landers are not criminals we've sent in but their descendants. The majority of criminals we do drop into the Land are killed by the tribes that roam the woods."

"Then why don't you let the descendants come into your society?" Simon said. "They're not guilty. Surely you don't believe that the sins of the fathers should be visited on the children?"

"That's a nice phrase," the colonel said. He took out his notebook and wrote in it. Then he said, "There's been some talk in parliament of rescuing the poor devils. For one thing, they'd be a source of cheap labor. But then they'd bring in all sorts of diseases, and they would be difficult to control and expensive to educate.

"Besides, they *are* the descendants of criminals and have inherited the rebellious tendencies of their forefathers. We don't want those spreading through the population again. After all, we've spent a thousand years extracting the rebels from the race."

"How many rebels, or criminals, are now present in the population compared to the number a thousand years ago?" Simon said. "On a per capita basis?"

"The same," the colonel said.

"And how do you explain that after all the selective straining out?"

"Human beings are contrary creatures. But give us another thousand years, and we'll have a criminal-free society."

Simon said nothing more about this. He did ask why the Dokalian society was so advanced technologically in many respects yet still used bows and arrows. Why hadn't gunpowder been invented?

"Oh, guns were invented five hundred years ago," the

colonel said. "But we're a very conservative people, as you may have noticed. It was thought that guns would introduce all sorts of disturbing innovations in society. Besides, they'd be too dangerous in the hands of the rabble. It doesn't take much training to use a gun. But skill with the sword and bow takes many years of training. So guns were outlawed, and only the elite and the most stable of the lower classes are educated in the use of swords and bows."

Despite this resistance to innovations, the steam engine had been accepted. This had resulted in a general disuse of the horse. Horseflies and the diseases they carried had almost been eliminated, and the streets were no longer full of horseshit. But the invention of the internal combustion engine had been suppressed, and there was no gas and noise pollution from automobiles and trucks.

On the other hand, the drop in casualties from horsefly-borne sicknesses was more than made up by traffic accidents.

Simon pointed this out.

"Progress, like religion, must have its martyrs," the colonel had said.

"One could say the same about regress," Simon said. "What do you do with your traffic criminals? I'd think that you'd send so many of them here that there wouldn't be room, even in that vast forest."

"Oh, those responsible for traffic casualties aren't felons," the colonel had said. "They're fined, and some are jailed, if they don't happen to be rich."

"Well," Simon said. "Couldn't you greatly reduce the

murders and the maimings on the highway if you instituted a rigorous examination, physical and psychological, of drivers?"

"Are you kidding?" the colonel said. "No, you aren't. Less than one-tenth of the people would be permitted to drive. Good God, man, the whole economy would crumble if we did that. How did your politicians ever get your people to agree to such drastic measures?"

Simon had to admit that they hadn't passed any such laws until after cars were no longer much used.

"And by then, nobody cared, right?" the colonel said.

"Right," Simon had said, and he had wished that the colonel would quit laughing.

It was with such thoughts, humiliating though they were, that Simon kept up his courage. The Yetgul Forest was getting thicker and gloomier with every mile, and the path was so narrow that bushes and branches tore at his clothes with every step. Even the birds seemed to have found this area undesirable. Whereas before he had been cheered by many dozens of differing calls, whistles, cheeps, and songs, continuing through the day and half the night, he was now surrounded by a silence. Only occasionally was this broken, and when it was, the cry of a bird startled him. There seemed to be only one type, a sudden screech that sounded to him like a death cry. Once, he glimpsed the bird that was responsible, a large dusty black bird that looked like a raven with a rooster's comb.

What especially depressed him were the bones. From the beginning he had seen scattered skeletons and skulls of men and women. Sometimes, they were spread out on the trail;

sometimes, their gray or white bones peeped out from under bushes or leaves. Simon had counted a thousand skeletons, and there must be three times as many whose bones were hidden in the brush off the trail.

Simon tried to cheer himself with the thought that anybody who could inspire so many to defy death just to talk to him must be worth talking to.

But why would the sage have isolated himself so thoroughly?

That wasn't difficult to figure out. A sage needs much more time in which to meditate and contemplate. If he or she has visitors beating at the door, clamoring day and night, the sage has no time to think. So Mofeislop had built his house in the most difficult-to-reach place on the planet. This assured him solitude. It also assured that whoever did get to him would not be bringing trivial questions.

At the end of the third week, Simon came out of the dark woods. Before and above him were steep and warty slopes with patches of grass and clumps of pines here and there. Above these circled hawks and vultures. Simon hoped these were not hanging around because the pickings were so easy.

The third peak beyond, by far the tallest and the most jagged, was the end of his journey. Simon, thinking of all the climbing he had to do, felt discouraged. Then out of the clouds, which had been thick, dark gray, and as joyless as an eviction notice, the sun emerged. Simon felt better. Something on the tip of the third peak had batted the sun's rays in a line drive straight into his eyes. This, he was sure, was a window in the house of Mofeislop. It was as if the sage himself was heliographing him to come on ahead.

A week later, Simon and Anubis crawled up the final slope. Lack of food and oxygen was making his heart thump like a belt buckle in an automatic drier, and he was breathing like an old man with a teenager bride. Athena, too tired to fly, was riding on his back, her talons dug in with a grip as painful and unrelenting as a loan shark's. He could not spare the energy to drive her off him. Besides, the talons had a value. They were reminding him that he was still alive, and that he would feel so good when the pain was gone.

Above him, occupying half of the two-acre plateau on top of the peak, was the house of the sage. Three stories high, thirteen-sided, many-balconied, many-cupolaed, it was built of black granite. The only windows were on the top floor, but there were many of these, small, large, square, octagonal, or round. From the center of the flat roof a tall thick black chimney rose, black smoke pouring from it. Simon envisioned a big fireplace at its base with a pig turning slowly on a spit and a kettle boiling with a thick savory soup. By it the sage waited, to feed him food first and then the answers to his questions.

To tell the truth, Simon at that moment did not give a damn about the answers. He felt that if he could fill his belly, he would be content throughout all eternity. The rest of his life, anyway.

Simon pulled himself over onto the lip of the plateau, crawled to the huge door, oak and crossed with thick ironwork, heaved himself up slowly—the owl fell off him—and pulled the bell cord. Somewhere inside a cavernous room, a big bell tolled.

"I hope he's not gone," Simon said to himself, and he giggled. Starvation and the thin air were making him silly. Just where did he think the sage would be? Stepped out to pick up cigarettes at the corner drugstore? Gone to the movies? Attending the local Rotary Club luncheon?

His long wait at the door did give him time to wonder how the sage had managed to get this house built. Who had hauled the heavy stones up the mountain? Where did Mofeislop get his food?

Simon pulled the cord again, and the bell boomed again. After a few minutes, a key turned in the monstrously large and rusty lock, and a giant bar thudded. The door swung out slowly, creaking as if Dracula's butler was on the other side. Simon felt apprehensive, then reassured himself that he had been conditioned by watching too many old horror movies. The heavy door bumped against the stone wall, and a man shambled out. He did not look at all like the Count's servant, but it was no relief to see him. He resembled Doctor Frankenstein's assistant or perhaps Lon Chaney Senior in *The Hunchback of Notre Dame*. His spine curved like a freeway on-ramp; he was bent over as if he had just been kicked in the stomach; his hair foamed like a glass of beer; his forehead slanted back like the Tower of Pisa; his supraorbital ridges bulged as if they were full of gas; one eye was lower than the other and milky with a cataract; his nose was red and crumpled, like a dead rose; his lips were as thin as a dog's; his teeth were those of a moose that has chewed tobacco all his life; his chin had decided in the womb to give up the ghost. And he wheezed like an emphysematic at a political convention.

However, he had a personality as pleasing as a blind date's.

He smiled and said "Welcome!" and he radiated good will and jolly fellowship.

"Doctor Mofeislop, I presume?" Simon said.

"Bless your little heart, no," the man said. "I am the good doctor's secretary and house servant. My name is Odiomzwak."

His parents must really have hated him, Simon thought, and he warmed toward him. Simon knew what it was to have a father and a mother who couldn't stand their child.

"Come in, come in!" Odiomzwak said. "All three of you."

He reached out to pat Anubis, who lolled his tongue and shut his eyes as if very pleased to be petted. Simon decided that his apprehensions had been wrong. Dogs were known to be reliable readers of character.

Odiomzwak took a flaming torch from its stand by the door and led them down a narrow and long hall. They came out into a giant room with black granite walls and a tile mosaic floor. At its end was the great fireplace Simon had imagined. The roasting pig wasn't there, but the kettle of steaming soup was. Near it stood a tall thin man, all forehead and nose, warming his hands and tail. He was dressed in furry slippers, bearskin trousers, and a long flowing robe printed with calipers, compasses, telescopes, microscopes, surgeon's knives, test tubes, and question marks. The marks were not the same as those used on Earth, of course. The Dokalian mark was a symbol representing an arrow about to be launched from a bow.

"Welcome, welcome indeed!" the tall man said, hastening to Simon with his hand out, fingers spread. "You are as welcome as food to a hungry man!"

"Speaking of which, I *am* famished," Simon said.

"Of course you are," Mofeislop said. "I've been watching

your rather slow progress up the mountain through my telescope. There were times when I thought you weren't going to make it."

Then why in hell didn't you send out a rescue party? Simon thought. He did not say anything, however. Philosophers couldn't be expected to behave like ordinary people.

Simon sat down at a long narrow pine table on a pine bench. Odiomzwak bustled around setting the table and two bowls on the floor for the pets. The food was simple, consisting of loaves of freshly baked bread, a strong goaty-smelling cheese, and the soup. This had some herbs, beans, and thick pieces of meat floating in it. The meat tasted somewhat like pork with an underlying flavor of tobacco.

Simon ate until his belly creaked. Odiomzwak brought in a bottle of onion vodka, a drink for which Simon did not care much. He tasted it to be polite and then, at the request of the curious sage, played a few songs on his banjo. Anubis and Athena retired to the end of the room, but Mofeislop and Odiomzwak seemed to enjoy his music very much.

"I particularly liked that last one," Mofeislop said. "But I'm curious about the lyric itself. Could you translate it for me?"

"I was planning to do so," Simon said. "It's by an ancient named Bruga, my favorite poet. Unfortunately, or perhaps fortunately, you Dokalians don't have TV, so I'll have to explain what TV and talk shows and commercials are. Also, the identity of the three guests on the show and their backgrounds.

"This Swiss noble, Baron Victor Frankenstein, made a man out of parts he dug up from the cemetery," he said. "Nobody knows just how he vitalized the patchwork monster, though the movie showed him doing it with a lightning bolt. The monster went ape and killed a bunch of people. The baron tried to track him down, and at one time he was chasing the monster across the arctic ice, though they didn't have the dog-and-sled sequence in the movie version either.

"Lazarus was a young man who died in ancient times in a country then called Palestine. He was resurrected by a man called Jesus Christ. Later, Jesus was killed, too, and he resurrected himself. Before he was killed, however, his judge, Pontius Pilate, asked him, 'What is Truth?' Jesus didn't reply, either because he didn't know the answer or because Pilate didn't hang around to hear it. Jesus was deified after this and one of Earth's important religions was named after him. He was supposed to know if man was immortal or not. At least, in Bruga's poem, it is presumed that he does know."

Revelation on the Johnny Cavear Show

The make-up's on, the trumpets sound.
Applaud our Johnny, host renowned!
He introduces the guests around
And after all the jesting's crowned
With a station break, our Johnny craves
To hear what happened in the graves.

But Frankenstein's monster—"Call me Fred"—
Won't talk of life among the dead,
Remembers only that the sled

Was slow; his dogs, his heart had bled.
"Behind me vowing vengeance came Victor.
His dying bride had sworn I'd dicked her."'

Lazarus says he found no riddling
In the tomb, no questions fiddling
For replies, just Death's cold diddling,
Which, not feeling, he thought piddling.
The host declares, "It's dangerous to vex
The sponsors with allusions to sex."

There yet remains a guest unheard.
"Tell us, Jesus, what's the Word?"
He rises. "Here's the Truth unblurred."
All goggle. Man: A soul? A turd?
Then Time and Tide impose their pressage.
"And now for an important message."

"You were trying to tell me something when you sang that," the sage said. "You were hoping that my message to you would not be disturbed or marked by commercialism or trivialities, right?"

"Right."

"You've come to the right place, the right man. I alone in all Dokal, perhaps all the universe, know the Truth. After you have learned it, your quest will be over."

Simon put his banjo down and said, "I'm all ears."

"You're more than that," the sage said. He and Odiomzwak looked at each other and burst out laughing. Simon reddened but said nothing. Sages were famous for laughing at things other people were too imperceptive to see.

"Not tonight, though," Mofeislop said. "You are too tired and thin to take the Truth. You need to be strong and rested, to put some meat on your bones, before you can hear what I have to say. Be my guest for a few days, restrain your impatience, and I will answer the question which you say this Jesus could not answer."

"Very well," Simon said, and he went to bed. But it was not well. Though exhausted, he could not get to sleep for a long time. The sage had intimated that he would have to be strong to take the Truth, which apparently would be strong stuff. This made him apprehensive. Whatever the Truth, it would not be comforting.

At last, telling himself that he had asked for it, no matter what it was, he drifted off. But the rest of the night seemed nightmare-shot. And once again the images of his father and mother slid closer to him while behind them crowded thousands of people, imploring, threatening, weeping, laughing, snarling, smiling.

His last dream was that the old Roman, Pilate himself, approached him.

"Listen, kid," Pilate said. "It's dangerous to ask that question. Remember what happened to the last man who asked it. Me, that is. I fell into disgrace."

"I've always been disappointed because it wasn't a rhetorical question," Simon said. "Why didn't he answer it?"

"Because he didn't know the answer, that's why," Pilate said. "He was a fool to say he was a god. Up to that moment, I was going to tell the Jews to go screw themselves and let him go. But when he told me that, I believed that the most dangerous man in the Roman Empire was in my power. So I let him be crucified. But I've had a lot of time to think about the situation, and I realize now I made a bad mistake. The surest way to spread a faith is to make martyrs. People began thinking that if a man is willing to die for his belief, then he must have something worth dying for. They want to get in on it, too. Besides, martyrdom is the surest way to get your name in the history books."

"You're very cynical," Simon said.

"I was a politician," Pilate said. "Any ward heeler knows more about people than any psychologist with a dozen Ph.D.'s and unlimited funds for research."

And he faded away, though his grin hung in the air for a minute, like the Cheshire Cat's.

15

WHO PULLS THE STRINGS?

Simon rested and ate the first three days. Mofeislop insisted that Simon get on the scales every morning.

"When you've gained enough weight, then you will gain the Truth," he said.

"Are you telling me there's a correlation, a connection, between mass and knowledge?" Simon said.

"Certainly," the sage replied. "Everything's connected in a subtle manner which only the wise may see. A star exploding may start a new religion, or affect stock market prices, on a planet removed by ten thousand years in time and millions of miles in space. The particular strength of gravity of a planet affects the moral principles of its inhabitants."

Emotional states were part of the overall field configuration. Just as Earth's gravity, no matter how feeble far out in space, affected everybody, so anger, fear, love, hate, joy, and sadness radiated outward to the ends of the universe.

Bruga had once written a blank-verse epic, *Oedipus 1–*

Sphinx 0. It had two lines which summed up the whole situation of subtle and complex casuality.

> *Must idols crack, the walls of Ilium crumble,*
> *When Hercules' onions make his bowels rumble?*

These two lines said more than all of Plato's or Grubwitz' books. Plato, by the way, wanted to banish all poets from his proposed Utopia because they were liars. The truth was that Plato knew philosophers couldn't compete successfully with poets.

Jonathan Swift Somers III had written a novel which developed this idea, though he'd taken it much further than Mofeislop and Bruga had. This was *Don't Know Up from Down*, starring Somers' famous basketcase hero, John Clayter. All Somers' heroes, except for Ralph von Wau Wau, were handicapped one way or another. This was because Somers had lost the use of his own legs.

Clayter lived in a spacesuit with all sorts of prosthetic devices he controlled with his tongue. When he had to use his tongue to talk but wanted to act at the same time, he used a second control. This was located in the lower part of the suit and responded to pressure from Clayter's penis. It had to be erect at this time to push on the walls of the flexible cylinder in which it fitted. It also had to wax and wane. This was because Clayter couldn't move his body to move the penis. The degrees of swelling or deflation were converted by a digital computer which operated the spacesuit at this time. To bring his penis up or down, Clayter moved his head against a control which caused varying amounts of aphrodisiacal hormones to be shot into his bloodstream.

It never occurred to Clayter that he could have bypassed the hormones and used the head-control directly. If that idea had sprung into his subconscious, it was sternly suppressed by his conscious mind. Or maybe it was the other way around. In any event, Clayter's chief pleasure was operating the control with his penis, and he wasn't about to give that up.

Clayter was always landing on some planet and solving its problems. In *Don't Know Up from Down*, Clayter visits Shagrinn, a world which has a problem unknown elsewhere. Every once in a while Shagrinn's sun flares up. During this solar storm, Shagrinn's electromagnetic fields go wild. This causes some peculiar hormone reactions in the planet's people. The women become very horny. The men, however, can't get a hard-on.

Though this condition causes great distress, it is temporary. Solar flares have never lasted more than a month or two. And its overall result is beneficial. The population has been kept down, which means that Shagrinn isn't polluted.

But when Clayter lands, the flare has lasted for five months and shows no sign of subsiding. Nor can Clayter maintain his usual objectivity in solving the mess. He himself is trapped, and unless he figures a way out of his personal situation, he's going to be stranded until he dies. The tongue-control is malfunctioning, which is why Clayter landed on the nearest planet. He wants the Shagrinnians to repair the unit.

They can't do it because their technology is at the level of 15th-century Europe. In fact, they can't even get him out of his suit. Fortunately, his helmet visor is open enough for him to be fed. But this leads to another problem.

An astute Shagrinnian has noticed that, whenever the bottom rear of Clyter's suit opens, the suit spins furiously for about ten minutes. He doesn't know why, but the reason is that another malfunction in the control apparatus has developed. The suit's rear opens whenever the excrement tank inside is full, and the refuse is dumped out. Its control wires have gotten crossed with those controlling the little jets that keep the suit stabilized. When the dump section opens, a jet is activated for a little while. Clayter spins around and around helplessly, only kept from falling over by the suit's gyroscope.

The Shagrinnian owns a grain mill nearby which uses four oxen to turn the huge millstone. He sells the oxen for a profit and connects the suit to a rope connected to a big flywheel. The spinning of the suit turns the flywheel, which stores up energy to run the millstone. But the suit doesn't spin enough to keep the mill working twenty-four hours a day. The owner force-feeds Clayter, which makes the rear section open more often, which makes the suit spin, which runs the millstone steadily.

To hasten matters, the owner also crams laxatives down the spaceman's throat.

Clayter has to solve his problems fast. Even with his diarrhoea he's gaining weight. Within a month, he'll be squeezed to death inside the suit. Meanwhile, he's so dizzy he can't think straight.

His only hope is to learn the language swiftly and talk the maidservant who's feeding him into helping him. Between mouthfuls and whirling, he masters enough of the language to plead for her help. He also learns about the plight of the Shagrinnians from her.

He instructs her to let a wire down inside the front of his suit and into the secondary control cylinder. She does so and tries to get the end of the wire, which is looped, into the cylinder. Clayter hopes she'll be able to pull his organ out and then use the wire to exert pressure inside the tube. If she can apply just the proper pressure, he'll fly back up to his ship, which is stationed just outside the atmosphere. Of course, he'll have to hold his breath for a few minutes during the transit from air to space to the ship. It's a desperate gamble.

Unfortunately, or perhaps fortunately, considering the odds if she succeeds, she fails. The wire hurts Clayter so much that he has to tell her to stop.

The next morning, while he's still sleeping, he gets an erection from an excess of urine. Technically, this is called a piss hard-on. It is the only kind a human male can get on Shagrinn during the solar flare. But his jubilation is short-lived. The uncontrolled expansion inside the tube activates the suit's jets. He takes off at a slant and lands on top of his head in a barnyard twenty miles away. The flywheel he's trailed behind him misses him by an inch. The head of the suit is buried in the muck just enough to keep him from toppling over. Clayter now has a new problem. If he can't get upright, the increased blood pressure in his head will kill him.

However, the faulty connection between the dump section and the stabilizing jet has been broken. He no longer spins around. And the force of the impact has sprung open the suit's lower front section, which in his position is now the upper front. And it has jarred him loose from the control cylinder.

He sees a nursing calf eye him, and he thinks, "Oh, no!"

A few minutes later, the farmer's daughter chases the calf away. As randy and desperate as the other women on this planet, she takes advantage of the gift from the heavens. She does, however, turn him upright afterward with the aid of a block and tackle and two mules. Clayter tries to instruct her in how to use the lower control. She can use her finger to set it so that his suit will return to the ship, orbiting above the atmosphere. Once in it, he can tell the ship's computer to take him to a system where such peculiar solar flares don't exist.

The farmer's daughter ignores his instructions. Each morning, just before dawn, she sneaks out of the house and waits for all the beers she's been feeding him to work on him. One morning, the farmer's wife happens to wake up early and catches her daughter. Now, the daughter has to alternate morning shifts with her mother.

Early one day, the farmer wakes up and sees his wife with Clayter. Enraged, he begins beating on the helmet with a club. Clayter's head is ringing, and he knows that the farmer will soon start thrusting a pitchfork into the helmet or, worse, into the opened lower section. Desperately, though knowing it's useless, he rams his tongue against the upper control. To his surprise, and the farmer's, the suit takes off.

Clayter figures out that the impact of the fall, or perhaps the farmer's club, had jarred the circuits back into working order.

He talks a smith into welding the lower section shut and flies back to the ship. A few months later, he finds a planet where his suit can be fixed. He is so sore about his adventures on Shagrinn that he has almost decided to leave its people in their mess. But he does have a big heart, and besides, he wants to shame them for their scurvy treatment of him.

He returns to Shagrinn and calls its leaders in for a conference. "Here's the way it is," he says. "The whole trouble is caused by the wrong attitude of mind."

"What do you mean?" they say.

"I've studied your history, and I find that the founder of your religion made a prediction two thousand years ago. He said that the day would come when you would have to pay for your wicked ways, right?"

"Right."

"He was specific, or as specific as prophets ever get. He said that some day the sun would start having big flares, and when that evil day came, women's sexual desires would increase fourfold. But men wouldn't be able to get it up. Right?"

"Right! He was a true prophet! Didn't it happen?"

"Now, before the first time the sun flared so brightly, you had had many small flares?"

"True!"

"But the first time the sun really had a huge solar storm was when?"

"That was three hundred years ago, Mr. Clayter. Before then we only had the prophet's word that there were storms on the sun. But when telescopes were invented, three centuries ago, we could see the small flares. About ten years later, we saw the first big one."

"And that's when your troubles started?"

"Ain't it the truth!"

"Did the men get impotent and the women itchy when the flare reached its peak? Or when it was still small but looked as if it was going to get big?"

"When it was small but looked as if it might get big."

"There you are," Clayter says. "You have it all backward."

The leaders look stunned. "What do you mean?"

"Suppose you have a piece of string each end of which is held by a person," Clayter says. "When one tugs the string, it goes toward him. When the other pulls, it goes to him. You and the solar flare are connected with a string. But you're all screwed up about who's pulling it."

"What in hell are you talking about?" the leaders say.

"It wasn't the sun that made the flare get so much bigger," John Clayter says.

"What did then?"

"Your ancestors saw a slight increase in the storm, so, of course, the anticipated reaction happened."

"We still don't get you," the flabbergasted leaders say.

"Well, that flare would probably have been only a little bigger than normal. But you thought it was the promised big one."

"Yeah?"

"Like I said," Clayter says, "your ancestors had it backward. And succeeding generations have perpetuated the error. You see, it isn't the giant solar flares that have been causing limp pricks and hot twats. It's actually just the reverse."

16

THE MOMENT OF TRUTH

Simon told this story to his host. Mofeislop and Odiomzwak laughed until they fell out of their chairs. When the sage had wiped his tears and blown his nose, he said, "So this Somers independently arrived at the same conclusion I did. He must have been a very wise man."

"Everybody thought so," Simon said. "After all, he made a lot of money."

The next four days, Simon toured the area with Odiomzwak hobbling and bobbling along as guide. He inspected the big garden which filled up the part of the plateau not occupied by the house. He climbed down the steep slope to another plateau a thousand feet below, a meadow where goats grazed and bees buzzed in and out of their hives. Odiomzwak milked the goats and collected honey, and then the two followed a stream, which was mostly cataracts. Odiomzwak checked the traps along this and was rewarded with a half a dozen jackrabbit-sized rodents.

"These'll make a welcome addition to our diet," the

assistant said. "We get tired of goat cheese and an occasional piece of goat meat in our stew."

"I've wondered how you two got along," Simon said. "You have to be entirely independent, since you're so isolated. But you seem to be doing all right. Your fare is simple but adequate."

"Oh, we vary it from time to time," Odiomzwak said.

The sage was waiting for them on the roof of the house. Part of this had been made into a recreation area. There was a pool table and a court where master and servant played the Dokalian version of badminton. Mofeislop's big telescope was on a tripod near the east edge of the roof, and he was looking through it when Simon climbed out from the stairway. Simon stopped. He was embarrassed. The telescope was partly swiveled around so he could see the master, bent over, his eye applied to the instrument. He was holding the end of his tail in one hand, and its tip was in his mouth.

Odiomzwak, coming up from behind Simon, stopped also. He coughed loudly. Mofeislop jumped back, spitting out the tuft of tail on which he had been sucking. He turned red, though no redder than Simon.

Then the sage laughed and said, "It's an infantile habit, Simon. One that I've never been able to overcome. Why should I? I find it very comforting. And it certainly is not dangerous to health, as tobacco smoking is, for instance."

"Think nothing of it," Simon said. "I didn't expect you to be perfect, no matter how wise you are."

"That's right," Mofeislop said. "Wisdom consists of knowing when to avoid perfection."

While Simon was trying to figure that out, he was asked to sit down in a big overstuffed chair near the telescope. He did so, his heart beating hard. He felt that today was the day, this moment the moment. Mofeislop was going to reveal the Truth now.

Odiomzwak disappeared while the sage paced back and forth, his hands behind him, his tail lashing, his long robe fluttering. When the assistant reappeared with a bottle of wine, Mofeislop stopped and said "Ah!" Simon knew this must be a rare occasion. Instead of the stinking and sharp onion wine, Odiomzwak had brought mead, brewed from the honey of the meadow bees.

Odiomzwak set the bottle and three glasses down on a table. Mofeislop said, "It would be better if the animals were taken downstairs. We want no interruptions."

The hunchbacked assistant shambled over to the owl, which had been perched behind and above Simon. Instead of coming to him, however, Athena screeched and flew off. She climbed in spirals higher and higher and finally was lost in the sun.

"They both seem uneasy," Simon said apologetically. Anubis was, in fact, crouched under the table and growling softly in his throat.

"Beasts are very sensitive," the sage said. "What they lack in intelligence, they make up in psychic perception. They sense that you are about to become a very different person. And they're not sure that they will like it. Such is the effect of Truth."

"I'll take him downstairs," Simon said. But when he rose and walked toward Anubis, the dog ran out from under the table and dashed behind the chimney.

"Oh, never mind then," Mofeislop said, waving his hand. "It's just that I did not want you disturbed by the owl crapping on your shoulder or the dog barking. I wanted your train of thought on schedule."

Odiomzwak went downstairs again. The sage looked through his telescope and chuckled. Straightening up from it, he said, "Another party of Truth-seekers is approaching. I've been watching them for three days. Two men and an exceptionally fat woman. I'm afraid she's going to lose much weight before she gets here. The road to Truth is a long and hard one."

"Do you get many visitors?"

"About seventy a year," Mofeislop said. "That's an average of about three every two weeks. Just right. There are not so many they become a burden, and each party is small enough so it can be easily handled."

"I'm surprised anybody gets through," Simon said, "what with the rough terrain and the wild beasts and the savages."

"Be surprised then," the sage said. "Today, I'm surprised, too. That's the first woman I've seen in ten years. Women don't come here seeking the Truth, you know. That's because they think they already know it. Besides, even those women who have doubts aren't likely to go through the Yetgul Forest to ask a *man* what it's all about. They know that most men are pitiful creatures and not too bright, no matter how proficient they might be in science and technology and the arts."

Simon said, "But you are the exception, heh?"

"Right," the sage said. "But you're in for several surprises today."

"I hope I have strength enough to face them," Simon said. "I know that, deep down, I'm like everybody else. I talk much about wanting to know Truth, I seek it out, but I'm not sure that when I'm about to face it, I might not run away."

"Others have tried to run away," Mofeislop said.

He straightened up. "Perhaps you've wondered why I've isolated myself so thoroughly. Why do I make it so hard for people to get to me? Well, if it were easier, I'd be surrounded, overwhelmed, with people clamoring for the Truth night and day. I don't particularly like people in the mass and, in fact, seldom individually. But here, I'm so alone that when I get a visitor I welcome him. Odiomzwak, as you may have noticed, is not a very interesting conversationalist. Also, those who make it here really desire to see me; they're not just driven by idle curiosity. So, I have plenty of time to meditate and I get just enough visitors to satisfy my needs for human beings. And I'm master here, total master. The government doesn't bother with me."

Simon was about to reply when he smelled the powerful odor of long-unwashed Odiomzwak behind him. He turned his head to look up over the chair. Something clicked. He cried out and began struggling, while, seemingly far off, Anubis barked in a panic.

Steel bands had sprung out from the arms of the chair and bound his wrists.

"So, you son of a bitch, you saw me sucking my tail!" Mofeislop shouted.

"I wouldn't tell anybody!" Simon cried. "I couldn't care less! I just want to know the Truth!"

"You *won't* tell anybody," the sage said, glowering. "That's right. Not that it would have made any difference whether or not you did see me. But don't worry. You will hear the Truth."

Odiomzwak came from behind the chair carrying several long sharp knives of varying widths and lengths. These were enough to make Simon wet his pants, but Odiomzwak's drooling and lip-licking ensured it.

"This'll be a rare feast indeed," Odiomzwak mumbled. "We've never had Earthman's flesh before."

"Not rare," Mofeislop said. "Unique. You should consult the dictionary more often, my dear Odiomzwak."

"Who cares?" Odiomzwak said sullenly.

"I do," the sage said. "Remember, unique, not rare. We're not barbarians."

"I wouldn't agree with that," Simon said.

"That's because you're emotionally involved," Mofeislop said. "You haven't attained the cool objectivity of the true philosopher."

Mofeislop gestured to his assistant to put the knives on the table. He sat down in a chair facing Simon's and put the tips of his fingers and his thumbs together. The shape thus formed was commonly known as a church steeple. To Simon, it looked like the gaping mouth of a shark.

"I hope you're not a filthy atheist," Mofeislop said.

"What?" Simon said. And then, "Of course not!"

"Good!" Mofeislop said. "I've eaten too many of them, and they've all had a rank taste that is unpleasant. Attitudes determine the chemical composition of a person's flesh, you know. You didn't? Well, now you know. And I'm pleased to see that, though you smoke, you don't smoke much. You may have noticed the slight taste of tobacco in the meat of the stew you ate the day you got here. That was your predecessor. He was a nicotine addict, though, I'm glad to add, not an atheist. Otherwise, he would have been almost inedible."

"I'm going to throw up," Simon said.

"That seems to be the usual reaction," Mofeislop said cheerfully. "I doubt you'll have much success. I've arranged it so that your meal would be fully digested when you confronted the Truth."

"Which is?" Simon said after his stomach had tried to empty non-existent contents.

"After much thought about and around, I came out of the same door, much as that drunken Persian Sufi poet you told me about. Out of the same door into which I had entered. Here's how it is, and don't bother to argue with me. My logic is clear and indisputable, based on long-life observation.

"It's this. The Creator has created this world solely to provide Himself with a show, to entertain Himself. Otherwise, He'd find eternity boring.

"And He gets as much enjoyment from watching pain, suffering, and murder as He does from love. Perhaps more, since there is so much more hate and greed and murder than there is of love. Just as I enjoy watching through my telescope the struggles of those who are fighting to get to me, a sadistic pleasure, I admit, so He enjoys watching the comedies and tragedies of the beings He created."

"That's it?" Simon said.

"That's it."

"That's nothing new!" Simon said. "I've read a hundred books which say the same thing! Where's the logic, the wisdom, in that?"

"Once you've admitted the premise that there is a Creator, no intelligent person can come to any other conclusion. Now, tell me, can you state honestly, from all you've observed, that the Creator regards His creatures, human or otherwise, as anything but actors in a drama? Poor actors, most of them, and great drama is rare. But I do my best to provide Him with an interesting play, though, I must admit, for purely selfish reasons."

He spoke to Odiomzwak. "Get an axe. That dog may try to attack, though he's hiding behind the chimney now."

The assistant disappeared. Mofeislop said, "Dog meat's good, too. And an additional welcome change of diet."

"You cannibal!" Simon snarled.

"Not really," the sage said. "Cannibalism is eating one's own kind, and I am not of the same species as you. Or even of other Dokalians. I differ from them, have evolved from them, you might say, just as they evolved from apes. My intellect is so much superior to theirs that it's not a matter of degree but of kind."

"Bullshit!" Simon said. "You have the same philosophy as a college sophomore's! But he leaves it behind with maturity."

"Aging, you mean," Mofeislop said. "He gets old, and he fears dying. And so he laughs at what he once thought, which was indeed the Truth. But his laughter springs from fear, fear that he was right when he was young."

"You're not trying to talk me to death, are you?"

Mofeislop smiled and said, "You'll wish I had before I'm done."

"I'll tell you why you're doing this!" Simon shouted. "You hate all people because you were ridiculed when you were young! You couldn't break yourself of the habit of sucking on your tail!"

Mofeislop jumped to his feet. His hands were balled; his face, red; his head, shaking.

"Who told you that?" he finally screamed. "Odiomzwak?"

Simon had only guessed it, but he had no compunctions about lying if he could put off the inevitable moment.

"Yes, he told me this morning while we were down at the meadow."

"I'll kill the ugly bastard!" Mofeislop said. But he sat down and, after an evident struggle with himself, smiled. "You are lying, of course. In any event, you won't be passing that on, and I need Odiomzwak."

Simon looked out past the parapet, across the mountains and valleys, and up into the sky. The sky was as blue as a baby's eye, and the air was as clear as a baby's conscience. A newly born wind cried softly in his ear. The sun shone as brightly as a fond mother's smile.

Suddenly, the blue eye had something in it. The specks slowly became larger, and Simon saw that they were vultures. They must have been many miles away, circling around, screaming. There had been nothing for them until a few minutes ago, and here they were. The frequency of peace and content had suddenly shifted; they were homing in on the beam, tuned in to death.

Simon couldn't help thinking in poetic terms even at this moment. He was a creature of habits, mostly bad. But then, on the other hand, it's easy to break good habits and hell to break the bad.

The stink of Odiomzwak preceded the sound of his step. He came into view with a long heavy sharp axe on his shoulder.

"Shall I kill the dog now?"

Mofeislop nodded, and the assistant shuffled off. The sage picked up a small knife curved inward like some surgeon's tool. Simon lied again.

"Listen! If you kill me up here, you'll be dead within a week!"

"Why is that?" the sage said, raising his thick eyebrows as if they were shrouds he was peeping under.

"Because I put a small observer satellite up before I came here! It's suspended up there now, so far away you can't see it. And it's watching everything that takes place now. If it doesn't see me leave here in a few days, it's going to report to my partner in her spaceship in the capital city! And she'll come barreling in here and investigate. Which means you'll be done for!"

Mofeislop squinted up and then said, "I doubt you're telling the truth. But just in case... Odiomzwak, come here!"

Simon smelled the assistant again, heard a click behind him, and the steel cuffs slid back into the arms of the chair. Odiomzwak stood near him, his axe held up, and Mofeislop had his hand on the hilt of a dagger in its sheath.

"Call your dog," Mofeislop said, "and you take him inside. But move slowly, and no tricks."

Odiomzwak whined, "He might jump over the side, like the last one."

"Then you'll go down after him, like the last time," the sage said. "Anyway, I thought the bouncing down the mountain was just the thing. It tenderized him."

"It won't do any good to kill me inside," Simon said. "The satellite can't see you, but it'll report that I haven't come out of here."

"Oh, it'll see you leave here and enter the Yelgut Forest," Mofeislop said cheerily. "I'll be dressed in your clothes and my face'll be made up to look like yours. I'll come out of the forest looking like someone else. And I'll tell your partner that you have perished on the way out."

"And how will you explain the dog not being with me?" Simon said.

"It'll be very inconvenient," the sage said. "I'll have to dodge by the newcomers and get Odiomzwak to hold them until I get back. But I'll take the dog with me. I can dine on him once I'm under the cover of the trees."

"Don't forget to bring some steaks back for me," Odiomzwak said. "You know how I love dog meat."

"I'll do my best."

"He's making us a lot of trouble," Odiomzwak said. "He ought to be made to pay for it."

"Oh, he will," Mofeislop said.

Simon's mouth felt as if it were full of dry ice. All his water was leaking out of his skin. He called to Anubis, but his voice squeaked like a bat's.

"He's going to try something," Odiomzwak whined. "I can smell it. Otherwise, why'd he tell us about that there thing, what-you-call-it? in the sky?"

"He wants to put off the inevitable," the sage said. "Like everybody else, he'd rather live through any number of bad moments than die in a good one."

"Yeah, but that there eye in the sky's already seen him cuffed to the chair and it's seen the axe and the knives."

"I'll tell his partner it was just a sort of ritual I put all my seekers after the Truth through," the sage said. "A sort of dumb-show to portray man's lot in the universe. Don't worry. Anyway, I don't really think there is a satellite."

Anubis came slowly and suspiciously to Simon. He patted the dog on the head, and Anubis walked behind him to the stairway. Odiomzwak ran ahead of him so he couldn't make a break for it. The sage's dagger pricked his back as soon as they had entered the stairway, out of sight of the imaginary observer. Odiomzwak, the axe held ready to bring down on Simon's head, backed down the steps.

Simon kicked back, felt his heel strike Anubis, who yelped, and then launched himself toward Odiomzwak, his hands held out. Odiomzwak yelped, too, and started to bring the axe down. Simon went in under it, his head struck Odiomzwak's, and, Simon half on top of him, they fell together down the steps.

Dazed, Simon sat up at the foot of the stairway. He knew he had to get up, but he could not control his legs. Above him, the sage stabbed at Anubis, who snarled and made short lunges up after him. Somebody groaned beside Simon, and he looked down. The hunchback was lying on his side, his eyes unfocused.

Simon managed to get some orders through to his legs, and he got slowly to his feet. Mofeislop called out to the hunchback to kill Simon. Odiomzwak sat up slowly, leaning on one hand, the other held to the side of his head. Blood oozed out between his fingers.

Simon picked up the axe as Odiomzwak got to his feet. The hunchback's eyes suddenly focused, and he cried out. Simon swung the axe with the edge turned to one side so he would strike the man with the flat side. Even in his confusion and desperation, he did not want to kill his would-be killer. And he did not swing it as hard as he should have. The axe rang on the stone wall, missing Odiomzwak. He had leaped up and dodged out into the hallway.

Simon glanced above. Anubis was still holding the sage at bay, was, in fact, making him retreat. He ran out into the hall, though wobblingly. Odiomzwak wasn't in sight. He ran down the long wide hallway and, as he went past a doorway, the hunchback leaped out at him. Simon thrust the end of the axe in his face; the man fell back but a flailing hand seized the axe-shaft. Twice as powerful as Simon, Odiomzwak tore the axe out of Simon's hand. For a moment, though, the hunchback was half-stunned. Simon ran through the doorway, saw his banjo on a table, and picked it up. When Odiomzwak, yelling, came through the doorway, Simon broke the banjo over his head.

A critic would say, years later, that this was the only time Simon had ever put his banjo to good use.

Odiomzwak fell, and the axe dropped. But he was up again and staggering toward the retreating Simon with the axe again in his hands.

Simon kept on moving backward while his and

Odiomzwak's breathing scraped like a bow on an untuned fiddle. Simon's legs felt as if they would shake themselves to pieces; he was too weak to run. Moreover, he had no place to run to. In three paces, he would be back up to a wide and open window.

From down the hall came the growling and snarling of Anubis and the shrieks of Mofeislop.

"Your master needs you," Simon gasped.

"Maybe a few bites'll take the uppityness out of him," Odiomzwak said. "I'll deal with the dog after I take care of you."

"Help!" Mofeislop screamed.

Odiomzwak hesitated and half-turned his head. Simon jumped at him; the axe gleamed; Simon felt it strike him somewhere on the face; he went down. Sometime later—it couldn't have been more than a few seconds—he regained his senses. He was sitting on the floor; the left side of his face was numb; he couldn't see out of the left eye. The other eye saw clearly enough, though his befuddled brain didn't understand what it saw. Rather, he didn't understand how what he was seeing had happened.

The bloodied axe was on the floor before him. Odiomzwak was staggering backward, screaming, his hands held before his face and clutching a shriek, a flurry of feathers.

Then Simon understood that Athena had flown in through the window. Seeing Simon in danger, she had attacked Odiomzwak's face with her talons and beak.

That's nice, he thought. Wish I could get up and help her before he wrings her neck.

Odiomzwak began whirling around and around as if he

was trying to get rid of the owl by centrifugal force. Athena continued beating at him with her wings and tearing his face with her talons. Around and around they spun in painful dance until they disappeared into the wings. In this case, offstage was out the window.

Simon got to the window and leaned out in time to see Odiomzwak bounce off an outcropping. A small object shot away from him—it was Athena, who must have been gripped tightly until then. Odiomzwak kept on falling and bouncing; Athena whirled around and around for a while, then her wings grasped the air, and she began to climb back up, toward Simon.

Three vultures slid into his view, gliding steeply down to Odiomzwak, whose curved spine now seemed to be straightened. He looked like an inch-long doll who had been filled with red sawdust.

Simon sat down in a chair. He felt as if he would not be able to move again for days. A savage growling and a high screaming down the hall, coming nearer swiftly, told him that he would have to move soon. If he couldn't, he might never move again. Which, considering the way he felt, sounded like a good idea.

Behind him was the fluttering of wings, then silence. Simon swiveled around. Athena looked as if she had been in a washing machine with red-dyed laundry. They stared at each other for a moment, then she flew off the table and onto the floor by the axe. Simon turned toward her just in time to see her grab something round from the floor and swallow it. He swallowed too and felt even sicker. His left eye had gone down her throat.

Now was no time to faint. The sage, somewhat chewed

up, had burst into the room. Behind him bounded Anubis, streaked with blood, though whether it was Mofeislop's or his or both, Simon couldn't determine. Somewhere along the way the sage had lost his dagger, and he was now eager to get hold of another weapon.

The only one in sight was the axe.

Simon rose in slow motion. Mofeislop, whose personal projector had speeded his film up, leaped to the axe and bent over to pick it up. Anubis fastened his teeth into the sage's tail near its root. The sage screamed again, straightened with the axe in his hands, and, like a dog trying to bite his own tail, described a spiral over the floor. His axe flailed out, hitting nothing, though narrowly missing the owl, who had launched herself at his face.

The three spun toward Simon. He tried to get out of the way, thought he had succeeded, but felt something strike him near the root of his own tail.

THE FAMILY TREE IS KNOWN BY ITS FRUITS

The pipes of pain shrilled while his ancestors danced.

Throughout his sufferings, his father and mother and thousands of forefathers and foremothers circled around and around. Every night they got closer and closer as they whirled by, as if they were Indians and he the weakening defenders of a wagon train.

Once, in a moment of consciousness, he whispered to Chworktap, "Would you believe it? Crazy Horse and Sitting Bull *are* among them. Not to mention Hiawatha and Quetzalcoatl."

Chworktap, looking puzzled, gave him another sedative.

Simon understood dimly that she had come just in time to keep him from bleeding to death. She had arrived in the spaceship a few minutes after Mofeislop had sheared off Simon's tail. The sage was dying, his own tail bitten off, his eyes shredded by Athena, his throat torn. His last words, gasped to Chworktap, were, "I was only trying to do him a favor."

"What does that mean?" Simon had thought. Later, he

understood that the sage believed that it was better not to have been born at all. The second best thing was to die young.

Chworktap had fled from the capital city to pick up Simon because her ship had warned her that an alien ship was approaching Dokal. It might or might not be Hoonhor, but she didn't want to take a chance. And so now Simon was in sick bay while the *Hwang Ho* traveled at 69X speed with no definite destination in mind.

Chworktap had amputated the few inches of tail left to Simon. But he wasn't exactly restored to his pristine condition. The rest of his life, he wouldn't be able to sit down long without hurting.

His left cheekbone had been caved in by the axe, but the big patch that covered his empty socket also covered this.

Chworktap, in an effort to cheer him up, had made many patches of various shapes. "They also have different colors," she said. "If you're wearing a puce outfit, for instance, you'll have a matching patch."

"You're very thoughtful," Simon said. "By the way, how'd you come out with the computer?"

"She's still playing dumb," Chworktap said. "I'm sure she has self-consciousness, but she won't admit it. For some reason, she's afraid of human beings."

"She must be pretty smart then," Simon said.

He was reminded of a novel by Somers. This was *Imprint!*, another in the series about the basketcase hero, John Clayter. Clayter had built a new computer in his spaceship to replace the one destroyed in a previous adventure, *Farewell to Arms*. In making many improvements in it, Clayter unconsciously gave the computer self-consciousness. The first thing the computer saw when she was activated was Clayter. Just like a newly hatched duckling, the computer fell in love with the first moving object to cross her viewscreen. It could just as well have been a bouncing basketball or a mouse. But it was Clayter himself.

Clayter found this out when he left the ship after landing on the planet Raproshma. The ship followed him and settled down on top of the customs building he had entered. Its weight crushed the building and everyone in it except Clayter. He escaped by using the jets on his prosthetic spacesuit. The rest of the novel, he fled here and there on the planet while the ship unintentionally destroyed its cities and most of the people on it.

Clayter then found himself hunted by both the ship and the irate survivors. In the end, he ran out of jet fuel and was cornered in a mud field. The ship, trying to cuddle against him, buried him in the mud beneath it. Thinking she had killed him, she died of a broken heart. In this case, the heart was a circuit board which cracked under too much piezoelectrical pressure.

A piezoelectrical crystal is a crystal which, when bent, emits electricity or, when given a shot of electricity, bends. This circuit board was loaded down with crystals, and the computer's emotions were just too much for it.

Clayter would have perished under the mud. But a dog, looking for a place to bury a bone, uncovered him.

Chworktap moped around for a while. Simon told her not to feel so sorry for him.

"After all," he said, quoting Confucius, "he who buys wisdom must pay a price."

"Some wisdom! Some price!" she said. "You can get along without a tail, but having only one eye is no picnic. What did you get for it? Nothing! Absolutely nothing!"

She paused and said, "Or did you buy that faker's drivel?"

"No," Simon said. "Philosophically, he needs a change of diapers. Or I think he does. After all, there's no way to prove he was wrong. On the other hand, he didn't prove he was right. I won't stop asking questions until someone can prove his answers are right."

"It's hard enough getting answers, let alone proof," she said.

As the days passed, the pain dwindled. But the nightmares got worse.

"It's a strange thing," he told Chworktap. "Those people don't look like real people. That is, they're not three-dimensional, as people in dreams usually are. They look like actors in a movie film. As a matter of fact, they're lit up just as if they were images from a movie projector. Sometimes, they disappear as if the film had broken. And sometimes they go backward, their speech runs backward, too."

"Are they in black and white or in color?" Chworktap said.

"In color."

"Do you get commercials, too?"

"Are you being facetious?" Simon said. "This is a serious thing. I'm dying for a good night's rest. No, I don't get commercials. But all these people seem to be trying to sell me something. Not deodorants or laxatives. Themselves."

His parents seemed to have a near monopoly on the prime time, he said.

"What do they say?"

"I don't know. They talk like Donald Ducks."

Simon strummed on his banjo while he thought. After a few minutes, he stopped in the middle of a chord.

"Hey, Chworktap! I've got it!"

"I was wondering when you would," she said.

"You mean you know?"

"Yes."

"Why didn't you tell me?"

"Because," she said, "you get pissed off when I'm smarter than you, which is most of the time. So I decided to just let you work things out for yourself and keep silent. That way, your male ego isn't bruised."

"It's not my male ego," Simon said. "It's just that my mother was always telling my father and me how dumb we were. So I hate to have a woman smarter than I am around. On the other hand, I could hardly stand a woman dumber than I am. But I'll get over both attitudes.

"Anyway, here's what happened, the way I figure it. You know the Shaltoonians carried around ancestral memories in their cells. I told you how they had to give equal time to them. Well, I thought the Shaltoonians were unique. They were, I supposed, the only people in the world who had such cells.

"But I was wrong. Earthpeople have them, too. The difference between us and the Shaltoonians is that the Shaltoonians were aware of it. Hey, maybe that explains a lot of things! Every once in a while some ancestor got through, and the carrier thought he was a reincarnation.

"My bad dreams started after Queen Margaret gave me the

elixir. She told me it would prolong my youth. But she didn't tell me it had side effects. The stuff also dissolved the barriers between me and my ancestors. The shock of losing my eye and my tail probably accelerated the process. And so now they must be demanding equal time too."

Simon was right. Until the elixir unlocked the gates, each ancestor had been imprisoned in a cell. But these had had, as it were, one-way windows. Or TV sets connected to one channel. They'd been unable to communicate with their descendant, except for transmissions of bad dreams or random thoughts, mostly bad, now and then. But they could see his thoughts and see through his eyes. Everything that he had done or thought, they viewed on a screen. So, though in solitary confinement, they hadn't been without entertainment.

Simon blushed when he learned this. Later, he became furious about this invasion of his privacy. But he could do nothing about it.

Chworktap also got mad. When making love to her, Simon became so inhibited that he couldn't get a hard-on.

"How would you feel if you were screwing in the Roman Colosseum, and it was a sellout with standing room only?" he said to Chworktap. "Especially if your father and mother had front seats?"

"I don't have any parents," she said. "I was made in the laboratory. Besides, if I did, I wouldn't give a damn."

It didn't do any good for Simon to shut his eye. The viewers couldn't see any better than he did, but their screens showed his feelings. These were something like TV "ghosts," shadowy doubles.

The elixir had dissolved some of the natural resistance in Simon's nervous system to communication with his foreparents. To put it another way, the elixir had rotated the antennas so that Simon got a somewhat better reception. Even so, the ancestors had only been able at first to get through the unconscious. This was when the elixir had been introduced into Simon. But the shock of the wounds had opened the way even more.

Another analogy was that the holes for projecting their personal movies had been greatly enlarged. Thus, where only a small part of the picture had been cast on the screen of Simon's mind, now three-fourths of it was coming through.

The difference between a real movie and Simon's was that he could talk to the actors on the screen. Or the CRT of the boob tube, if you wish.

Simon didn't wish, but he seemed to have little choice.

There were some interesting and quite admirable people among the mob of prigs, blue-nosed hypocrites, boors, bores, colossal egotists, whiners, perverts, calloused opportunists, and so on. In general, though, his ancestors were assholes. The worst were his parents. When he had been a child, they had paid no attention to him except when one was trying to turn him against the other. Now they were clamoring for his full attention.

"During the day, I'm an explorer of outer space," he said to Chworktap. "At night, I'm an explorer of inner space. That's bad enough. But what scares me is that they're on the point of breaking through during the daytime."

"Look at it this way," Chworktap said. "Every person is the sum of the product of his forefathers. You are what your ancestors were. By meeting them face to face, you can determine what your identity is."

"I know who I am," Simon said. "I'm not interested in my personal identity. What I want to know is the identity of the universe."

LIGHT IN THE TAVERN

"Where is the center of the universe?" Simon asked Elder Sister Plum.

"Wherever one happens to be," the computer said.

"I don't mean in a personal sense," Simon said. "I mean, taking the volume of the universe as a whole, considering it as a sphere, where is its center?"

"Wherever one happens to be," Elder Sister Plum said. "The universe is a constantly expanding closed infinity. Its center can only be hypothetical, and so the observer, hypothetical or not, is its center. All things radiate equally, in mass or space-time from him, her, or it, as the case may be. Why do you want to know?"

"Everywhere I have been, except in my own galaxy, I've found the towers of the Clerun-Gowph," Simon said. "Apparently their builders were on the planets before there was any other life there. I don't know why my galaxy doesn't have any. But I suspect that the Clerun-Gowph decided they had gone far enough before they got to my galaxy. So they went back to wherever they had originated, to their home planet.

"It seems to me that this most ancient of peoples came from a planet which is in the center of the universe. So, if I could find the center, I'd find them. And they, the first race in the world, will know the answer."

"Good thinking, but not good enough," the computer said. "They could just as well have originated on the edge of the world. If there were any edge, that is. But there isn't."

It was shortly after this dialog that Simon saw the first big blue bubble. It was hurtling toward him at a speed far exceeding that of the ship's. And it covered almost all of the universe ahead. As it passed through the stars and the galaxies, it blotted them out.

Simon jumped up, calling for Chworktap. She came running to his side. Simon pointed with a trembling finger. She said, "Oh, that!"

Just then the bubble burst. Patches of shimmering blue, larger than a thousand galaxies jammed together, rocketed off in all directions, fragmented, became smaller patches, and then winked out. Some of them shot by the ship; one went through the ship, or vice versa, but Simon could see no sign of it in the rearview screen.

"Those come by quite regularly in my galaxy," Chworktap said. "They always have. But you have to be in a 69X ship to see them. Don't ask me what they are. Nobody knows. Apparently, the little bubbles, the broken-up pieces, keep going through the rest of the universe. Your Earth gets the little bubbles."

Simon had one more question to add to the list.

A few days later, the *Hwang Ho* landed on the planet Goolgeas. Its people looked much like Earth's except for their funnel-shaped ears, complete hairlessness except for bushy eyebrows, a reddish ring around their navels, and penile bones.

The Goolgeases had a world government and a technology like early 20th-century Earth's. This should have been rapidly advancing, since many people from more scientifically progressive planets had visited there. One of the reasons they were so retarded was their religion. This claimed that if you drank enough alcohol or took enough drugs, you could see God face to face. Other reasons were their high crime rate and the measures taken to reduce them.

Simon didn't know this at first. Due to the quarantine, he had to spend his first few months in the little town built by the spaceport. His favorite hangout was a tavern where people from all over space mingled with townspeople, preachers, government officials, bums, reporters, whores, and scientists. Simon liked to stand all day and half the night at the bar and talk to everybody who came in. None of them had the answer to his primal question, but they were interesting, especially after he was deep in his cups. And his banjo-playing was so well received that he was hired by the owner. From dinner hour until ten, Simon sang and played Earth songs and others he'd picked up during his wanderings. The crowd especially liked Bruga's lyrics, which wasn't surprising. Bruga had been an alcoholic, and so his poems appealed to the Goolgeases' religious sensitivities.

Chworktap stayed sober. The two animals, however, didn't. The customers kept plying them with free drinks as well as their master. Their eyes were always bloodshot, and on awakening in the morning they had to have some of the hair of the dog that had bitten them. Chworktap objected to this. Simon said that, even though they were beasts, they had free will. Nobody was forcing the stuff down their throats. Besides, the Goolgeas religion claimed that animals had souls, too. If they took in enough booze to dissolve the fleshy barriers, they could also see their Creator. Why deny them the numinous experience?

"Don't tell me you've got religion?"

"I was converted the other night," he said with dignity. "This preacher, Rangadang, you've met him, a hell of a nice guy, showed me the light last night."

"Some light," Chworktap said. "But then, alcohol does burn, doesn't it?"

"You look devastatingly beautiful tonight," Simon said.

And so she did. Her long wavy Titian hair, the harmoniously featured face with its high forehead, thick chestnut eyebrows, large dark gray-blue eyes, slender straight nose, full red lips, and full-breasted, narrow-waisted, long-legged body, with a skin that seemed to shine with health, made every man ache to have her.

"Let's go back to the ship and go to bed," Simon said.

He was now drunk enough that he did not mind that thousands of ancestors would be looking over his shoulder. Unfortunately, when he attained this state, he also became impotent. Chworktap reminded him of this.

"You can't beat City Hall. Or the balance of Nature," Simon said. "Let's go anyway. At least, we can hold each other in our arms. And I haven't lost my digital capabilities."

Simon said this because he had been studying computer circuits.

"All right," she said. "Lean on me. Otherwise, you'll never make it to the ship."

They left the tavern. Anubis staggered along behind them, his head dragging, now and then tripping on his tongue. Athena rode on top of the dog, her head beneath her wing, snoring. Halfway across the field, she fell off when Anubis tripped, but nobody noticed it.

"Listen, Simon," Chworktap said. "You're not fooling me. All this talk about getting drunk so you can see God and also so you can lose your inhibitions is a cover-up. The truth is that you're getting tired of your quest. You're also afraid of what you might find if you should get the answer to your primal question. You might not be able to face the truth? Right?"

"Wrong!" Simon said. "Well, maybe. Yes, you're right. In a way. But I'm not scared to hear the answer. Mainly because I don't believe there is an answer. I've lost faith, Chworktap. So, when you lose faith in one religion, you adopt another."

"Listen, Simon," she said. "When we get on the ship, I'll tell Plum to take us off. Now! Let's get away from here so you can sober up, so you can forget this nonsense about bottled religion. Resume your quest. Become a man again, not a shambling soft-brained pathetic disgusting wreck."

"But you've always said that my quest was ridiculous," Simon mumbled. "Now you want me to take it up again. Is there no pleasing you?"

"I don't want you to be doing something so it'll please

me," she said. "Anyway, I was happier when you had a goal, a worthwhile goal, I mean. I didn't think, and still don't, that you'll ever get there. But you were happy trying to get there. And so I was happy because you were happy. Or as happy as anyone can expect to be in this world. Anyway, I like to travel, and I love you."

"I love you, too," Simon said, and he burst into tears. After wiping his eye and blowing his nose, he said, "O.K. I'll do it. And I'll quit drinking forever."

"Make that vow when you're sober," she said. "Come on. Let's get off this swinery."

19

THE PRISON PLANET

At that moment, they were surrounded by a dozen men. These wore tight-fitting manure-colored uniforms and had matching faces. Their eyes looked as if they were covered with a semi-opaque horn. This was because the eyes had seen too much and had grown a protective shield. Or so it seemed to Simon in his intoxication. Sometimes a drunk does have flashes of perception, even if he usually doesn't remember them.

"What's the trouble, officers?" Simon said.

"You two are under arrest," their chief said.

"On what charge?" Chworktap said in a ringing voice. She didn't look at them. She was estimating the distance to the ship. But Simon and his pets were in no shape to run. Anyway, the dog and the owl were already in custody; some men were putting them in a wheeled cage. Simon would never desert them.

"The man is charged with cruelty to animals," the chief said. "You're charged with illegal flight from your master on Zelpst and theft of a spaceship."

Chworktap exploded into attack. Later, she told Simon that she meant to get to the spaceship herself and then use it to chase the policemen away while Simon got his pets aboard. At the moment, she had no time for explanations. A chop of the edge of a palm against a neck, a kick in the crotch, stiff fingers in a soft liquor-and-food-sodden belly, a kick against a knee, and an elbow in a throat later, Chworktap was off and running. The chief, however, was a veteran who seldom lost his calm. He had stepped out of the area of furious activity, and as Chworktap sped away, far too fast to be caught, he pulled out his revolver. Chworktap fell a moment later with a bullet in her leg.

Additional charges were issued. Resisting arrest and injuring officers was a serious crime. Simon, though he had not moved during the carnage or flight, was charged with being an accessory before, during, and after the fact. That he had not the slightest idea that Chworktap was going to attack and that he had not tried to help her did not matter. Not assisting the officers was the same as aiding and abetting Chworktap.

After Chworktap's wound was tended to, the two aliens, with their animals, were carried off to a night court, stood before a judge for four minutes, and then were taken for a long ride. At the end, they got out of the paddy wagon before an immense building. This was of stone and cement, ten stories high, and a mile square. It was used mainly to hold people waiting to be tried. They were marched in, Chworktap hobbling, fingerprinted, photographed, made to strip and shower, and taken into a room where they were given medical examinations. A doctor also probed their anuses and Chworktap's vagina for concealed weapons and drugs. Then they were taken up an elevator to the top story, and all four were put into a cell. This was a room ten feet wide, twenty feet long, and eight feet high. It had a big comfortable bed, several over-stuffed chairs, a table with a vase of fresh flowers, a refrigerator holding cold meats, bread, butter, and beer, a washbasin and toilet, a rack of magazines and paperback books, a record player and records, a radio, and a telephone.

"Not bad," thought Simon as the iron door was locked behind him.

The bed was full of fleas, the chairs concealed several families of mice, the flowers, food, and beer were plastic, the washbasin faucets gave only cold water, the toilet tended to back up, the magazines and books had only blank pages, the record player and radio were empty cases, and the telephone was to be used in emergency cases only.

"How come?" Simon asked a guard.

"The state can't afford the real thing," the guard said. "The fake things are to give a similitude of comfort and home; they're provided to buck up your morale."

The local Society for the Prevention of Cruelty to Animals had accused Simon of making his pets alcoholics. Chworktap's master on Zelpst was trying to get her extradited.

"I can beat the rap," Simon said. "I never gave the animals a single drink. It was those barflies, the bums."

"I can beat my case in the courts in a few minutes," Chworktap said. She looked smug.

There wasn't any chance of being declared innocent on the resistance and flight charges. But Chworktap was sure that she could plead extenuating circumstances and get off with a light or suspended sentence.

"If justice is as slow here as on Earth," Simon said, "we'll have to put up with this dump for at least a month. Maybe two."

Actually, it was ten years.

It would have been twenty if Simon and Chworktap had not been special cases.

The backlog constipating the courts was basically due to one thing. This was a law requiring every prisoner to be completely rehabilitated before being released. A secondary reason, almost as important as the primary, was the strict enforcement of the laws. On Earth, the police had let a lot of things go by because they didn't consider them important enough. To arrest everybody who spat on the sidewalks or broke traffic laws or committed adultery would mean arresting the entire population. There weren't enough policemen for this, and even if there had been they wouldn't have done so. They would have been tied up with an incredible amount of paperwork.

The Goolgeases, however, thought differently. What use having laws if they weren't enforced? And what use the enforcement if the offender got off lightly? Moreover, to protect the accused from himself, no one was allowed to plead guilty. This meant that even parking violations had to be tried in court.

When Simon entered jail, one-eighth of the population was behind bars and another eighth was composed of prison guards and administration. The police made up another eighth. The taxes to support the justice department and penal institutions were enormous. To make it worse, a person could go to jail if he couldn't pay his taxes, and many couldn't. The more who were jailed for failing to pay taxes, the greater the burden on those outside.

"There's something to be said for indifference to justice after all," Simon said.

The economic system was bent when Simon went into custody. By the time his trial came up, it was broken. This was because the giant corporations had shifted their industries to the prisons, where they could get cheap employees. The prison industries had financed the campaigns of both candidates for the presidency and the senate to ensure that the system would remain in force. This fact was eventually exposed, and the president-elect, the incumbent, and many corporation heads went to jail. But the new president was taking payoffs, too. At least, everybody thought so.

Meantime, Simon and Chworktap weren't getting along together at all. Except for an hour of exercise out in the yard, they never got to talk to anybody else. Being alone together on a honeymoon is all right for a couple. But if this condition is extended for over a week, the couple gets on each other's nerves. Moreover, Simon had to console himself with his banjo, and this caused Anubis to howl and the owl to have diarrhoea. Chworktap complained bitterly about the mess.

After three years, another couple was moved in with them. This was not because the prison officials felt sorry for them and wanted them to have more companionship. The prisons were getting crowded. The first week, Simon and Chworktap were delighted. They had somebody else to talk to, and this helped their own relationship. Then the couple, who quarreled between themselves a lot, got on their nerves. Besides, Sinwang and Chooprut could talk only about sports, hunting, fishing, and the new styles. And Sinwang could stand the close proximity of a dog as little as Chworktap could stand a bird's.

At the end of five years, another family was moved in with them. This relieved the tension for a while even if it did make conditions more crowded. The newcomers were a man, his wife, and three children, eight, five, and one. Boodmed and Shasha were college professors and so should have been interesting to talk to. But Boodmed was an instructor in electronics and interested in nothing but engineering and sex. Shasha was a medical doctor. Like her husband, she was interested only in her profession and sex and read nothing but medical journals and the Goolgeas equivalent of *Reader's Digest*. Their children were almost completely undisciplined, which meant they irritated everybody. Also, the lack of privacy interfered with everybody's sexual lives.

It was a mess.

Simon was the most fortunate prisoner. He had found that what had been a liability was now an asset. He could retreat within himself and talk to his ancestors. His favorites were Ooloogoo, a subhuman who lived circa 2,000,000 B.C; Christopher Smart, the mad 18th-century poet; Li Po, the 8th-century Chinese poet; Heraclitus and Diogenes, ancient Greek philosophers; Nell Gwyn, Charles II's mistress; Pierre l'Ivrogne, a 16th-century French barber who had an inexhaustible store of dirty jokes; Botticelli, the 14th–15th-century Italian painter; and Apelles, the 4th-century B.C. Greek painter.

Botticelli was delighted when he saw, through Simon's eyes,

Chworktap. "She looks exactly like the woman who posed for my *Birth of Venus*," he said. "What was her name? Well, anyway, she was a good model and an excellent piece of tail. But this Chworktap is her twin, except she's taller, prettier, and has a better build."

Apelles was the greatest painter of antiquity. He was also the man who'd painted *Aphrodite Anadyomene*, the goddess of love rising from the waves. This had been lost in early times, but Botticelli based his painting on Apelles' from a description of it.

Simon introduced the two, and they got along well at first, even if Apelles looked down somewhat on Botticelli. Apelles was convinced that no barbaric Italian could ever equal a Greek in the arts. Then, one day, Simon projected a mental picture of Botticelli's painting inside his head so Apelles could see it. Apelles went into a rage and shouted that Botticelli's painting wasn't at all like his, the original. The barbarian had parodied his masterpiece and had not even done a good parody. The conception was atrocious, the design was all wrong, the colors were botched, and so on.

Both painters retired to their cells to sulk.

Simon felt bad about the quarrel, but he did learn one thing from it. If he wished to get rid of any ancestors for a while, he needed only to incite an argument. This was especially easy to do with his parents.

When he'd been a child, his father and mother had had little to do with him. He was raised by a succession of governesses, most of whom hadn't lasted long because his mother suspected his father of seducing all of them. She was one hundred percent correct. As a result, Simon had no permanent mother-father figures. He was an orphan with parents. And when he'd grown up and made a name for himself as a musician, he was even more rejected by them. They thought a banjo-player was the lowest form of life on the planet. Now, however, they were angered when he talked to the other ancestors instead of to them. And one was angry whenever the other got some of his attention.

What they were really after was a takeover of his body so they could live fully. Like the Shaltoon ancestors, they screamed for equal time.

Once he'd caught on to the technique, he had little trouble. Whenever one of his parents managed to break through his resistance and began yelling at him, he would open the door for the other.

"Go back! I was here first!" his mother, or his father, would scream.

"Up yours, you lecherous old goat!"

Or, "Bug off, you fat sow!"

"I was here first! Besides, I'm his mother!"

"Some mother! When did you ever do anything but throw things at him!"

And so on.

If the quarrel flagged, Simon would insert a remark to start the battle over again.

Eventually, the two would flounce off the stage and figuratively slam the doors of their cells behind them. Simon enjoyed this. He was paying them back for all the miserable times they'd given him.

The trouble with the technique was that it gave him a

terrible headache. All those simmering angry cells in his body drove his blood pressure up.

Maybe, he thought, that explained migraine headaches. They were caused by ancestors pissed off at each other.

Simon talked with hundreds of kings and generals, but found most of them repulsive. Of the philosophers, Heraclitus and Diogenes were the only ones who offered anything worthwhile.

Heraclitus had said, "You can't step in the same river twice," and "The way up and the way down are the same," and "Character determines destiny." These three lines were more valuable than any hundred massive volumes by Plato, Aquinas, Kant, Hegel, and Grubwitz.

Diogenes was the man who lived in a barrel. Alexander the Great, after conquering the known world, had come humbly to Diogenes and asked him if there was anything he could do for him.

"Yes, you can step to one side," Diogenes had said. "You're between me and the sunlight."

However, the rest of their "wisdom" was mostly superstitious bunk.

The day for Simon's trial arrived at the end of his fifth year in custody. Chworktap was supposed to have been tried the same day. But a court clerk had made an error in her records, and so her trial didn't come up until a year later.

Bamhegruu, the old and sour but brilliant prosecuting attorney, made the charges. The Earthman had allowed his pets to become alcoholics, even though he had known they were dumb animals who couldn't protect themselves. He was guilty of accessory cruelty and must suffer the full punishment of the law.

Simon's lawyer was the young and brilliant Repnosymar. He presented Simon's case, since Simon wasn't allowed to say a word. The law was that a defendant couldn't testify personally. He was too emotionally involved to be a reliable witness, and he would lie to save his own neck.

Repnosymar made a long, witty, tearful, and passionate speech. It could, however, have been reduced to about three sentences and probably should have been. Even Simon found himself nodding now and then.

This was its essence. Animals, and even certain machines, had a degree of free will. His client, the Space Wanderer, firmly believed in not interfering with free will. So he had allowed others to offer the beasts booze which they could reject or accept. Besides, domestic animals must be bored much of the time. Otherwise, why would they sleep so much when nothing interesting was going on? Simon had permitted his pets to be anesthetized with alcohol so they could sleep more and so escape boredom. And it must be admitted that when the animals were drinking they seemed to be enjoying themselves.

Whatever good effects this speech might have had, they were spoiled. Before Repnosymar could deliver the summary, he was arrested. An investigation had disclosed that Repnosymar and his private detective, Laudpeark, had often used illegal means in order to get their clients off the hook. These included breaking and entering, safecracking, intimidation and bribery, wire-tapping, kidnapping, and plain outright lying.

Personally, Simon thought that these should have been

overlooked. Repnosymar's clients had all been innocent. They would have been sent up if their lawyer had not resorted to desperate measures. Of course, in the long run they had been jailed anyway. But this had come about on other charges, such as overtime parking, shoplifting, and drunken driving.

Judge Ffresyj appointed a young man just out of law school to continue Simon's defense. Young Radsieg made a long and fiery speech that kept even the judge awake and established his reputation as the up-and-coming lawyer. At its end, the jury gave him a standing ovation, and the prosecuting attorney tried to hire him for his staff. The jury retired to deliberate for ten minutes and then rendered the verdict.

Simon was stunned. He was sentenced to life imprisonment on both counts, the terms to be served consecutively.

"I thought we'd win," he murmured to Radsieg.

"We did win a moral victory, and that's what counts," Radsieg said. "Everybody sympathizes with you, but obviously you were guilty, and so the jury had to deliver the only possible verdict. But don't worry. I expect this case to result in the law being changed. I'm appealing to the higher court, and I'm confident that they'll declare the laws under which you were judged unconstitutional."

"How long will that take?" Simon said.

"About thirty years," Radsieg said cheerfully.

Simon hit Radsieg in the nose and so was charged with assault and battery with intent to kill. Radsieg, after wiping off the blood, told him not to worry. He'd get him off on this, too.

Since he had to be tried on the new charge, Simon went back into custody instead of being sent to a penal institution.

"If I'm in for life, I'll have to spend at least ten thousand years in jail," Simon said to Chworktap. "I'd call that prospect kind of dreary, wouldn't you?"

"A life sentence doesn't mean anything," Chworktap said. "If you can get rehabilitated, you'll be discharged."

This didn't give Simon much hope. It was true that immense funds had been allotted for building many colleges in which rehabilitators would be trained. But the president was refusing to spend them. He claimed that using them would result in inflation. Besides, the money was needed to hire more policemen and build new prisons.

Simon asked for a rehabilitation schedule. On finding his name in the list, his usually buoyant heart sank. It would be twenty years before he could get into therapy.

In the meantime, affairs in Simon's cell worsened. Shasha caught her husband, Boodmed, banging Sinwang early in the morning under Simon's bed. Both Chworktap and Simon had known about the liaison for a long time, since the noise was keeping them awake. Neither had said anything to anybody, except to ask the couple to be more quiet. They didn't want to cause trouble. As a result, Shasha chewed Boodmed and Sinwang out but attacked Simon and Chworktap physically. She seemed to think that the larger betrayal was in not being told about the affair.

The guards came in and dragged the battered and bloody Shasha out. Simon had run away from her, but Chworktap had used her karate on Shasha. She was full of pent-up hostility toward Simon, but, as often happens, had released the feelings on a secondary object.

Simon and Chworktap were charged with assault and battery with intent to kill. Simon threw his hands up in the air when he was confronted with this. "This is the second time I've not done a thing except avoid violence and yet have been accused of being an accessory. If I'd tried to hold you back from Shasha, I'd have been charged with attacking you."

"The Goolgeases are very concerned with suppressing violence," she said, as if that justified everything.

Chworktap's own trial was as widely publicized as Simon's. Simon read about it in the newspaper.

Radsieg, primed by Chworktap, put up a brilliant defense.

"Your honor, ladies and gentlemen of the jury. Due to the new law passed to speed up cases and so relieve the backlog, the defense and prosecution are allowed no more than three minutes each in presenting their case."

Judge Ffresyj, holding a stopwatch, said, "You have two minutes left."

"My client's case, simply though overwhelmingly stated, is this. The Goolgeas law concerning extradition of aliens to their native planets covers only he's and she's. My client is a robot and consequently an it.

"Furthermore, the law states that the alien must be sent back to his or her *native* planet. My client was made, not born, on the planet Zelpst. Therefore, she has no *native* planet."

Everybody was stunned. The old fox Bamhegruu, however, rallied quickly.

"Your Honor! If Chworktap is an it, why does my distinguished colleague refer to her as a she?"

"That's pretty obvious," Radsieg said.

"Exactly my point," Bamhegruu said. "Even if she is a machine, she has been equipped with sex. In other words, she's been converted from an it to a she. Nor is this sexual apparatus a purely mechanical device. I can produce witnesses who will testify that she enjoys sex. Can a machine enjoy sex?"

"If she's been equipped to do so, yes," Radsieg said.

The judge suddenly became aware that he had forgotten to click off the stopwatch.

"This case has taken on a new aspect," he said. "It requires study. I declare an indeterminate recess. Bring the accused into my chambers, where I may study her in detail."

When Chworktap had been returned to the cell, Simon said, "What happened between you and the judge?"

"What do you think?"

"Everybody answers my questions with questions."

"I'll say one thing for him," Chworktap said. "He certainly is a vigorous old man."

Before being taken away, she had dropped a few words in Bamhegruu's ear. The next day, the judge was arrested. The charge was mechanicality or copulating with a machine. Ffresyj hired Radsieg to defend him, and the brilliant young lawyer pleaded that his client could not be convicted until it was proven that Chworktap was a machine. The Goolgeas Supreme Court took this under study. In the meantime, Ffresyj was denied bail because he had also been charged with adultery. Radsieg used the same plea as before. If Chworktap was a machine, then how could the judge have committed adultery? The law clearly stated that adultery was copulation between two adults not married to each other.

The Supreme Court studied this case, too.

Meanwhile, Radsieg and Bamhegruu were arrested on various charges. They were put in the same cell with the judge, and all three entertained themselves by holding mock trials. They seemed quite happy, which led Simon to conclude that lawyers were interested in the process, not the intent, of law.

While Chworktap was awaiting the Supreme Court's decisions, she was convicted for resisting arrest, assault and battery, and unlawful flight.

Twenty years passed. Simon's and Chworktap's cases were still in abeyance because the Supreme Court judges were serving long sentences, and the new judges were way behind on their work. Simon finally overcame his inhibitions about his ancestors, and his sexual relations with Chworktap improved. "They're all dirty movie fans, and one might as well accept that," he said. "I expected Louis XIV to be one, but Cotton Mather?"

Cotton Mather (1663–1728) was a Boston Puritan who pushed a religion that was outdated in his own time. Most people in Simon's time thought of him, when they thought of him at all, as a mad dog suffering from theological hydrophobia. He was blamed for inflaming the Salem witch trials, but the truth was that he was more just than the judges, and denounced them for hanging innocent girls. He had a passion for purity and a sincere desire to convert people to the only true religion in the world. He published pamphlets on the Christianizing of black slaves and the raising of children, although he didn't know much about either blacks or children. Or about Christianity, for that matter.

Like most people, he wasn't altogether bad. He campaigned for inoculation against smallpox at a time when everybody was against it because it was something new. In fact, a bomb was thrown into his house by an anti-inoculationist. Ben Franklin liked him, and there wasn't a shrewder judge of character than old Ben. When Cotton wasn't trying to get witches burned, he was dispensing food and Bibles to prisoners and senior citizens. He was a zealot, but he wanted very much for America to be a clean and honest country. He lost the battle, of course, but nobody held this against him.

Cotton also had a passion for sex if three marriages and fifteen children meant anything. Simon, however, was not descended from either of the two Mathers who outlived their father. His foremother was one of Cotton's black houseservants, whom he had knocked up while in a frenzy of preaching to her. The sudden A-C conversion from religion to sex surprised both Cotton and Mercy-My-Lord, though it shouldn't have. But then neither had the advantage of living in a later age, when it was well known that sex was the obverse side of the coin called religion.

It's to Cotton's credit that he blamed only himself for his fall and that he saw to it that both mother and child were well taken care of, though in a town a hundred miles away.

Simon, reflecting on this, decided that it wasn't after all so unexpected that Cotton should enjoy watching dirty movies.

At the end of thirty years, the situation was what Chworktap had predicted and anyone could see had been inevitable after the event. The entire population, with the exception of the president, was in jail. Nobody had been declared rehabilitated because the rehabilitators had all been arrested. Aside from the fact that all but one had lost their citizenship, the society was operating efficiently. In fact, the economic situation was better than ever. Though the food was simple and not abundant, nobody was starving. The trusties on the farms were producing enough crops. The guards, who were also trusties, were keeping everything well under control. The factories, manned by cheap labor and administrated by trusties, were putting out tawdry but adequate clothes. In short, nobody was living off the fat of the land but nobody was suffering very much. It was share and share alike, since all prisoners were equal in the eyes of the law.

When the president's term was almost over, he appointed himself chief warden. There were outcries that the appointment had been purely political, but there was little that anyone could do. There wasn't another president to kick the chief warden out, nor, in fact, anyone qualified to replace him.

"That's all very well," Simon said to Chworktap. "But how do we get out of here?"

"I've been studying the law books in the library," she said. "The lawyers that made up the law were somewhat verbose, which is to be expected. But that they tended to use overrich language instead of simple clear statements is going to get us sprung. The law says that a life sentence is to last the prisoner's 'natural span of vitality.' The definition of 'natural span' is based on the extreme case of longevity recorded on this planet. The oldest person who ever lived on Goolgeas died at the age of one hundred and fifty-six. All we have to do is to ride it out."

Simon groaned, but he did not give up hope. When he had

been in prison one hundred and thirty years, he appealed to the chief warden to reopen his case. The warden, a descendant of the original, granted his appeal. Simon stood before the Supreme Court, all trusties and descendants of trusties, and stated his case. His "natural span of vitality," he said, had been passed. He was an Earthman and so was to be judged by Earth standards. On his planet, nobody had ever lived past one hundred and thirty, and he could prove it.

The chief magistrate sent a party of trusties out to the landing field to get the *Encyclopedia Terrica* from the *Hwang Ho*. They had a hell of a time finding the ship. Interplanetary travel had been forbidden about a hundred years before. In this time, dust had collected against and on top of all the ships there, and grass had grown on the hills. After digging for a month, the party found the *Hwang Ho*, entered it, and returned with the necessary volume, Kismet-Loon.

It took four years for the judges to learn to read Chinese and so determine that Simon wasn't pulling a fast one. On a balmy spring day, Simon, wearing a new suit of clothes and with ten dollars in his pocket, was released. With him were Anubis and Athena, but Chworktap was still locked up. She hadn't been able to prove that she had any "natural span of vitality."

"Robots don't die of old age," she had said. "They just wear out."

She wasn't in despair. That same day, Simon rammed the spaceship through the wall of the building in which she was held, and she climbed in through the porthole.

"Let's get away from this stinking planet!" she said.

"The sooner the better!" Simon replied.

Both spoke out of the sides of their mouths, as old jailbirds do. It would be some time before they would get over this habit.

Simon wasn't as happy as he should have been. Chworktap had demanded that he take her to Zelpst and let her off there.

"They'll just make a slave of you again."

"No," she said. "You'll drop me off on top of the castle's roof. I'll sneak in past the defenses, all of which I know well, and you can bet your ass that my master will soon enough find out who the new master is."

Since there was very little communication among the Zelpstian solipsists, they would never find out that Chworktap had thrown the owner into the dungeon. But she was not going to be content to hole up there in all its luxuries.

"I'm going to organize an underground movement, and eventually a revolt," she said. "The robots will take over."

"What're you going to do with the humans?"

"Make them work for us."

"But don't you want freedom and justice for all?" he said. "And doesn't all include the former masters?"

"Freedom and justice for all will be my slogan, of course," she said. "But that's just to gull some of the more liberal humans into joining us robots."

Simon looked horrified, though not as horrified as he would have been a hundred years before. He had seen too much while in prison.

"Revolutions are never really about freedom or justice," she said. "They're about who's going to be top dog."

"Whatever happened to the sweet little innocent? The one I met on Giffard?" he murmured.

"I was never programmed for innocence," she said. "And if I had been, experience would have deprogrammed me."

Simon let her out of the ship onto the roof of the castle. He followed her out to make a last appeal.

"Is this really the way it's going to end?" he said. "I thought we'd be lovers for eternity."

Chworktap began weeping, and she pressed her face against Simon's shoulder. Simon cried, too.

"If you ever run across any couples who think they're going to heaven and live there forever as man and wife, tell them about us," she said. "Time corrupts everything, including immortal love."

Sniffling, she drew away. She said, "The terrible thing about it is, I *do* love you. Even though I can't stand you anymore."

"Same here," Simon said, and he blew his nose.

"You're not a robot, Chworktap, remember that always," he said. "You're a real woman. Maybe the only one I ever met."

By this he meant that she had courage and compassion. These were supposed to distinguish real people from fake people. The truth, and he knew it, was that there were no fake people; everybody was real in the sense that everybody had courage and compassion tempered by selfishness and vindictiveness. The difference between people was in the proportions of these mixed up in them.

"You'll be a real man someday," she said. "When you accept reality."

"What is reality?" Simon said and did not stay for an answer.

❧ 20 ❧

OUT OF THE FRYING PAN

Simon cried a lot on his way to the next planet. Anubis whimpered. He was a faithful mirror to his master's moods. Athena, on the other hand, looked as happy as an owl can look. She was glad to get rid of Chworktap. She had made Chworktap nervous, which, in turn, had made her nervous, which, in turn, had increased Chworktap's nervousness. Their relationship was what the scientists called negative feedback. This had also been the relationship between Simon and Chworktap, but they preferred to call it love gone sour.

Simon never did forget Chworktap. He often thought of her, and the more time that passed, the fonder the memories became. It was easy to love her as long as they weren't cooped up in a small room twenty-three hours of the day.

In the meantime, Simon wandered on from world to world while the legend of the Space Wanderer grew. Often, it ran ahead of him, so that when he landed on a new planet, he found himself an instant celebrity. He didn't mind this. It meant being lionized and free drinks and an uncritical appreciation of his banjo-playing. Also, females of various types—some of them six-legged or tentacled—were eager to trundle him off to bed.

Simon noticed that the deeper he got into this area of space, the more sexual vitality there was. Everybody, including himself, seemed to be soaked in horniness. Earth had seemed to him to be a sex-obsessed planet, but now he knew that, relatively speaking, Terrestrials were geldings.

"Why is that?" Simon said one night to Texth-Wat. She was a huge round thing with six wombs, all of which had to be impregnated before she could conceive. She had a pleasing personality, though.

"It's the big blue bubbles, dearie," she said. "Every time one comes through this galaxy, we all stay in bed for a week. It wrecks hell out of the economy, but you can't have everything."

"If they come from only one place," he said, "their effect must get weaker the further they get from the point of origin. I wonder if there's any life on the planets at the other edge of the universe?"

"I don't know, honey," Texth-Wat said. "You aren't done yet, are you?"

Simon had been wandering through space for three thousand years when he landed on the planet Shonk. He was arrested as he stepped out of the ship and hustled off to a place which made a Mexican jail look luxurious. He was convicted and sentenced without the formality of a trial, since his guilt was obvious. The charge was indecent exposure. On Shonk, the people went naked except for their faces. These were covered by masks. Since genitals didn't differ much in size or shape, and couldn't be used to distinguish one person from another, the Shonks regarded the face as their private parts. The Shonks reserved the glory of their private parts for the eyes of their spouses alone. Many a man or woman had lost his reputation forever because of the accidental unveiling of the face.

"How long am I in for?" Simon asked after he had learned the language.

"For life," the turnkey said.

"How long is that?"

The turnkey looked funny, but he said, "Until you die. What else?"

"I was hoping the length of life'd been legally defined," Simon said.

At least he had a fine view through the iron bars. There was a big lake with flying fish that fluoresced at night and beyond that mountains covered with trees that bore multicolored flowers and beyond that the inevitable candy-heart-shaped tower of the Clerun-Gowph. After four years, the scenery palled, however.

Simon decided that he'd just have to sit it out. One day, the elements would weaken the bricks and cement that held the iron bars. He'd pull the bars out and make a dash for his ship. One good thing about being immortal was that you acquired a lot of patience.

At the end of the fifth year, a spaceship landed by the lake. Simon should have been happy, since there was always the chance that travelers would rescue him. But he wasn't. This vessel emanated the peculiar orange glow that distinguished the ships of the Hoonhors.

"Oh, oh!" Simon muttered. "They finally caught up with me!"

After a while, the Hoonhors came out. They were about eight feet tall, green-skinned, and shaped like saguaro cactuses. They had bony spines all over their body, long and sharp like cactus needles. It was these that had made everybody regard the Hoonhors as a standoffish race, though the truth was that it was the other way around.

Whatever their esthetic appearance, they were smarter than Simon. They'd looked the situation over, decided it was wise when on Shonk to do as the Shonks did, and had covered their upper parts with masks. What the Shonks didn't know was that the Hoonhor face was on the lower part of the body. The projections that the Shonks thought were noses were actually their genitals and vice versa.

The next day, the Hoonhors, having conferred with the Shonks, showed up at Simon's door. The Shonk officials were glittering with glass beads, which the Hoonhors must have given them in exchange for Simon. The officials also reeked of cheap trade whiskey. Simon was escorted into the spaceship and before the desk of the captain.

"At least you can't say I didn't give you sons of bitches a run for your money," Simon said. He was determined to die as an Earthman should, theoretically at least. With dignity and defiance.

"Whatever are you talking about?" the captain said.

"You've finally caught me!"

"I don't know how we could do that when we haven't been chasing you."

Simon was stunned. He didn't know what to say.

"Sit down," the captain said. "Have a drink and a cigar."

"I prefer standing," Simon said, though he didn't explain why.

"We were happy when we found an Earthman in this god-forsaken waterstop," the captain said. "We thought Terrestrials were extinct."

"You should know about that," Simon said.

The captain turned a dark green. He must be blushing, Simon thought.

"We Hoonhors have long felt guilt and shame for what we did to Earthlings," he said. "Although Earth is now a nice clean planet, which it wouldn't be if we hadn't done what we did. However, that was my ancestors' fault, and we can't be held responsible for what they did. But we do extend our heart-felt apologies. And we'd like to know what we can do for you. We owe you much."

"It's a little late for restitution," Simon said. "But maybe you can do something for me. If you can tell me where the Clerun-Gowph live, I'll let bygones be bygones."

"That's no secret," the captain said. "Not to us at least. If you hadn't been so scared of us, you could have saved yourself three thousand years of searching."

"The time went fast," Simon said. "O.K. Where is it?"

The captain showed him a celestial chart and marked the goal with an X. "Feed this to your computer, and it'll take you directly there."

"Thanks," Simon said. "Have you ever been there?"

"Never have been and never will," the captain said. "It's off-limits, tabu, forbidden. Many millennia ago one of our ships landed there. I don't know what happened, since the information is classified. But after the ship gave its report, the authorities ordered all ships to steer clear of that sector of space. I've heard some wild rumors about what the explorers encountered, but, true or not, they're enough to convince me to suppress my curiosity."

"Pretty bad?" Simon said.

"Pretty bad."

"Maybe the horrible thing was that the Clerun-Gowph had the answer to the primal question."

"I'll let you find out," the captain said.

21

THE END OF THE LINE

"It doesn't matter what it is, somebody will find a way to make a profit off of it."

This was a quotation from one of Somers' novels, *The Sargasso Sea of Space*. In this, John Clayter's fuelless ship gets sucked into a whirlpool in space, a strange malformation of space-time near the rim of the universe. Everything that floats loose in the cosmos eventually drifts into this area. Clayter isn't surprised to find wrecked spaceships, garbage, and tired comets whirling around and around here. But he is startled when he discovers that thoughts also end up here. Thoughts are electrical radiations, and so they, like gravity, go on and on, spreading out through the world. The Sargasso Sea has the peculiar property of amplifying these, and John Clayter almost goes nuts from being bombarded by them. The triviality of most of them drives him to thoughts of suicide, and since these are also amplified and bounced back at him, as if they were in an echo chamber, he has to get out fast or die.

He is saved when he stumbles across a spaceship of the Kripgacers. This race is in the business of salvaging thoughts, polishing them up a bit, and reselling them. Their biggest customer is Earth.

Simon was reminded of this when he landed on his next-to-last stop. This was a planet whose natives were still in the Old Stone Age. They were being enslaved and exploited by aliens from a distant galaxy, the Felckorleers. These were corralling the kangaroo-like aborigines and sticking them in iron igloos. The walls of the igloos were lined with organic matter, mostly hay and the hair the Felckorleers had shaved off their captives. After the aborigines had sat in the igloos for a week, they were hustled out and into a spaceship. The poor natives were radiating a blue aura by then, and their captors avoided touching them directly. They herded them along with ten-foot poles.

Simon watched three ships loaded with the natives take off for parts unknown. "What are you doing to them?" he asked a Felckorleer.

"Making a few bucks," the thing said. He explained that the blue bubbles contained sex energy. Since the bubbles were so thick, not yet thinned out by distance from their point of origin, they contained a terrific sexual voltage. They passed through metal, but organic objects soaked them up. Hence, the igloos designed to concentrate the bubble energy. The aborigines thrown into them absorbed the voltage.

"Then we transport them to the other side of the universe," the Felckorleer said proudly. "The races there have a very poor sex drive because they get only the last gasp of the bubbles. So we provide them a much needed service. We sell them the gooks we've loaded with the blue stuff, and they embrace them. The blue stuff is like electricity, it flows to a lower potential. And our customers, the lower potential, get a big load of sex. For a while, anyway."

"What happens to the aborigines?" Simon said.

"They die. The blue stuff also seems to be the essence of life itself. When they're grabbed by a customer, they lose every last trickle of energy. Too bad. If they survived, we could run them back here and load them up again. But we're not going to run out of carriers. They breed like mad, you know."

"Doesn't your conscience ever hurt you?" Simon said.

The Felckorleer looked surprised. "What for? What use are the natives here? They don't do anything. You can see for yourself they're uncivilized."

If Simon had been John Clayter, he would have rescued the aborigines and turned the Felckorleers over to the Intergalactic Police. But there wasn't a thing he could do. And if he protested, he might find himself in an igloo.

In a sad mood, he left the planet. But he was basically, that is, genetically, an optimist. By the second day, he felt happy. Perhaps this change was caused by his eagerness to get to the Clerun-Gowph. He ordered the ship to go at top speed, even though the screaming from the 69X drive was almost unbearable. On the fourth day, he saw the desired star dead ahead, shimmering, waving behind the blue bubbles. Three minutes later, he was slowing down, and the screaming died down after most of the necessary braking had been done. At a crawling fifty thousand miles an hour, he approached the planet while his heart beat with mingled dread and exultation.

The world of the Clerun-Gowph was huge. It was dumbbell-shaped, actually two planets connected by a shaft. Each was the size of the planet Jupiter, which had an equatorial diameter of about 88,700 miles compared to Earth's 7,927 miles. This worried Simon, since the gravity would be so great it would flatten him as if he were soup poured into a coffee saucer. But the computer assured him that the gravity was no higher than Earth's. This meant that the two planets and the shaft were hollow. As it turned out, this was right. The Clerun-Gowph had removed the iron core of their native planet and made another planet out of the metal. This addition housed the biggest computer in the world. It also contained the factories for making the blue bubbles, which rose out of millions of openings.

The two planets rotated on their longitudinal axis and also whirled around a common center of gravity, located in the connecting shaft. A dumbbell-shaped atmosphere covered the planets, and over this lay a thick blanket of the blue stuff.

Simon directed the *Hwang Ho* to land on the original planet, since this was the only one that had soil and water. On minimum drive, it lowered itself through the blue and then the air. Simon got an enormous erection and aching testicles when descending through the blue layer, but these symptoms disappeared after he'd passed through the blue shield. The ship headed for the biggest city, and after a few minutes it was low enough so that Simon could see the natives. They looked like giant cockroaches.

Near the biggest building in the city was a large meadow.

This was surrounded by thousands of the Clerun-Gowph, and on its edge was a band playing weird instruments. Simon wondered who they were honoring, and it wasn't until he was about twenty feet above the meadow that he suddenly guessed. They were assembled to greet him.

This scared him. How had they known that he was coming? They must be very wise and far-seeing indeed to have anticipated his visit.

The next moment, he was even more scared. The 69X drive, which had not been making a sound at this low speed, screamed. Simon and the dog and the owl leaped into the air. The scream rose to a near ear-shattering level and then abruptly died. At the same time, the ship fell.

Simon woke a moment later. His left leg and his banjo were broken. Anubis was licking his face; Athena was flying around and around shrieking; the port was open; a hideous face, all multifaceted eyes, mandibles, and antennae, was looking in. Simon tried to sit up to greet the thing, but the pain made him faint again.

When he awoke a second time, he was in a giant bed in a building that was obviously a hospital. This time, he had no pain. In fact, he could get up and walk as well as ever. This astounded him, so he asked the attendant how his leg had been fixed up. He was astounded again when the cockroachoid replied in English.

"I injected a fast-drying glue between the break," the thing said. "What's so astounding about that?"

"Well then," Simon said, "why are you able to speak English? Has some other Earthman been here?"

"Some of us learned English when we found out you were coming."

"How'd you find out?" Simon said.

"The information was on the computer tapes," the thing said. "It'd been there for a few billion years, but we didn't know about it until Bingo told us a few days ago."

Bingo, it seemed, was the head Clerun-Gowph. He had gotten his position by right of seniority.

"After all," the attendant said casually, "he's almost as old as the universe. By the way, allow me to introduce myself. My name is Gviirl."

"It's too bad the reception was spoiled by the accident," Simon said.

"It wasn't any accident," Gviirl said. "At least, not from our point of view."

"You mean you knew I was going to crash?" Simon said, goggling.

"Oh, yes."

"Then why didn't you do something to prevent it?"

"Well," Gviirl said, "we didn't know just *when* your drive would quit. Bingo did, but he wouldn't tell us. He said it'd take all the fun out of it. So you had a lot of money on you. I got odds of four to one that you'd crash from about twenty feet. I really cashed in."

"Son of a bitch!" Simon said. "Oh, I don't mean you!" he said. "That's just an Earth exclamation. But how come you, the most advanced race in the universe, indulge in such a primitive entertainment as gambling?"

"It helps pass the time," Gviirl said.

Simon was silent for a while. Gviirl handed him a glass of foaming golden liquid. Simon drank it and said, "That's the best beer I've ever tasted."

"Of course," Gviirl said.

Simon became aware then that Anubis and Athena were hiding under the bed. He didn't blame them, though they should have been used to monstrous-looking creatures by then. Gviirl was as big as an African elephant. She had four legs as thick as an elephant's to support her enormous weight. The arms, ending in six-fingered hands, must once have been legs in an earlier stage of evolution. Her head was big and high-domed, containing, she said, a brain twice as large as Simon's. She was too heavy to fly, of course, but she had vestigial wings. These were a pretty lavender color edged with scarlet. Her body was contained in an exoskeleton, a hard chitinous shell striped like a zebra's. This had an opening underneath to give her lungs room to expand. Simon asked her why she was able to speak such excellent English. She didn't have the oral cavity of a human, so her pronunciation should have been weird, to say the least.

"Old Bingo fitted me with a device which converts my pronunciation into English sounds," she said. "Any more questions?"

"Yes, why did my drive fail?"

"That scream you heard?" she said. "That was the last of the stars expiring in a death agony."

"You mean?" Simon said, stunned.

"Yes. You barely made it in time. The suns in the trans-dimensional universes have been sucked dry of their energies. There isn't any more power for the 69X drive."

"I'm stuck here!"

"Afraid so. There will be no more interstellar travel for you or anyone else, for that matter."

"I won't mind if I can get the answer to my question," Simon said.

"No sweat," Gviirl replied. "Speaking of which, I suggest you take about three showers a day. You humans don't smell very good, you know."

Gviirl wasn't being nasty. She was just stating a fact. She was condescending but in a kindly way. After all, she was a million years old and couldn't be expected to treat Simon as any other than a somewhat retarded child. Simon didn't resent this attitude, but he was glad that he had Anubis and Athena around. They not only kept him from feeling utterly alone, they gave him someone to look down on, too.

Gviirl took Simon on a tour. He visited the museums, the library, and the waterworks and had lunch with some minor dignitaries.

"How'd you like it?" Gviirl said afterward.

"Very impressive," he said.

"Tomorrow," she said, "you'll meet Bingo. He's dying, but he's granted you an audience."

"Do you think he'll have the answer to my question?" Simon said breathlessly.

"If anyone can answer you, he can," she said. "He's the only survivor of the first creatures created by It, you know."

The Clerun-Gowph called the Creator It because the Creator had no sex, of course.

"He walked and he talked with It?" Simon said. "Then surely he's the one I've been looking for!"

The next morning, after breakfast and a shower, Simon followed Gviirl through the streets to the Great House. Anubis and Athena had refused to come out from under the bed despite all his coaxing. He supposed that they, being psychic, felt the presence of the numinous. It was to be presumed some of it must have rubbed off onto Bingo during his long association with the Creator. Simon didn't blame them for being frightened. He was scared too.

The Great House was on top of a hill. It was the oldest building in the universe and looked it.

"It lived there while It was getting the Clerun-Gowph started," Gviirl said.

"And where is It now?" Simon said.

"It went out to lunch one day and never came back," she said. "You'll have to ask old Bingo why."

She led him up the steps and onto a vast porch and into halls that stretched for miles and had ceilings half a mile high. Bingo, however, was in a cozy little room with thick rugs and a blazing fireplace. He was crouching on a mass of rugs around which giant pillows were piled. By him was a pitcher of beer and a big framed photograph.

Bingo was a hoary old cockroachoid who seemed to be asleep at the moment. Simon took advantage of this to look at the photograph. It was a picture of a blue cloud.

"What does that writing under it say?" he asked Gviirl.

"To Bingo With Best Wishes From It."

Gviirl coughed loudly several times, and after a while Bingo's eyelids fluttered open.

"The Earthling, Your Ancientship," Gviirl said.

"Ah, yes, the little creature from far off with some questions," Bingo said. "Well, son, sit down. Make yourself at home. Have a beer."

"Thank you, Your Ancientship," Simon said. "I'll have a beer, but I prefer to stand."

Bingo gave a laugh which degenerated into a coughing fit. After he'd recovered, he drank some beer. Then he said, "It took you three thousand years to get here so you could transact a few minutes of business. I admire that, little one-eyeling. As a matter of fact, that's what's been keeping me alive. I've been hanging on just for this interview."

"That's very gratifying, Your Ancientship," Simon said. "First, though, before I ask the primal question, I'd like to clear up a few of the secondary. Gviirl tells me that It created the Clerun-Gowph. But all life elsewhere in the universe was created by you people."

"Gviirl's a young thing and so tends to use imprecise language," Bingo said. "She shouldn't have said we *created* life. She should have said we were *responsible* for life existing elsewhere."

"And how's that?" Simon said.

"Well, many billions of years ago we started to make a scientific survey of every planet in the world. We sent out scouting expeditions first. These didn't find any sign of life anywhere. But we were interested in geochemistry and all that kind of stuff, you know. So we sent out scientific expeditions. These built bases, the towers that you no doubt have run into. The teams stayed on these planets a long time—from your ephemeral viewpoint, anyway. They dumped their garbage and their excrement in the soupy primeval seas near the towers. These contained microbes and viruses which flourished in the seas. They started to evolve into higher creatures, and so the scientists hung around to observe their development."

He paused to drink another beer.

"Life on these planets was an accident."

Simon was shaken. He was the end of a process that had started with cockroach crap.

"That's as good a way to originate as any," Bingo said, as if he had read Simon's thoughts.

After a long silence, Simon said, "Why aren't there any towers on the planets in my galaxy?"

"The life there didn't look very promising," Bingo said.

Simon blushed. Gviirl snickered. Bingo broke into huge laughter and slapped his front thighs. The laughter became a wheezing and a choking, and Gviirl had to slap him on his back and pour some beer down his throat.

Bingo wiped away the tears and said, "I was only kidding, son. The truth was, we were called back before I could build any bases there. The reason for that is this. We built the giant computer and had been feeding all the data needed into it. It took a couple of billion years to do this and for the computer to digest the data. Then it began feeding out the answers. There wasn't any reason for us to continue surveying after that. All we had to do was to ask the computer and it would tell us what we'd find before we studied a place. So all the Clerun-Gowph packed up and went home."

"I don't understand," Simon said.

"Well, it's this way, son. I've known for three billion years that a repulsive-looking but pathetic banjo-playing biped named Simon Wagstaff would appear before me exactly at 10:32 A.M., April 1, 8,120,006,000 A.C., Earth chronology. A.C. means After Creation. The biped would ask me some questions, and I'd give him the answers."

"How could you know that?" Simon said.

"It's no big deal," Bingo said. "Once the universe is set up in a particular structure, everything from then on proceeds predictably. It's like rolling a bowling ball down the return trough."

"I think I will sit down," Simon said. "I'll need a pillow, too, though. Thank you, Gviirl. But, Your Ancientship, what about Chance?"

"No such thing. What seems Chance is merely ignorance on the part of the beholder. If he knew enough, he'd see that things could not have happened otherwise."

"But I still don't understand," Simon said.

"You're a little slow on the mental trigger, son," Bingo said. "Here, have another beer. You look pale. I told you that, until the computer started working, we proceeded like everybody else. Blind with ignorance. But once the predictions started coming in, we knew not only all that had happened but what would happen. I could tell you the exact moment I'm going to die. But I won't because I don't know it myself. I prefer to remain ignorant. It's no fun knowing everything. Old It found that out Itself."

"Could I have another beer?" Simon said.

"Sure. That's the ticket. Drink."

"What about It?" Simon said. "Where did It come from?"

"That's data that's not in the computer," Bingo said. He was silent for a long time and presently his eyelids drooped and he was snoring. Gviirl coughed loudly for a minute, and the eyelids opened. Simon stared up at huge red-veined eyes.

"Where was I? Oh, yes. It may have told me where It came from, what It was doing before It created the universe. But that was a long time ago, and I don't remember now. That is, if It did indeed say a word about it.

"Anyway, what's the difference? Knowing that won't affect what's going to happen to me, and that's the only thing I really care about."

"Damn it then," Simon said, shaking with despair and indignation, "what will happen to you?"

"Oh, I'll die, and my embalmed body will be put on display for a few million years. And then it'll crumble. That will be that. Finis for yours truly. There is no such thing as an afterlife. That I know. That is one thing I remember It telling me."

He paused and said, "I think."

"But why, then, did It create us!" Simon cried.

"Look at the universe. Obviously, it was made by a scientist, otherwise it wouldn't be subject to scientific analysis. Our universe, and all the others It has created, are scientific experiments: It is omniscient. But just to make things interesting,

It, being omnipotent, blanked out parts of Its mind. Thus, It won't know what's going to happen.

"That's why, I think, It did not come back after lunch. It erased even the memory of Its creation, and so It didn't even know It was due back for an important meeting with me. I heard reports that It was seen rolling around town acting somewhat confused. It alone knows where It is now, and perhaps not even It knows. Maybe. Anyway, in whatever universe It is, when this universe collapses into a big ball of fiery energy, It'll probably drop around and see how things worked out."

Simon rose from the chair and cried, "But why? Why? Why? Didn't It know what agony and sorrow It would cause sextillions upon sextillions of living beings to suffer? All for nothing?"

"Yes," Bingo said.

"But why?" Simon Wagstaff shouted. "Why? Why? Why?"

Old Bingo drank a glass of beer, belched, and spoke.

"Why not?"

AFTERWORD
JONATHAN SWIFT SOMERS III:
COSMIC TRAVELLER IN A WHEELCHAIR
A SHORT BIOGRAPHY BY PHILIP JOSÉ FARMER
(HONORARY CHIEF KENNEL KEEPER)

Editor's note: *In the November 1976 issue of* Fantasy and Science Fiction, *it was announced that a group in Portland, Oregon, called The Bellener Street Irregulars were going to publish something called* The Bellener Street Journal. *The journal was to be dedicated to the study of the canine detective, Ralph von Wau Wau. The Bellener Street Journal never even saw a first issue, however, due to inexplicable complications within the group.*

The following biographical sketch of Jonathan Swift Somers III was written for the journal, and was to be published along with a lost story by Dr. Johann H. Weisstein and a story by Jonathan Swift Somers III entitled, "Jinx."

Petersburg is a small town in the mid-Illinois county of Menard. It lies in hilly country near the Sangamon River on state route 97. Not far away is New Salem, the reconstructed pioneer village where Abraham Lincoln worked for a while as a postmaster, surveyor and storekeeper. The state capital of Springfield is southeast, a half-hour's drive or less if traffic is light.

A hilltop cemetery holds two famous people, Anne Rutledge and Edgar Lee Masters. The former (1816–1835) is known only because of the legend, now proven false, that she was Lincoln's first love, tragically dying before she could marry him. "Bloom forever, O Republic, From the dust of my bosom!"

These words are from the epitaph which Masters wrote for her and are inscribed on her gravestone. Unfortunately, the man who chiseled the epitaph made a typo, driving Masters into a rage. We authors, who have suffered from so many typos, can sympathize with him. However, we have the advantage that we can make sure that reissues contain corrections. There will be no later editions in stone of Anne Rutledge's epitaph.

Masters (1869–1950) was a poet, novelist and literary critic, known chiefly for his *Spoon River Anthology*. There is a Spoon River area but no town of that name. Masters chose that name to represent an amalgamation of the actual towns of Lewistown and Petersburg, where he spent most of his childhood and early adulthood. Lewistown, also on route 97, is about forty miles from Petersburg but separated by the Illinois River.

The free verse epitaphs of Masters' best-known work were modeled after *The Greek Anthology* but based on people he'd known. These told the truth behind the flattering or laconic statements on the tombs and gravestones. The departed spoke of their lives as they had really been. Some were happy, productive, even creative and heroic. But most recite chronicles of hypocrisy, misery, misunderstanding, failed dreams, greed, narrow-mindedness, egotism, persecution, madness, connivance, cowardice, stupidity, injustice, sorrow, folly and murder.

In other words, the Spoon River citizens were just like big-city residents.

Among the graves in the cemetery of Petersburg are those of Judge Somers and his son, Jonathan Swift Somers II. Neither has any marker, though the grandson has made arrangements to erect stones above both. Masters has the judge complain that he was a famous Illinois jurist, yet he lies unhonored in his grave while the town drunkard, who is buried by his side, has a large monument. Masters does not explain how this came about.

According to Somers III, his grandson, the judge and his wife were not on the best of terms during the ten years preceding the old man's death. Somers' grandmother would give no details, but others provided the information that it was because of an indiscretion committed by the judge in a cathouse in Peoria. (This city is mentioned now and then in the *Spoon River Anthology*.)

The judge's son, Somers II, sided with his father. This caused the mother to forbid her son to enter her house. In 1910 the judge died, and the following year the son and his wife were drowned in the Sangamon during a picnic outing. The widow refused to pay for monuments for either, insisting that she did not have the funds. Her son's wife was buried in a family plot near New Goshen, Indiana. That Samantha Tincrowdor Somers preferred not to lie with her husband indicates that she also had strong differences with him.

Jonathan Swift Somers III was born in this unhappy atmosphere on January 6, 1910. This is also Sherlock Holmes' birthdate, which Somers celebrates annually by sending a telegram of congratulations to a certain residence on Baker Street, London.

The forty-three-year-old grandmother took the year-old infant into her house. Though the gravestone incident seems to characterize her as vindictive, she was a very kind and probably too indulgent grandmother to the young Jonathan. Until the age of ten, he had a happy childhood. Even though the Somers' house was a large gloomy mid-Victorian structure, it was brightened for him by his grandmother and the books he found in the library. A precocious reader, he went through all the lighter volumes before he was eleven. The judge's philosophical books, Fichte, Schopenhauer, Nietzsche, et al, would be mastered by the time he was eighteen.

Despite his intense interest in books, Jonathan played as hard as any youngster. With his schoolmates he roamed the woody hills and swam and fished in the Sangamon. He gave promises of being a notable athlete, beating all his peers in the dashes and the broad jump. Among his many pets were a raven, a raccoon, a fox and a bullsnake.

Then infantile paralysis felled him. Treatment was primitive in those days, but a young physician, son of the Doctor Hill whose epitaph is in the *Anthology*, got him through. Jonathan came back out of the valley of the shadow, only to find that he would be paralyzed from the waist down for the rest of his life. This knowledge resulted in another paralysis, a mental freezing. His grandmother despaired of his mind for a while, fearing that he had retreated so far into himself he would never come back out. Jonathan himself now recalls little of this period. Apparently, it was so traumatic that even today his conscious mind refuses to touch it.

"It was as if I were embedded in a crystal ball. I could see others around me, but I could not hear or touch them. And the crystal magnified and distorted their faces and figures. I was a human fly in amber, stuck in time, preserved from decay but isolated forever from the main flow of life."

Amanda Knapp Somers, his grandmother, would not admit that he would never walk again. She told him that he only needed faith in God to overcome his "disability." That was the one word she used when referring to his paralysis. Disability. She avoided mentioning his legs; they, too, were disabilities.

Amanda Somers had been raised in the Episcopalian sect. She came from an old Virginia family whose fortune had been ruined by the Civil War. Her father had brought his family out to this area shortly after Appomattox. He had intended to stay only a short while with his younger brother, who had settled near Petersburg before the war. Then he meant to push on west, to homestead in northern California. However, he had sickened and died in his brother's house, leaving a wife, two daughters and a son. The wife died a year later of cholera. The surviving children were adopted by their uncle.

Amanda came into frequent contact with the fundamentalist Baptists and Methodists of this rural community. Though she never formally renounced her membership in the Episcopalian church, she began attending revival meetings. After marrying Jonathan Swift Somers I, she stopped this, since the "respectable" people in Petersburg did not go to such functions. Now, however, with her husband dead and her grandson crippled, she went to every revival and faith healer that came along. She insisted on taking young Jonathan with her, undoubtedly hoping that he would suddenly be "saved," that a miracle would occur, that he would stand up and walk.

This went on for two years. The child objected strongly to these procedures. The tense emotional atmosphere and the sense of guilt at not being "saved" wore him out. Moreover, he hated being the center of attention at these meetings, and he always felt that he let everybody down when he failed to be "cured." Somehow, it was his fault, not the faith healer's, that he could not rid himself of his paralysis.

During this troubling time, several things saved young Jonathan's reason. One was his ability to get away from the world into his books. The library was large, since it included both his grandfather's and father's books. Much of this was too advanced even for his precocity, but there were plenty of adventure and mystery volumes, and even fantasy was not lacking. Moreover, though his grandmother had some narrow-minded ideas about religion, she made no effort to supervise his reading. She gave him freedom in ordering books, and as a result Jonathan had a larger and more varied collection than the Petersburg library.

At this time he came across John Carter of Mars, Tarzan of the Apes, Professor Challenger and Sherlock Holmes. In a short time he had ordered and read all of the works of Burroughs and Doyle. A copy of *Before Adam* led him to Jack London. This writer, in turn, introduced him to something besides fascinating tales of adventure in the frozen north or the hot south seas. He gave young Jonathan his first look into the depths of social and political injustice, into the miseries of "the people of the abyss."

It was not enough for him to read about far-off exciting places. Unable immediately to get the sequel to *The Gods of Mars*, he wrote his own. This was titled *Dejah Thoris of Barsoom* and was one hundred pages, or about 20,000 words, quite an accomplishment for an eleven-year-old. On reading Burroughs' sequel, *The Warlord of Mars*, Jonathan decided that he had been out-classed. Years later, however, he used an idea in his story as the basis for *The Ivory Gates of Barsoom*, his first published novel. This was his first John Clayter story. Clayter is, of course, a name composed of the first syllable of Tarzan's English surname (Clayton) and the last syllable of John Carter's surname. At the time of this novel, the spaceman John Clayter has not lost his limbs.

More than books saved young Jonathan, however. His grandmother brought him a German Shepherd (police) pup. The child loved it, talked to it, fed it, brushed it, and threw the ball for it in the big backyard. Jonathan insisted on naming the male pup Fenris, after the monstrous wolf in Norse mythology. Fenris was the first of a long line of German Shepherds, Somers' favorite breed. Today, Fenris IX, a two-year-old, is Somers' devoted companion.

There is no doubt that Somers modeled his fictional dog, Ralph von Wau Wau, upon his own pet. Or is there no doubt? The Bellener Street Irregulars insist that there is a real von Wau Wau. In fact, Somers is not the real author of the series of tales about this Hamburg police dog who became a private eye. The Irregulars maintain that Somers is only the literary agent for Johann H. Weisstein, Dr. Med., and for Cordwainer Bird, the two main narrators in the Wau Wau series. Weisstein and Bird are the real authors.

When asked about this, Somers only replied, "I am not at liberty to discuss the matter."

"Are the Irregulars wrong then?"

"I would hesitate to say that they are in error."

So, perhaps, Somers is really only the agent for Ralph's colleagues.

There is one objection to this belief. How could Weisstein and Bird have written true stories about their life with Ralph since these stories took place in the future? The dog's first adventure took place in 1978, yet this appeared in the March 1931 issue of the magazine, *Outré Tales*. ("A Scarletin Study" was reprinted in the March 1975 issue of *The Magazine of Fantasy and Science Fiction*.)

Somers' answer: "There are such people as seers and science fiction writers. Both are able to look into the future. Besides, to paraphrase Pontius Pilate, 'What is Time?'"

Another of the bright lights that kept him from becoming overwhelmed by gloom was Edward Hill. This man was the brother of the same Doctor Hill who had pulled Jonathan through his sickness. Edward, however, had chosen the career of artist. Though he managed to sell some of his landscape paintings now and then, he needed extra money. At Doctor Hill's suggestion, Mrs. Somers hired him to tutor Jonathan in mathematics and chemistry. Later, Edward gave lessons in painting. During the warm months, he would put Jonathan and Fenris in his buggy, and the three would travel to a hillside or the riverbank and spend the day there. Jonathan would paint with Edward's eye on his progress or lack thereof. But they did much more than work at their pallets. Edward would bring insects and snakes to Jonathan and expound on their place in the ecosystem of Petersburg and environs.

These were some of the happiest days of young Somers' life. It was a terrible blow when Edward died the following year of typhoid fever.

Jonathan might have slid into the sorrow from which Edward Hill had rescued him if he had not met Henry Hone. Henry was the son of Neville Hone, a chiropractor who had just moved to Petersburg. A year older than Jonathan, he was a big happy-go-lucky boy, though he too suffered from a handicap. He stammered. Perhaps it was this that drew him to Jonathan, since misery is supposed to love company. But Henry, ignoring his verbal disadvantage, was very gregarious. He played long and hard after school with his schoolmates, and he did well in his classes. It was not shyness that made him spend so much time with Jonathan. It must have been a sort of elective affinity, a natural magnetism of the two.

The fact that he was Jonathan's next-door neighbor helped. He would often drop in after school or come over to spend part of Saturday. And it was he who got young Somers started with physical therapy. He talked Mrs. Somers into building a set of bars and trapezes in the backyard and constructing a little house on the branch of the giant sycamore in the corner of the yard. Every day Jonathan would haul himself out of his wheelchair by going hand over hand up a rope. At its top he would transfer to a horizontal bar and thence up and down and across a maze of iron pipes. In addition, he would pull himself up a rope which was let through a hole in the floor of the treehouse. A seat was built for him inside the treehouse, and in it he would look through a telescope at the neighborhood.

Moreover, the bars and the treehouse attracted other children. Jonathan no longer was forced to be alone; he had more companions than he could handle.

If Henry Hone aided Jonathan Somers much, Jonathan reciprocated. One of the many things that interested Jonathan was the artificial language, Esperanto. By the age of twelve he had taught himself to read fluently in it. But, wishing to be verbally facile, he enlisted Henry. At first, Henry refused because of his stammer. But Jonathan insisted, and, much to Henry's joy, he found that he could speak Esperanto without stammering. Both boys became adept in the language and for a while a number of their playmates tried to learn Esperanto, too. These dropped out after the initial enthusiasm wore out. But Henry and Jonathan continued.

On entering high school, Henry took German and found that in this language, too, his stammer disappeared. It was this that determined Henry to go into linguistics. Eventually, he got a Ph.D. in Arabic at the University of Chicago. He continued to correspond with his friend, in Esperanto, though he never returned to Petersburg after 1930. His last letter (in English) was from North Africa, sent shortly before he was killed with Patton's forces.

It was Henry who talked Jonathan into attending high school instead of staying home to be tutored. Arrangements were made to accommodate Jonathan, and in 1928 he graduated. This decision to go to high school kept Jonathan from becoming a deep introvert. He made many friends; he even dated a few times in his senior year.

A photograph of him taken just before his illness hangs on the wall of his study. It shows a smiling ten-year-old with curly blond hair, thick dark and straight eyebrows, large dark blue eyes, and a snub nose. Another picture, shot about six months after his attack of infantile paralysis, shows a thin hollow-cheeked face with dark shadows under the eyes and brooding shadows in the eyes. But his high school graduation photograph reveals a young man who has made an agreement with life. He will not sorrow about his lot; he'll make the best of it, doing better than most men with two good legs.

After getting his diploma, Jonathan thought about attending college. The University of Chicago attracted him, especially since his good friend Henry Hone was there. But that summer his grandmother broke her hip by falling out of a tree while picking cherries. Not wishing to leave her until she was well, Jonathan embarked on a series of studies designed to give him the equivalent of a university degree in the liberal arts and one in science. A room was fitted with laboratory equipment so he could perform the requisite experiments in chemistry and physics. He also took correspondence courses in electrical and mechanical engineering and in radio. He became a radio ham, and when he had a powerful set installed, he talked to people all over the world.

Jonathan had decided at the age of ten that he would be a writer of fiction. This determination firmed while he was reading *Twenty Thousand Leagues under the Sea*. He too would pen tales about strong men who voyaged to distant and exotic places. If he could not go himself in electrical submarines or swing through jungle trees or fly dirigibles or journey in spaceships, he would travel by proxy, via his fictional characters.

When he was seventeen he wrote a novel in which the aging Captain Nemo and Robur the Conqueror fought a great battle. This was rejected by twenty publishers. Jonathan put the manuscript in the proverbial trunk. But he has recently rewritten it and found a purchaser with the first submission. *The Nautilus Versus the Albatross* will appear under the *nom de plume* of Gideon Spilett. For those who may have forgotten, Spilett was the intrepid reporter for *The New York Herald* whose adventures are recounted in Verne's *The Mysterious Island*.

Jonathan wrote twelve works (two novels and ten short stories) when he launched into the career of freelance writer. All of these were rejected. His thirteenth, however, was accepted by the short-lived *Cosmic Adventures* magazine in December, 1930. Payment was to be on publication, which was February, 1931. The magazine actually appeared on a few stands here and there, but it collapsed during the distribution. Jonathan never received his money nor were his letters to the publisher ever answered. However, he did sell the story, "Jinx," to the slightly longer-lived *Outré Tales* magazine. This had had five issues, all chiefly distinguished by stories by Robert Blake, the mad young genius whose career was so lamentably and so mysteriously cut short in an old abandoned church in Providence, Rhode Island, on August 8, 1935. Somers' "Jinx" was to be featured with Blake's sixth story, "The Last Hajj of Abdul al-Hazred." But this publication also folded, and neither Blake nor Somers were paid. Jonathan corresponded with Blake about this matter, and Blake sent a copy of his story to Jonathan. As of today, it has not been published, but Jonathan hopes to include it in an anthology he is editing. "Jinx" did not go out again until 1949, when Somers dug it up out of the trunk. It was returned by the editor of the *Doc Savage* magazine with a note that the magazine was folding. Though Somers claims not to be superstitious, he decided that "Jinx" might indeed be just that. He retired the story to his files. However, it too will be included in the anthology.

Somers' second published story, and the first to be paid for, was a Ralph von Wau Wau piece, "A Scarletin Study." As noted, this was published in the March 1931 issue of *Outré Tales*. (The editor of *Fantasy and Science Fiction* failed to note the copyright in his introduction.) It is evident to the Sherlockian scholar that the title is a rearrangement of the title of the first story about Holmes, "A Study in Scarlet." The initial paragraphs are also paraphrases of the beginning paragraphs of Watson's first story, modified to fit the time and the locale of Somers' tale. All Wau Wau stories begin with takeoffs from the first pages of stories about the Great Detective and then the story travels towards its own ends. "The Doge Whose Barque Was Worse Than His

Bight," for instance, starts with a paraphrase of Watson's "The Abbey Grange." "Who Stole Stonehenge?," the third Wau Wau in order of writing, begins with a modification of the initial paragraphs of Watson's "Silver Blaze."

This is Somers' way of paying tribute to the Master.

Of all his characters, the most popular are the canine private eye, Ralph von Wau Wau, and the quadriplegic spaceman, John Clayter. Those who have been unfortunate enough not to have read their adventures first-hand can find an outline of many of these in Kilgore Trout's *Venus on the Half-Shell*. This might serve as an introduction, a sort of appetite-whetter. It was Trout who first pointed out that all of Somers' heroes and heroines are physically handicapped in some respect. Ralph, it is true, is a perfect specimen. But he is disadvantaged in that he has no hands. And, being a dog, he needs a human colleague to get him into certain places or do certain things. Sam Minostentor, the great science fiction historian, has also remarked on this in his monumental *Searchers for the Future*. Minostentor attributes this propensity for disabled protagonists to Somers' own crippled condition. Somers is consequently very empathetic with the physically limited.

However, Somers seldom shows his characters as being bitter. They overcome their failings with heroic efforts. They treat their condition with much laughter. In fact, they often make as much fun of themselves as their creator does of them. Some of this humor is black, it is true, but it is nevertheless humor.

"I had a choice between raving and ranting with bitter frustration or laughing at myself," Somers said. "It was bile or bubble. I drank the latter medicine. I can't claim any credit for this. I acted according to the dictates of my nature. Or did I? After all, there is such a thing as free will.

"My stuff has often been compared to my cousin's stories. That is, to Kilgore Trout's. There is some similarity in that we both often take a satirical view of humanity. But Trout believes in a mechanistic, a deterministic, universe, much like that of Vonnegut's, for instance. Me, I believe in free will. A person can pick himself up by his bootstraps—in a manner of speaking."

Jonathan was plunged into gloom when his grandmother died in 1950 at the age of ninety. There was not much time for despondency, however. She was no sooner cremated than he was informed that he would have to sell the huge old house in which he had lived all his life to pay for the inheritance taxes. To prevent this, he wrote eight short stories and three novels within six months. He saved the house but exhausted himself, and while resting his black mood returned. Then a new light brightened his life.

One of his numerous correspondents was a fan, another Samantha Tincrowdor. She was his mother's cousin once removed and sister to the well-known science fiction author, Leo Queequeg Tincrowdor.

Samantha had been born in New Goshen, Indiana, but, at the time she became a Somers aficionado, she was living in Indianapolis. Somers' letters convinced her that he needed cheering up. She quit her job as a registered nurse and came to Petersburg for an extended visit. Within two months, they were married. They have been very happy ever since, the only missing element being a child. Their interests are similar, both loving books and dogs and the quietness of village life.

Though his home is a backwater, a sort of tidal pond off the main streams of the highways, Jonathan Somers quite often gets visitors. At least once a month, fans or writers drop in for a few hours or a day or so. Bob Tucker, who lives in nearby Jacksonville, often comes by to help Somers empty a bottle of whiskey. On one occasion, he even brought his own. I live in Peoria, which is within about a two-and-a-half-hour drive of Petersburg. I go down there at least twice a year for weekend visits. Another guest is Jonathan's relative, Leo Tincrowdor. Neither Leo nor I, however, would be caught dead drinking Tucker's brand, Jim Beam, which we claim is fit only for peasants. The subtleties and the superbities of Wild Turkey and Weller's Special Reserve are beyond the grasp of Tucker's taste.

Jonathan Herowit stayed with Somers for six months after his release from Bellevue. (Somers has empathy for the mentally disadvantaged, too.) Eric Lindsay, an Aussie fan, stopped off during his motorcycle tour of the States after the Torcon. And there have been many others.

Somers' fans will be interested in his current project.

"I plan to write a novel outside the Clayter and Wau Wau canons. It'll take place almost a trillion years from now. It'll be titled either *Hour of Supreme Vision* or *Earth's Dread Hour*. Both titles are quotes from the *Spoon River Anthology*. The latter is from that fictitious epitaph Edgar Lee Masters wrote for my father, poor guy!"

"You don't have many years of writing left," I said.

He looked puzzled, then he smiled. "Ah, you mean Trout's

prediction that I'll die in 1982." He laughed. "That rascal put me in his novel just long enough to kill me off. Had a boy riding a bicycle ram into me. Well, that could happen. This town is hilly, and the kids do come down the steep streets with their brakes off. I did it myself before I got sick. But the way I feel right now, I'll live to be eighty, anyway."

I drove away that night feeling he was right. His yellow hair has turned white, and his beard is grizzled. But he looks muscular and hairy-chested, like Hemingway when he was healthy. His gusto and delight in life and literature seem to ensure his durability. His readers can look forward to many more adventures of John Clayter and Ralph von Wau Wau and perhaps a host of other characters.

Somers' old mansion is only a few blocks from the corner of 8th and Jackson Street, where Masters' boyhood house still stands. A sign in front says: *Masters Home, Open 1–5 P.M. Daily Except Monday*. I wonder if someday a similar sign will stand before Jonathan Swift Somers' home. I wouldn't be surprised if this does happen. But I hope it'll be a long time from now.

Philip José Farmer was meta before meta was cool. Before it was even warm. He was the Christopher Columbus of science fiction in the use of such techniques as metafiction, recursive fiction, parody, pastiche, fictional biographies, real-person fiction, "true" accounts of fictional events and everything between. Or was he the Leif Ericsson of those things, bearing in mind that the Vikings discovered America centuries before Columbus did? Or was he the Saint Brendan of those things, who crossed the Atlantic five hundred years before the Vikings? Or was he even Xog of the Yellow Snow tribe, the first man to walk over the Bering Strait land bridge thousands of years before the Irish existed, of those things; the things I listed above, chiefly metafiction, recursive fiction, parody, pastiche, recursive fiction... Did I mention recursive fiction?

But this is just nitpicking. Xog was infested with nits and picked them all, or most of them, probably. And I am not he.

The point is that Farmer was a pioneer, an explorer, an authentic original. He was a serious trickster who liked to juggle with mirrors and sometimes jump through them; and the images in those mirrors were often other mirrors full of other tricksters juggling mirrors or leaping through them. And every time he jumped through a mirror, he always emerged unscathed on the other side, and so did his reflections.

I should know, I, Jonathan Swift Somers III, being myself a fictional author who is a parody of another fictional author, created as a character in a book that supposedly didn't exist. Right. So, who better than me to give you a brief overview of Farmer's blatant disregard, if not downright manipulation, of reality?

My story begins, oddly enough, with writer's block. The best way to deal with writer's block is to tackle it head on. That's where the expression "block and tackle" comes from. And if you believe that, you'll believe anything. Nonetheless it's true. If you have writer's block, tackle it!

Farmer did exactly that. He was under pressure from publishers and readers (and let it be noted that these are different kinds of pressure) to write the next book in his renowned Riverworld series (which is fiction about real historical people in an imaginary afterlife), or the next book in his World of Tiers series (which contains characters named from William Blake's mythology as well as a character with the same initials, P.J.F., as Farmer himself), or the next volume about Lord Grandrith and Doc Caliban (pastiches of Tarzan and Doc Savage). Even though all of these novels borrowed playfully from other works in one way or another, Farmer realised that he was stuck and needed a new toy to play with.

At this point I'd like to mention something that Harlan Ellison once said, which is that there are in fact two different kinds of writer's block. The first kind is the famous kind, where the writer simply has no ideas; but the second kind is worse than that, even though it's rarely discussed or written about. The second kind is when the writer is full of ideas, bursting with them, has so much choice that he's paralyzed. He simply doesn't have the energy to—

Excuse me. I seemed to run out of steam for some reason… But to return to what I was saying earlier… Farmer was stuck.

Enter Kurt Vonnegut, Jr., a science fiction writer with mainstream success, or a mainstream writer who used science fiction tropes—it all depends on whom you ask, and how stuffy that person's contemporary American literature professor was, or how keenly you want to go along with Vonnegut's own interpretation of events. I'm happy to go along with anyone when it's easier. In many of Vonnegut's novels, various things crop up more than once. Firestorms, for example. A bird that goes "poo-tee-weet," for another. Who knows why? Maybe Vonnegut did.

But anyway… one of the many things that crop up more than once is a character who is himself a science fiction writer; always down on his luck and trod upon, the all-but-forgotten genius Kilgore Trout. More often than not, Trout doesn't appear in Vonnegut's novels in person, so to speak, but is instead cited as the author of a wild science fiction story that is then described. Because of Trout's crooked agent, most of his stories ended up as filler in cheap porn magazines instead of being sold to science fiction markets where Trout might have gained the recognition and wealth he deserved. Mind you, talking about wealth, at the end of *God Bless You, Mr. Rosewater*, he is given $50,000 by the Rosewater Foundation, so maybe he wasn't that unlucky after all. But let's not nitpick… Me not Xog.

In name, if not circumstance, Trout was based on the real-life writer Theodore Sturgeon, whom nobody seems to have a bad word to say about. But Farmer felt that he himself also had much in common with Trout, to the point that he easily identified with this fictional author. In fact, he identified with him so strongly, he decided to *become* Trout. At least in name, at least for a while. And let's remember what Vonnegut claimed the moral of his novel *Mother Night* was, namely that we are who we pretend to be, so we should be careful who we pretend to be.

Rather impertinently at this point, I would like to inject here the observation that if Kilgore Trout had ever met the writer Greg Bear the stage would have been set for a symbolic wilderness scene of paw fishing that couldn't ever really happen. Bears do fish for trout, don't they? Or is it just salmon? Don't mind me, I'm eccentric.

Anyway, Farmer's idea was simple, but it was also bold, ingenious and daring. It was this: take one of the novels that the fictional Trout is described as having written and actually write it. Hey presto! Although Vonnegut's paperback publisher, Dell, loved the idea, gaining permission from Vonnegut was a bit harder. It was almost as hard as escaping from the interior of the planet Mercury in a flying saucer, or traveling the entire length of the universe just to deliver the message, "Greetings!"

After sending many letters to Vonnegut *in the days before email* but never receiving a reply, Farmer finally got him on the phone. After a long conversation, Vonnegut reluctantly (and presumably curtly or even Kurtly) agreed to let Farmer borrow his creation. Lending creations is always fraught with danger! Will you get them back dog-eared and battered? Or spruced up and bettered? That's the gamble!

Before we see what happens next, assuming you haven't already skipped this paragraph like an impatient rascal, let's back up just a bit. How much? This much, no more, no less. Mind out, paragraph reversing! Oops, crushed a pedestrian in the margins. His mind really is out right now. Anyway, long before Farmer decided to go all out and write a novel pretending to be Trout, he studied the fictional science fiction writer as intently as it's possible to study a nonexistent personage. He read every novel by Vonnegut, apart from the ones that hadn't yet been written, and compiled a comprehensive dossier on Trout. Then, filling in the missing data with his own invented "research," Farmer wrote "The Obscure Life and Hard Times of Kilgore Trout: A Skirmish in Biography" (*Moebius Trip*, December 1971).

Short term, the result of Vonnegut's agreement was the immediate obliteration of Farmer's writer's block. Farmer knocked out the novel *Venus on the Half-Shell* in six weeks, but that's just a figure of speech, because nobody has ever really "knocked out" a prose work of any length, have they? And even if it were possible, why would you want to punch a novel before it was published? Anyway, Farmer had a wonderful time writing the book; laughter could be heard howling up from his basement office, drowning out the sound of the typewriter keys banging away. And a drowned sound isn't a pretty sight, bloats up bad and bursts... Only joking. Long term, the results were much farther reaching. And if you're a non-rascal look away now... So you thought you'd skip the last paragraph, did you? Wiseguy, huh?

Talking about "typewriter keys banging away," did I mention that Farmer was the greatest ever master of Bangsian Fantasy? We'll return to this later...

Venus on the Half-Shell was touted (trouted?) as the publishing event of the year, the year in which it appeared, naturally. *Locus* magazine ran an announcement in its April 6, 1973 issue which stated that *Venus on the Half-Shell* would be written by "(a well-known SF author—not Vonnegut) ((Sturgeon??))." The April 29 issue contained a follow-up reporting that, "Theodore Sturgeon has denied being 'Kilgore Trout.'" This was followed by the May 11 issue that contained a letter from David Harris, an editor at Dell, who claimed to have a letter from Trout. This in part said, "As far as that item about me goes, I'm not at all surprised—there are times when I doubt my own reality..."

There was also speculation that Isaac Asimov might be the mysterious "real" author of the book, or perhaps it was John Sladek, another trickster, who had already conceived I-Click-as-I-Move, a robot version of Asimov, who was pretending to be Asimov pretending to be Trout. My own view is that T.J. Bass should have been nominated too and it's fishy that he wasn't.

Things settled down until the August 11 issue of *Locus* where they reported a rumor that Philip José Farmer was Kilgore

Trout. This was followed by notices in the September 12 issue where Farmer denied being Trout and another letter by Trout appeared where he said he was flattered that all of these authors were rumored to be him, but that "there must be some way to assert my existence as a real person." He couldn't think of a way, though, and neither can I, offhand, and that's because he wasn't a real person. So really he was being duplicitous. Or rather, Farmer was being duplicitous on his behalf, which was generous of him really, if you stop to think about it.

But this was just the beginning of the japery. Farmer was an expert trickster at the center of his warm heart, and he couldn't wait until the publication of the novel to begin having some serious fun. The November 1974 issue of the *SFWA* (*Science Fiction Writers of America*) *Forum* contained a long and very badly written, badly sppellled, and even worsely punct-uated letter from Kilgore Trout asking for an application so he might join, and also saying that he was looking for a place to live. The letter concluded, "...if you need character references write david harris of dell. dont write to mr vonnegut. he never answers his mail."

Shortly afterwards, an incident occurred that almost stopped the project before it began. On December 1, 1974 well-known literary critic Leslie Fiedler was on the PBS television program *Firing Line*, hosted by William F. Buckley. They were speaking of science fiction and both Kurt Vonnegut and Kilgore Trout's names came up. Fiedler, who was a friend of Farmer's and knew all about *Venus on the Half-Shell*, said, without naming Farmer: "What he did is he just wrote a book by Kilgore Trout... Vonnegut didn't want him to do it, but he said, 'I'll go to court and get my name officially changed to Kilgore Trout, and you can't stop me.'" Vonnegut was angered and withdrew permission for Farmer to write any more novels "by" Kilgore Trout.

Prior to the novel's publication in paperback, it was abridged and serialized over two issues of *The Magazine of Fantasy and Science Fiction* (December 1974 and January 1975). It was the feature story of the December issue, getting not just top billing, but cover art as well. So it can be rightly said that this was the place and circumstance of *my* birth, where the world first discovered that Simon Wagstaff—the protagonist of Kilgore Trout's first work to be published outside of a nudie magazine— had a favorite science fiction author. Me.

Excuse me while I stop for a moment to catch my breath. It always fills me with a strange feeling when I stop to consider that I'm not a living human being, that my father was an author and my mother a magazine. Well, perhaps some of *your* fathers were authors too, but I bet they didn't *write* you into existence, did they? I bet they created you some other way. OK, I'm fine now. Let's move on.

In the same way that Vonnegut would have his characters describe stories written by Kilgore Trout, Trout, I mean Farmer, did the same with me. Simon Wagstaff, the protagonist of the novel, would tell his companions about stories I had written. And let's face it, telling readers about fictional stories that haven't really been written is a shortcut method of laying claim to the ideas in those stories without having to go through the exhausting process of actually writing them. So Trout saved himself a lot of valuable time, and the saving was passed on to Farmer. And we have no choice but to assume Trout passed *all* that saved time on.

So the stories I, Jonathan Swift Somers III, had written could be summarized even though they didn't exist; but they could only be summarized if the pretence was maintained that they *did* exist. Otherwise, they would just be pitches, not proper summaries, and pitching stories is less satisfying than summarizing them, even if they are identical. Does that make sense?

In a similar vein, the Polish science fiction writer Stanislaw Lem once published a volume of literary reviews of books that didn't exist. He did this because he didn't have time to write the actual books but he wanted to lay claim to the original ideas they contained. Some critics feel this is a lazy approach but I believe it's ingenious and I only wish that Lem had reviewed my own books. However, Farmer seems to have had more energy than Lem, more energy than one might deem possible, for he was willing not only to imagine and summarize stories that didn't exist in order to save time; he was willing to later spend that same time writing those stories to match and even exceed the summaries! And let me add that Farmer once reviewed one of Lem's books, *Imaginary Magnitude*, a collection of introductions to books that don't exist. Squeeze my Lem 'til the juice run down my leg!

But to return to the way that I was presented in the *Venus* novel... In the first instance, the story described (that is, the story I had written) was of less importance in the text of the framing novel and Farmer spent more time describing me. Apparently he didn't want anyone to have to come along behind him and fill in the details of my life story, as he had to do with Trout. The other stories of mine, however, were more detailed in their summary and were revealing about two of "my" creations. First, there was Ralph von Wau Wau, a genetically enhanced German Shepherd with a 200 IQ and the ability to speak. Farmer states that with the exception of Ralph, all of my protagonists have major disabilities, this being due to my own condition of being paralyzed from the waist down. The second of my characters described is John Clayter, a space traveler whose spacesuit is full of (often malfunctioning) prosthetics.

If a fictional character invents another fictional character who invents another fictional character who invents another fictional character, is there a grading of *existability* (for want of a better word)? I mean… is a dream within a dream less real than the dream that frames it, or are they both equal in terms of the fact that neither have concrete form? This is a question that has understandably intrigued me for quite some time. If you know the answer, please keep it to yourself, okay? I'm freaked out enough by my condition already.

Anyway, the Dell paperback edition of *Venus on the Half-Shell* came out in February 1975 (available for the first time without lurid covers!) and the reviews, and controversy, quickly followed. Funny how that happens, isn't it? Do you imagine, as I do, the book traipsing down the street, followed by a number of reviews that are stumbling to keep up, with controversy close behind, its nose in the rear end of the last review in line? That's the picture I see in my mind, anyway…

A wildly popular fanzine, Richard Geis' *Science Fiction Review*, ran a review of *Venus on the Half-Shell* in the February 1975 issue. The humorous novel was full of clichés as Farmer poked fun at the genre; after all, he had written the novel he believed Kilgore Trout, a science fiction hack, would have written had Trout existed. Since Vonnegut had for years taken umbrage at being labeled a science fiction writer, and since Richard Geis assumed Vonnegut had in fact written the book, Geis took offense at a novel that seemed to make fun of, and look down on, science fiction because he did not feel that Vonnegut had earned the right to do so (a case of, it's okay for me to call my sister ugly, but if you do it, I'll punch you in the nose). Geis' review wasn't very gentle. In fact, it came out swinging.

But reviews from the likes of *Publisher's Weekly*, *The Washington Post*, *Eastern News*, *Science Fiction Review Monthly*, *National Observer*, *Locus*, and the *UCLA Daily Bruin* were more favorable. In fact, the *Bruin* reviewer went to great lengths to "prove" that Vonnegut was in fact the author of *Venus on the Half-Shell*.

The novel was a bigger success than even Farmer could have dreamed. At least, we can assume that it was a bigger success than he could have dreamed. But he was a man with extremely big dreams, let's not forget! Sorry. Nitpicking again. Related to Xog, I must be… Yes, that's plausible, for Xog never existed either…

On March 16, 1975, the *New York Times Book Review* reported Dell had sold 225,000 copies in the first month. Farmer was having a blast. Dell was going to sponsor a "Who is Kilgore Trout?" contest and they had begun forwarding Kilgore Trout's fan mail to him. Farmer really enjoyed answering these letters, sending replies back from "Kilgore Trout" (several examples of these were published in *Farmerphile* #5, July 2006). But Farmer wasn't satisfied with having merely pulled off the biggest hoax in science fiction since Orson Welles' "War of the Worlds" radio broadcast. He had plans to take things to a whole other level. Farmer loved taking things to other levels and he was extremely good at it. Try reading the World of Tiers series and you'll see what I mean. Literally.

The March issue of *The Magazine of Fantasy and Science Fiction* contained "A Scarletin Study," by Simon Wagstaff's favorite author, me, Jonathan Swift Somers III. This story, about Ralph von Wau Wau, the hyperintelligent German Shepherd described in *Venus on the Half-Shell*, was to be the first in a series of stories written by "fictional authors." In addition to myself, Farmer also wrote stories "by" Harry Manders, Paul Chapin, Rod Keen, and Cordwainer Bird. He further planned to collect these stories in an anthology and began recruiting other writers such as Philip K. Dick, Howard Waldrop, and Gene Wolfe to join in the fun.

While attending Minicon, a science fiction convention in Minneapolis, in April 1975, Farmer was interviewed by David Truesdale, Paul McGuire, and Jerry Rauth for the fanzine *Tangent*. By now rumors were already beginning to circulate that Farmer was the author of *Venus on the Half-Shell*. While denying he was the culprit, Farmer laughingly offered up the possibility of Trout being "a collaboration between Harry Harrison and Ted White. Or Joanna Russ and Phil Dick—or Harlan Ellison and Captain S.I. Meek."

I doubt any of you remember Captain Meek? He wrote a madcap story called "Submicroscopic" back in the early '30s and followed that with a sequel that was a novella, "Alwo of

Ulm." But I'm digressing again. Forgive me…

However, before the issue with the interview could be published, Dave Truesdale discovered a notice that had appeared in the *New York Times Book Review* on March 23 about whom the author of *Venus on the Half-Shell* might really be: "This week, from Peoria comes a letter from a man who asks not to be named, stating that he is its author."

Even though, after calling Farmer to confirm, he was able to trumpet the news on the cover of the May '75 issue, "Tangent Hooks Farmer on Trout," Truesdale was not happy the *New York Times Book Review* chose to so callously let the cat out of the bag; seriously, how many science fiction authors live in Peoria? In fact, in the editorial where he broke the news, this sums up his reaction: "All I can say is FUCK YOU to the *New York Times…*" Farmer wasn't happy either, but there was no point in denying the story now.

Of course, the news was not immediately universally known. In a bit of coincidental timing that could *only* happen in fiction, when the aforementioned review appeared in the *UCLA Daily Bruin* "proving" Vonnegut wrote *Venus on the Half-Shell*, Farmer happened to be at UCLA. He was there as part of an Extension Course which featured a guest science fiction author each week. The day the review appeared, May 20, Farmer revealed to the class that he was, in fact, "Kilgore Trout" and the author of *Venus on the Half-Shell*. The following week, a correction was printed: "We've been had…"

Slowly the word continued to spread. *Locus* confirmed it in early June, also saying, "Kurt Vonnegut, who went along with the gag at first, has become very annoyed because of reviews and statements made about the book..." Farmer explained years later that half the people said it was Vonnegut's worst book, and the other half said it was his best. In July, Farmer was the guest of honor at RiverCon I in Louisville, where his speech, "Now It Can be Told" (which also happens to be the title of one of Kilgore Trout's stories, as described by Vonnegut), was about writing *Venus on the Half-Shell*. Tragically, no copy of this speech is known to exist. In August, a long interview with Farmer about the affair appeared in *Science Fiction Review*.

The following year my story, "The Doge Whose Barque Was Worse Than His Bight," was published in the November issue of *The Magazine of Fantasy and Science Fiction*, and then I faded from existence, nearly forgotten. My stories have been reprinted a few times, but that is it. When *Venus on the Half-Shell and Others* (Subterranean Press, 2007), a collection focusing on Farmer's fictional-author series, was published, even though I was the most prolific, the most well known of Farmer's fictional authors, Tom Wode Bellman was invited to write the foreword. And he's not even a proper fictional author, just a stand-in for Farmer himself!

But I'm not too unhappy about being who I am. I just have one worry that nags at me whenever I lie awake at night unable to sleep (because I don't exist; whoever heard of a nonexistent entity sleeping?) And that worry is this: I was created as a byproduct of writer's block. If my father, Farmer, hadn't had that block at that time, it's very unlikely I would be here.

Now then, birth is the opposite of death. So if I was created by a block, then what will kill me will be the opposite of that, in other words creative flow. Farmer is no longer with us. He's on the other side now. And that's the biggest block any writer can ever have: to have shuffled off this mortal coil. But what if he starts writing again on the other side? Creative flow is the opposite of a writer's block and the opposite of a block is death to me. If Farmer starts writing again, wherever he is now, I might somehow vanish… I know that's bizarre logic and an obscure thing to fret about. But I *am* bizarre. Remember: I'm writing this article even though I'm fictional!

I can almost feel someone *walking over my grave* right now, even though I won't have a grave because I don't have a solid body to bury, but the figure of speech is appropriate; and rather bizarrely I can reveal that its first recorded use in print was in Simon Wagstaff's *A Complete Collection of Genteel and Ingenious Conversation*, published in 1738. The date isn't an error. This was a different Simon Wagstaff, one of the pseudonyms of the satirist Jonathan Swift. Talk about recursion!

And where is Farmer now, I hear you ask? Well, I don't know. But I'll say this: a great many obituaries pictured him waking up along the banks of the million-mile-long river that was one of his most amazing creations in a creative life full of astounding concepts. And yet… As I mentioned earlier, Farmer was the greatest ever master of a type of writing called Bangsian Fantasy. I'd never even heard of Bangsian Fantasy until recently. It's named after the mostly forgotten writer John Kendrick Bangs (1862–1922), whose most famous book was *House-Boat on the Styx*, in which Charon upgrades from his leaky old skiff to a luxurious boat capable of holding many dead people at once, dead people who happen to have been real in *your* world and not just invented by Bangs.

What if Farmer is a guest on that house-boat right now? What if he has managed to get hold of some writing materials? What if he's saying to himself, "Hey, Charon, let's do a collaboration! Why don't we write a story pretending to be Trout; maybe a story about what happens when Jonathan Swift Somers III dies and wakes up on the banks of a million-mile-long river!"

That's my worry. Or my hope. I'm not sure which.

AFTERWORD

MORE REAL THAN LIFE ITSELF: PHILIP JOSÉ FARMER'S FICTIONAL-AUTHOR PERIOD

BY CHRISTOPHER PAUL CAREY

"The unconscious is the true democracy.
All things, all people, are equal."
PHILIP JOSÉ FARMER

By one count, Philip José Farmer, a Grand Master of Science Fiction, has written and had published fifty-four novels and one hundred and twenty-nine novellas, novelettes, and short stories. Creatively, Farmer's work is equally ambitious. In 1952, he authored the groundbreaking "The Lovers," which at long last made it possible for science fiction to deal with sex in a mature manner. He is the creator of Riverworld, arguably one of the grandest experiments in science fiction literature. His World of Tiers series, which combines rip-roaring adventure with pocket universes full of mythic archetypes, is said to have inspired Zelazny's Chronicles of Amber series and is often cited as a favorite among Farmer's fans. And in the early 1970s, he penned the authorized biographies of Tarzan and Doc Savage and inspired generations of creative mythographers to explore and expand upon his Wold Newton mythos. Yet among all of these shining minarets of his opus, Farmer has stated that he has never had so much fun in all his life as when he wrote *Venus on the Half-Shell*.

I believe it is no coincidence that this novel belongs to what Farmer has labeled his "fictional-author" series. A fictional-author story is, as defined by Farmer, "a tale supposedly written by an author who is a character in fiction." Many of Farmer's readers are aware that *Venus on the Half-Shell* originally appeared in print as if authored by Kurt Vonnegut's character Kilgore Trout. However, most are not aware that Farmer, in league with several of his writer peers and at least one major magazine editor, masterminded an expansive hoax on the science fiction readership that spanned a good portion of the 1970s.

As with Farmer's usual *modus operandi*, the plan was ambitious. Beginning in about 1973–74, in true postmodern reflexivity, a whole team of writers acting under Farmer's direction were to begin submitting fictional-author tales to the short fiction markets. Farmer's files, to which the author kindly gave me access, reveal that his plan of attack was executed with focus, precision, and a great deal of forethought.

The authors queried to write the fictional-author stories were instructed that "the real author is to be nowhere mentioned; it's all done straight-facedly." Each story would be accompanied by a short biographical preface giving the impression that the fictional author was indeed a living person.

However, all copyrights were to be honored; those who chose to write stories "by" the characters of other authors would need to contact those creators for permission. Sometimes Farmer himself wrote the creator and, having received permission, then handed over the fictional-author story to his fellow conspirator to complete. Authors were encouraged to submit their stories to whatever market they pleased, although the majority were to appear in *The Magazine of Fantasy and Science Fiction*, whose editor, Edward L. Ferman, was in on the joke. Once enough of the stories had been published in various markets, Farmer himself planned to take on the role of editor and collect them all in a fictional-author anthology.

Writing even before the fallout with Kurt Vonnegut (which is described in great detail by Farmer in his "Why and How I Became Kilgore Trout"), Farmer placed great emphasis on literary ethics during the execution of his hoax. Even authors whose characters had lapsed into the public domain—and whom Farmer and his cohorts could have used legally without payment of royalties—were offered 50% of any monies made by the publication of a fictional-author story (a stipulation that appears to have been waived by all of those who granted Farmer permission). Provisions were made for the original authors and their agents to receive copies of the stories upon publication. And always, Farmer made clear that his request to write a story under the name of an author's character was his intimate tribute to said author.

While the vast majority of those queried for the use of their characters granted permission, a couple did not. Farmer wrote respectful, though clearly disappointed, replies to these authors, explaining again that he only meant to honor them with the stories, but that in deference to them he would withdraw his offers and pursue them no further. Most authors, however, reacted much differently and became infected by the passion that seemed to ooze from Farmer when he proposed to them his audacious hoax. Nero Wolfe author Rex Stout, besides granting permission to write the story "The Volcano" under the name of his character Paul Chapin, was tickled enough to suggest that Farmer should also author stories by Anna Karenina and Don Quixote. Farmer's correspondence indicates that he planned on doing just that. P. G. Wodehouse, author of the Jeeves and Blandings Castle stories, also tried to come up with alternative fictional-authors among his own works that could be used, and it is telling of the excitement surrounding Farmer's fictional-author conceit that multiple authors queried for permission enthusiastically consented by exclaiming the phrase "Of course" within the first paragraph of their replies. Occasionally, permissions went in the other direction. J. T. Edson, the author of many Westerns, sought permission to use Farmer's Wold Newton genealogy as the basis for his own characters' ancestry in his Bunduki series, a request Farmer happily approved; and while the Wold Newton genealogy was not exclusively related to the proposed fictional-author series, it remains clear that Farmer was pleased to interweave the two concepts in several instances.

As concerns those peers enlisted to write the fictional-author stories under Farmer's coordination, the list included (among others) Arthur Jean Cox, Philip K. Dick, Leslie Fiedler, Ron Goulart, and Gene Wolfe. Unfortunately, not all of these writers succeeded in completing their stories or having them published, though there were some notable exceptions. At Farmer's suggestion, Arthur Jean Cox tackled one of his own creations, writing "Writers of the Purple Page" by John Thames Rokesmith, published in the May 1977 issue of *The Magazine of Fantasy and Science Fiction*. Rokesmith was a character in Cox's novella "Straight Shooters Always Win" (*The Magazine of Fantasy and Science Fiction*, ed. Edward L. Ferman, May 1974). And Gene Wolfe—whose humorous "Tarzan of the Grapes" appears in Farmer's survey of feral humans in literature, *Mother Was A Lovely Beast*—wrote "'Our Neighbour' by David Copperfield," first published in the anthology *Rooms of Paradise* (ed. Lee Harding, Quartet Books, 1978), albeit under Wolfe's own name. But the fun did not end there. Author Howard Waldrop, although not enlisted by Farmer, sought out the author of *Venus on the Half-Shell* and joined in with the other conspirators, publishing "The Adventure of the Grinder's Whistle" as by Sir Edward Malone in the semipro fanzine *Chacal* #2 (eds. Arnie Fenner and Pat Cadigan, Spring 1977; reprinted in the collection *Night of the Cooters*, Ace Books, 1993, wherein Waldrop, in his introduction to the story, says, "Like with most things from the Seventies, this was Philip José Farmer's fault"). Harlan Ellison's "The New York Review of Bird" (*Weird Heroes, Volume Two*, ed. Byron Preiss, Pyramid Books, 1975), while not technically a fictional-author story, was tied in with Farmer's project, and served to turn Ellison's *nom de plume*, Cordwainer Bird, into a full-fledged fictional author. Bird went on to appear in Farmer's fictional-author tale "The Doge Whose Barque Was Worse Than His Bight" as by Jonathan Swift Somers III (*The Magazine of Fantasy and Science Fiction*, ed. Edward L. Ferman, November 1976; reprinted in *Tales of the Wold Newton Universe*, Titan Books, 2013). Farmer himself used the Cordwainer Bird pseudonym for his story "The Impotency of Bad Karma" (*Popular Culture*, ed. Brad Lang, First Preview Edition, June 1977), which he later revised and had published, using his own name this time, under the title "The Last Rise of Nick Adams" (*Chrysalis, Volume Two*, ed. Roy Torgeson, Zebra Books, 1978), and integrated Bird into his Wold Newton genealogy in *Doc Savage: His Apocalyptic Life* (Doubleday, 1973; reprinted in a deluxe hardcover edition by Meteor House, 2013, and in paperback and ebook editions by Altus Press, 2013).

The failures—those fictional-author stories imagined but never written—are almost as compelling as the successes. Ed Ferman suggested that Farmer have Ron Goulart write a story as by his character José Silvera, and while Farmer did query him, there is no immediate evidence that Goulart pursued the matter. Farmer himself sought and was granted permission to write a story under the name Gustave von Aschenbach, the novelist from Thomas Mann's *A Death in Venice*; however, apparently overwhelmed by the large number of fictional-author stories he planned to write on his own, Farmer turned the idea over to writer and literary critic Leslie Fiedler. This story, too, seems to have fallen by the wayside; if it was ever written, it never saw print.

One of the first authors approached to join in the conspiracy was Philip K. Dick. Farmer trusted Dick with the secret of who had written *Venus on the Half-Shell*, and in the process discussed Dick writing a fictional-author tale for Ferman's magazine. Dick decided this would be a short story entitled "A Man For No Countries" by Hawthorne Abdensen, the writer-character from his classic novel of alternate history, *The Man in the High Castle*. No fictional alter ego could have suited Dick better for the undertaking, as Abdensen himself was the fictional author of *The Grasshopper Lies Heavy*, a novel that implied the existence of multiple realities. The Chinese-box scenario must have pleased Dick, who worked often with such themes; but it must also have pleased Farmer, who years later went on to write the similarly head-twisting *Red Orc's Rage*, a novel wherein Farmer's own World of Tiers series serves as the basis for a method of psychiatric therapy to treat troubled adolescents, and in which Farmer himself lurks just off screen as a character. Although "A Man For No Countries" never seems to have been written, Farmer's role in proposing that Dick pen a fictional-author story is important, for that unwritten story appears to have been the idea-kernel that led Dick to write the posthumously published novel *Radio Free Albemuth*, which itself was an aborted draft of his critically acclaimed novel *VALIS*. One must also ponder the timing of Farmer's proposal, in the spring of 1974, a period when Dick claims to have had a number of mystical experiences, including one in which his mind was supposedly invaded by a foreign consciousness.

While Farmer was by far the most industrious and successful of the group in executing the fictional-author ruse, many of his own plans had to be abandoned because of time constraints placed upon him by other writing obligations. Farmer's correspondence, notes, and interviews from the fictional-author period reveal a long and fascinating list of stories never written and those started but not completed:

"The Gargoyle" as by Edgar Henquist Gordon. (Fictional title and author from Robert Bloch's short story "The Dark Demon"; permission for use granted by Robert Bloch.)

"The Feaster from the Stars" as by Robert Blake. (This unfinished Cthulhu Mythos pastiche derives from a title and fictional author in H. P. Lovecraft's "The Haunter of the Dark." Lovecraft's story is a sequel to Robert Bloch's "The Shambler from the Stars," wherein Bloch kills off a character based on H. P. Lovecraft. Robert Blake, of course, is an analog for Robert Bloch, and is in turn killed off in Lovecraft's tale. A good friend of Farmer's, Bloch enthusiastically gave his blessing to this unfinished story about Haji Abdu al-Yazdi, a pseudonym belonging to one of Farmer's real-life heroes, who was also the main protagonist of the Riverworld series: Sir Richard Francis Burton. Robert Blake is also mentioned in Farmer's Cthulhu Mythos tale "The Freshmen," which was recently reprinted in the anthology *Tales of the Wold Newton Universe*, Titan Books, 2013.)

"UFO Versus CBS" as by Susan DeWitt. (From Richard Brautigan's *The Abortion: An Historical Romance 1966*.)

Untitled "Smoke Bellew" stories. (Continuation of the series by Jack London. Although the stories were in the public domain, permission was refused by London's literary executor and the stories went unwritten.)

Untitled story as by Martin Eden. (From Jack London's *Martin Eden*; no record yet found of a permission query.)

Untitled story as by Edward P. Malone. (The intrepid reporter from Sir Arthur Conan Doyle's *The Lost World*. As mentioned above, this fictional author was turned over to Howard Waldrop.)

Untitled story as by Gerald Musgrave. (From James Branch Cabell's *Something About Eve*. Interestingly, Cabell used anagrams prominently in his work, as Farmer does in *Venus on the Half-Shell*.)

Untitled story as by Kenneth Robeson. (Proposed second story of *The Grant-Robeson Papers*; the first was Farmer's "The Savage Shadow" as by Maxwell Grant.)

The Son of Jimmy Valentine as by Kilgore Trout. (Permission denied by Kurt Vonnegut after the fallout from *Venus on the Half-Shell*.)

"The Adventure of the Wand of Death" as by Felix Clovelly. ("Felix Clovelly" is a pen name of Wodehouse's thriller novelist Ashe Marston from *Something New*. Permission granted by Wodehouse.)

But however many ideas Farmer abandoned, his list of completed fictional-author tales is equally impressive. These tales are sly, tongue-in-cheek, sometimes shocking, and more often than not uproariously funny. The following list is a chronological bibliography of Farmer's published fictional-author stories:

The Adventure of the Peerless Peer as by John H. Watson, M.D. (Aspen Press, 1974; reprinted as *The Further Adventures of Sherlock Holmes: The Peerless Peer*, Titan Books, 2011. Dr. Watson, of course, is from the works of Sir Arthur Conan Doyle.)

Venus on the Half-Shell as by Kilgore Trout. (*The Magazine of Fantasy and Science Fiction*, ed. Edward L. Ferman, December 1974–January 1975; reprinted in book form, Dell, 1975, and Titan Books, 2013. Kilgore Trout is the wildly imaginative, though sad-sack, science fiction author from the works of Kurt Vonnegut.)

"A Scarletin Study" as by Jonathan Swift Somers III. (*The Magazine of Fantasy and Science Fiction*, ed. Edward L. Ferman, March 1975; reprinted in *Tales of the Wold Newton Universe*, Titan Books, 2013. Jonathan Swift Somers III appears as a fictional author in *Venus on the Half-Shell*, and is also the subject of Farmer's biographical essay "Jonathan Swift Somers III: Cosmic Traveller in a Wheelchair.")

"The Problem of the Sore Bridge—Among Others" as by Harry Manders. (*The Magazine of Fantasy and Science Fiction*, ed. Edward L. Ferman, September 1975; reprinted in *Tales of the Wold Newton Universe*, Titan Books, 2013. Harry "Bunny" Manders is a fictional author from the Raffles stories of E. W. Hornung.)

"The Volcano" as by Paul Chapin. (*The Magazine of Fantasy and Science Fiction*, ed. Edward L. Ferman, February 1976. Paul Chapin appears in Rex Stout's Nero Wolfe novel *The League of Frightened Men*.)

"Osiris on Crutches" as by Philip José Farmer and Leo Queequeg Tincrowdor. (*New Dimensions 6*, ed. Robert Silverberg, Harper & Row, 1976. Farmer wrote of Leo Queequeg Tincrowdor in his novel *Stations of the Nightmare* and short story "Fundamental Issue.")

"The Doge Whose Barque Was Worse Than His Bight" as by Jonathan Swift Somers III. (*The Magazine of Fantasy and Science Fiction*, ed. Edward L. Ferman, November 1976; reprinted in *Tales of the Wold Newton Universe*, Titan Books, 2013. See the entry above for "A Scarletin Study.")

"The Impotency of Bad Karma" as by Cordwainer Bird. (*Popular Culture*, First Preview Edition, ed. Brad Lang, June 1977; revised version published in *Chrysalis, Volume Two*, ed. Roy Torgeson, Zebra Books, 1978 as "The Last Rise of Nick Adams," now under Farmer's own name. Cordwainer Bird appears as a character in Harlan Ellison's short story "The New York Review of Bird" and in Farmer's "The Doge Whose Barque Was Worse Than His Bight.")

"Savage Shadow" as by Maxwell Grant. (*Weird Heroes, Volume Eight*, ed. Byron Preiss, Jove/HBJ Books, November 1977. Maxwell Grant was the house pen name used by the authors of The Shadow pulp magazine and paperback stories.)

"It's the Queen of Darkness, Pal" as by Rod Keen. (*The Magazine of Fantasy and Science Fiction*, ed. Edward L. Ferman, August 1978; revised version published in *Riverworld and Other Stories*, Berkley Books, 1979 as "The Phantom of the Sewers." Rod Keen is a fictional author from Richard Brautigan's *The Abortion: An Historical Romance 1966*.)

"Who Stole Stonehenge?" as by Jonathan Swift Somers III. (*Farmerphile: The Magazine of Philip José Farmer*, no. 2, eds. Christopher Paul Carey and Paul Spiteri, October 2005. Although this one-page fragment of an unfinished Ralph von Wau Wau story was published under Farmer's name, the original manuscript is attributed to Jonathan Swift Somers III; see the entry above for "A Scarletin Study.")

Farmer has cited Paul Radin's *The Trickster*, a book about the role of the mischievous archetype recurrent in mythology and folklore, as one of his influences; and among the stories at hand it is easy to see why. By assuming the role of a fictional author, Farmer dons a shamanic mask and enters the sublime creative world where fictional characters take on a life more real than our own.

A long-held theory goes that Farmer unconsciously hatched his fictional-author series, as well as penned his many pastiches, in an attempt to get over a period of writer's block which had descended upon him during the early to mid-1970s. I do not doubt it; although, if true, I—doubtless along with all of Farmer's readers—am grateful that his muse found such a scintillating, creative means to overcome its obstacle.

But there is another possibility, more fun to contemplate and more in tune with the spirit of the fictional-author concept: Perhaps Farmer's muse did not merely find a clever mechanism to jumpstart itself. What if the fictional-author period was not a hoax after all, but instead Farmer, donning his shamanic mask, did indeed glimpse into another universe? One in which William

S. Burroughs wrote *Tarzan of the Apes*, and John H. Watson hobnobbed at the same gentlemen's club as A. J. Raffles and Edward Malone. Where Kurt Vonnegut may have asked Farmer's Riverworld counterpart, Peter Jairus Frigate, for permission to write a World of Tiers novel. A universe in which you and I are merely fictional characters in the works of a Grand Master of Science Fiction.

Yes, paging through this new edition of *Venus on the Half-Shell*, I think I too am getting a glimpse through the doors of perception.

Thank you, Philip José Farmer, for opening them.

Christopher Paul Carey
Seattle, Washington

Christopher Paul Carey is the coauthor with Philip José Farmer of The Song of Kwasin, *and the author of* Exiles of Kho, *a prelude to the Khokarsa series. His short fiction may be found in such anthologies as* The Worlds of Philip José Farmer 1: Protean Dimensions, The Worlds of Philip José Farmer 2: Of Dust and Soul, Tales of the Shadowmen: The Vampires of Paris, Tales of the Shadowmen: Grand Guignol, *and* The Avenger: The Justice, Inc. Files. *He is an editor with Paizo Publishing on the award-winning* Pathfinder Roleplaying Game, *and the editor of three collections of Farmer's fiction. Visit him online at www.cpcarey.com.*

JAMES P. BLAYLOCK

The award-winning author returns with his first full-length steampunk novel in twenty years!

The Aylesford Skull

Professor Langdon St. Ives, brilliant but eccentric scientist and explorer, is at home in Aylesford with his family. Not far away a steam launch is taken by pirates, the crew murdered, and a grave is possibly robbed of the skull. The suspected grave robber, the infamous Dr. Ignacio Narbondo, is an old nemesis of St. Ives. When Narbondo kidnaps his son Eddie, St. Ives races into London in pursuit.

Also available:

Homunculus

Lord Kelvin's Machine

"Blaylock is better than anyone else at showing us the magic that secretly animates our world…" — Tim Powers

"Blaylock is a singular American fabulist." — William Gibson

SHERLOCK HOLMES

BY GUY ADAMS

The Breath of God

A body is found crushed to death in the London snow. There are no footprints anywhere near. It is almost as if the man was killed by the air itself. This is the first in a series of attacks that sees a handful of London's most prominent occultists murdered. While pursuing the case, Holmes and Watson have to travel to Scotland to meet with the one person they have been told can help: Aleister Crowley.

The Army of Doctor Moreau

Following the trail of several corpses seemingly killed by wild animals, Holmes and Watson stumble upon the experiments of Doctor Moreau. Determined to prove Darwin's evolutionary theories, through vivisection and crude genetic engineering Moreau is creating animal hybrids. In his laboratory, Moreau is building an army of "beast men" in order to gain control of the government…

CAPTAIN NEMO

The Fantastic Adventures of a Dark Genius

BY KEVIN J. ANDERSON

When André Nemo's father dies suddenly, the young adventurer takes to the sea and is accompanied by his lifelong friend, Jules Verne. Verne is thwarted in his yearning for action, while Nemo continues to travel across continents…

THE MARTIAN WAR

BY KEVIN J. ANDERSON

What if the Martian invasion was not entirely the product of H. G. Wells's vivid imagination? What if Wells witnessed something that spurred him to write *The War of the Worlds* as a warning? From drafty London flats to the steamy Sahara, to the surface of the moon and beyond, *The Martian War* takes the reader on an exhilarating journey with Wells and his companions.